BOZOPHOBIA

BOZOPHOBIA

scott parson

Whiskey Shallows

Press

Whiskey Shallows Press
eBook Edition 2018
Paperback Edition 2018

ISBN 978-0-9996378-1-4

Cover and interior design: Slade Withers
Front cover image: Sonja www.fotosearch.com
Back cover image: mfilippo www.fotosearch.com
Find out more about the author at www.scottparson.com

For Lisa, Vergil, and Maggie –
my everyday circus

BOZOPHOBIA

chapter one

THE BIG TOP TAVERN SITS just off the old main drag at the south end of Chumleyville. It's the kind of place vocational drinkers can get that special kind of darkness at midday they find so attractive.

But inside at the moment, a single customer had the place to himself. The guy, alone and in the shadows at the end of the bar, sat spinning his drink in the wet rings on the wooden surface.

"I'm thinking," said the guy in the dark, "maybe it's better for everyone if Franklin got himself knocked off, too. What do you think?"

"That's the bourbon talking." Red, owner and sole bartender, polished glassware and stacked it on the service rail.

"Possibly," said the guy in the dark, staring into his glass, "but you can't beat it for eloquence."

"What'd be the good of killing off Franklin?"

"He wouldn't always be getting in the way every time I meet someone."

"Live and let live I always say. Besides, you never know when he'll come in handy. Finish him off and then it's, 'Oops! Sure wish I had Franklin here.'"

"Haven't so far. How many years has it been? Maybe it's time for him to go."

"I'm just saying." Red shrugged. "You want me to call somebody?"

"You know any women up for some recreational self-medication?" The guy in the dark rattled the ice in the empty glass. He set it down and pushed it toward Red, who came over and picked it up, ready to dash out the ice and start fresh.

"Don't toss those out. That ice is already broken in."

Red put the glass down, bare-handed a few more cubes in on top and splashed bourbon over them.

The guy in the dark was smoking. The glow of the cigarette revealed a white-gloved hand. The guy bent his face down, looking into the glass.

"Welcome to the team, guys." He swirled the glass and said to Red, "It's important you make the rookies feel welcome."

"You sure you don't want me to call somebody?"

"Who've you got in mind?"

The front door swung open, scorching the dark with a slash of late afternoon daylight. A tall newcomer stood silhouetted in the doorway. A woman.

The door banged shut behind her, restoring the refuge of stopped time. Their eyes adjusted to the renewed darkness. They could see the newcomer was big-hipped, wearing a skirt and jacket that could be lavender or gray. Hard to tell in the bar's dim lighting. The jacket strained at its one button fastened across her midriff. She wore dark tights, her feet mashed into black, unhappy heels. In heavy makeup, she had the look of a woman on the hunt. She surveyed the room then weaved her way through the empty tables up to the bar. She planted herself on a stool at the middle of the bar, her back to the door.

Red studied the newcomer while the newcomer studied the guy in the dark while the guy in the dark studied his drink.

"White Russian. With a cherry," said the woman in a voice husky with smoke and whiskey, her eye still on the guy in the dark.

She laid her purse and mobile phone on the bar, pushing money toward Red.

"I'm meeting some clown here today. Showing him a little piece of real estate," said the woman, still watching the guy in the dark.

"This clown a yours. Got a name?" asked Red.

"Didn't give me a name."

"What's he look like?"

"Don't know. Didn't tell me how to recognize him. All he said was to meet him here. For Happy Hour."

Red, mixing her drink, gestured with his elbow. "Only clown in the place."

"So, maybe it's him?"

"I doubt it." Red turned toward the guy in the dark. "Hey, Franklin. You supposed to meet somebody?"

"Gladys," offered the woman.

"Gladys?" Red asked the guy in the dark.

"I've had my minimum daily allowance of excruciating heartbreak for the day. But thanks for asking."

"Not him." Red put down a napkin and placed her drink on it. "I'm guessing Lucy put him off women for a while."

"Lucy?"

"He came in saying she threw him over for some other clown. He's been sitting there drinking ever since."

"Just until she forgets me," said Franklin, the guy in the dark.

Gladys took a sip and asked, "Shouldn't that be the other way around?"

"I always pour it in my lap when I drink it the other way around."

"My ex was a clown." Gladys shifted to get her whole bottom onto the seat. She sipped again, studying Franklin.

Franklin wore a bald, white pate ringed with a fringe of wild, blue hair over white, arched eyebrows, bulbous nose, and a big, red, greasepaint smile.

An actual clown.

She leaned back to check the shoes. Huge, with the toe tips balanced on the bar rail.

"Oh," said Gladys, eyes wide, lips pursed. "*Excusez-moi.*"

Franklin's costume was a patchwork jumpsuit of clashing patterns, gaudy colors, and a floppy red collar. It was grimy, scorched, and lacerated front and back. His makeup had been rubbed away in spots.

Franklin gave a quick nod to Gladys and took another drag on his cigarette. He rolled the ash off in the mouth of the ceramic clown-faced ashtray in front of him on the bar. He sucked at the bourbon.

"Rough day at the circus?" Gladys stirred her drink. "I gotta ask. You have much luck with women, looking the way you're looking?"

"Only the one. She hated clowns." Franklin took another drag of his smoke. "Doesn't anymore. Hooray for me."

Gladys lifted her glass, saluting the air between them. "To the bottomless bourbon therapy for broken hearts."

"Nah. Just until I finish all the liquor. Hey, Red. Have I finished all the liquor yet?"

Overhead, above the great long mirror, the big clown-faced clock chuckled the hour. They all looked up.

"I can't stand to wait," said Gladys. "I have a formula. One drink every ten minutes for one hour. Cuts wait time to zero."

Red tried doing the arithmetic on his fingers but had to ask, "How's that work?"

"By drink number six, I can't remember who the hell stood me up." Gladys slapped the bar, barking a throaty laugh. "Time flies right by. I hate waiting. Time and most men are too short."

"I've been here—" Franklin clipped his cigarette in one corner of his mouth, pushing up his sleeves to check his wrists, then stopped. "Forgot. Clown's first rule. Never work with anything that's got a funnier face than you."

Gladys checked her own watch, then twisted around to check the front door. She leaned in toward Red.

"Any chance this Lucy of his showing up?"

Red leaned in toward Gladys. "Look at him. Would you?"

Gladys stirred her drink again, sucked the straw dry, and tapped it against the glass rim.

"So, who's this Lucy who's got you sitting here in the dark, crying in your beer?"

"Bourbon."

"Bourbon." Gladys raised her glass at the correction. "Childhood sweetheart?"

A scrapbook slid out of the shadows at Gladys, stopping near her elbow resting on the bar. She put down her drink to flip through its pages.

The scrapbook was a memorial to a single, bloody crime spree. It bulged with newspaper clippings, pictures and articles cut from magazines, pages printed off the internet, snapshots, postcards, and matchbooks.

"That's gruesome." Gladys pushed the scrapbook back down the bar to Franklin. "Yours? If you'll forgive my asking."

"Lucy's," said Franklin. "You ever hear of the Baggy Pants Slasher?"

"The clown killer?"

"The killer of clowns," Franklin corrected her, waggling a gloved finger.

Gladys gave out with a *pish*. "Not in this neck of the woods."

"A week ago, this place was wall-to-wall clowns." Red waved his hand out to the empty tables. "Now, none a them'll show their painted puss around 'cause a that guy," said Red, pointing to the scrapbook.

◆ ◆ ◆

Until a week ago, the Big Top had for years been the place to go for clowns. Painted up to look like a circus tent, the Big Top sat between an auto parts place in an oversized Quonset hut on one side, and a cinder block building divided up into a plumbing supply store, a laundromat, and church thrift shop on the other. Dangling out front of the tavern hung a large, sheet metal clown quaffing beer from a foamy mug.

The blue-and-white canvas peak over the roof, and the windows filled up with neon announced the presence of beer, cocktails, and clowns, promising communal hilarity.

Red Bottoms loved three things—clowns, drinking, and clowns drinking. Not necessarily in that order. The Big Top let Red have them all in one place. Wall-to-wall clowns. That's how Red wanted it. The dabblers, the journeymen, and the kinds of clowns who weren't always welcome in the local clown alleys. Especially the ones who had bet everything on a pair of big shoes, rubber nose, and painted smile. Clowns who were still waiting for the dice to stop rolling.

It helped that clowns, the regulars, had turned the place into their own kind of union hall. The kind of place to wait for work, keep spirits up when times were bad, and share the booty when times got better.

It cut down on the more genteel trade. But that was fine with Red, as long as the knuckleheads who filled up his place paid their bar tabs with negotiable currency, not with buttons, lick-and-stick tattoos, or used kazoos.

It was the kind of crowd that turned the Big Top into a slummer's paradise and a rite of passage for freshman drinkers. First timers needed guts and a sense of humor. If they could be a good-natured stooge and smile through their first time, the regulars took up a collection to buy their new patsy a second drink. They'd never be a stranger after that.

Back before the Baggy Pants Slasher, calls came in at all hours from people looking for clowns. Never all that particular, callers trusted Red to steer them right.

Like the call late last week. When the phone rang behind Red everyone in the place looked up.

"Big Top," answered Red. "Yeah. We got clowns."

That set off the riot of cavorting, ball-walking, hand-standing, club-juggling, and unicycling.

Red ignored them, wedging the phone between his ear and shoulder so he could write on the notepad by the register.

"Yeah. Yeah. Got it." Red hung up the phone and tore off the page.

Starchy, a whiteface in a pointed hat and flowing bow-tie, launched himself along the bar, sliding past Red, snatching the note. He sat up, cross-legged, and read.

"Midnight bachelorette party!"

Red grabbed back his note, only to lose it to Wiggins, a bald, character clown who waved the note over his head.

"You know what that means!" shouted Wiggins, putting a hand to his ear, waiting.

"Baby lotion Twister!" they shouted back, lunging as one, elbowing each other to grab at the note.

Red plucked the note from Wiggins and fought off the crowding clowns with the soda gun, hosing them down with its needle-hard spray, the gas cranked up for just such emergencies.

"C'mon, Red," whined Wiggins, flinging water from his face and wringing out his pizza-paddle tie.

"You already got one." Red looked across the room and shouted, "Franklin!"

Franklin sat against the wall, his big shoes propped up on the table. The shoes parted so he could look between them at Red. Franklin went back to batting at the inflated rubber glove dangling from his nostril by an air-filled finger.

Red came over and put the note in Franklin's hand. Franklin studied it as all the other clowns watched.

"Trade ya." Blinkers, another character clown, rested his chin on the table, peeking from between Franklin's heels.

"What've you got?"

"Senior Day at the shoe store out at the mall. Nothing but grandmas and grandkids. Guaranteed." Blinkers wiggled his eyebrows.

Franklin didn't hesitate. He leaned forward and handed over the note. Blinkers shot out the door, leaving a swirl of bar napkins, swizzle sticks, and pretzel pieces fluttering in the draft.

Nothing left for everyone else but get back to their drinks.

"Franklin." Red shook his head and sighed the deep, fatherly sigh he used on the whole collection of miscreants.

Franklin looked up at Red, the glove still dangling. "What?"

"You'd rather surround yourself with a bunch a women more'n twice your age, stuffed into their support hose?"

Franklin gave Red a shrug, still tapping the inflated glove dangling from his nostril. "Doesn't matter. My age. Twice my age. Aged in a cave with the rest of the cheese. As long as I'm wearing this face, I'm just another clown to the whole bunch of them."

That stopped conversation and drew every eye in the place.

Red's frown deepened.

"You know what I mean," said Franklin, facing the rest of the clowns, aggravated by the combined ignorance in the room. "You all know what I mean."

Which earned him a shower of peanuts.

"Come on! When it comes to clowns, there's only two kinds of women. Bozophobes and bozophiles. I'm nothing but one more painted face to them." Franklin stretched to see over Red's shoulder, eyeballing the rest of the clowns. "That goes for every one of you."

Which earned him another shower of peanuts.

"You won't meet either kind sitting around here with your finger up your nose." Red pointed at the rubberized intrusion fixed up Franklin's schnozz.

Franklin tugged on the inflated finger. It came free with a pop. "Not technically *my* finger."

"I don't say this often, but I'm making an exception in your case. Get out from behind that face. Take it off once in a while. Walk around. Be a civilian."

"If a real woman really wants to reach the really real me," said Franklin, pointing to his face, "she can prove it by going through this." He stretched his mouth and eyebrows, giving them a classic clown face. In case they missed the point.

"It might help if you stopped treating women like they're jokes."

"Hey! When they stop treating me like a clown."

Which earned him yet another shower of peanuts.

"You might've found the one, special Mrs. Franklin Slapshoes MacGillicuddy right there under your nose. Instead, Blinkers'll get what you could've had all to yourself."

Franklin stuck the finger of the ballooned glove back up his nose and gave it a *thonky* whack, bouncing it off his forehead.

◆ ◆ ◆

Blinkers turned up early at the Hudson Hotel, anxious to get started on what any clown could reasonably expect to be a nighttime romp with a collection of college-aged inebriates in bikinis. Instead, he found a construction site. No cars in the parking lot, no lights on over the pool, and a hurricane fence with the padlock on the gate dangling open, its shank cut.

A *ka-chugging* rattle started up.

"Hey, hey, hey!" Blinkers held up his bottle of baby lotion. "Who's ready for a little Twister?"

A work light snapped on.

Blinkers squinted against the sudden glare. He walked toward the sound of the rattling slush on the other side of the broken ground laid out with a wire mesh grid and rebar, edged with a border of two-by-fours.

The sound came from under a dirty canvas tarp.

Blinkers lifted the tarp. Underneath, a large, portable cement mixer turned, the soggy sound of cement churning in its spinning barrel.

A cat's curiosity is nothing compared to that of a clown. Blinkers had to stick his head inside the barrel for a quick look-see.

Gloved hands reached out of the dark and shoved Blinkers all the way into the rotating mixer, leaving him to gurgle and spin, his legs kicking. The gloved hands pushed with a rake to fold the rest of Blinkers into the mixer barrel going around and around and around.

When Blinkers quit gurgling, his legs limp, the gloved hands hauled on the lever, tilted the spinning barrel, pouring Blinkers and the wet cement into the mesh grid. Using a long-handled float, the gloved hands smoothed the cement around Blinkers, leaving nothing but his round rubber nose and the big, bulbous tips of his shoes showing. A gloved finger drew a dead clown face around the nose, marking an X for each eye.

The mixer stopped and the lights went out.

◆ ◆ ◆

"That's your name? MacGillicuddy? For real?" Gladys asked Franklin.

"Nah. Red calls you that if he's got a point to make and can't remember your real name. Am I right?"

"Real names are over-rated," Red shrugged. "Extra baggage for a clown, you ask me."

"So. Your girl—" Gladys started.

"His ex-girl." Red swiped at an imaginary wet spot, looking ready for some real conversation.

"—ex-girl is the Baggy Pants Slasher. And you're sitting here wearing a clown suit?" Gladys gathered up her purse, phone, and drink, shifting over next to Franklin.

"I think I see your problem." Gladys turned back to Red. "Hey, Red, top me off. And go easy on the stupid sauce in this next one. The clown here's starting to make sense."

Gladys hiked herself up onto the stool, tipping slightly to land her backside squarely, scooching to settle herself.

Close up, Franklin could see through the caked foundation of her makeup that Gladys was older. Her hair a shocked mop, wild and silver, could be a wig. Her face and figure already starting to round out. Franklin recognized her.

"You're the clown junkie from the shoe store."

"That was you? Small world." Gladys patted Franklin's arm. "Relax. The way you look right now ain't stirring up the crazy-juice for me." She pointed to the pack of cigarettes in front of Franklin. "Anyone ever tell you those things'll kill you?"

"Many, many, many times."

"Then you won't miss one."

Franklin tapped out a cigarette for her and flicked her a light. She drew delicately, streaming smoke from her nostrils. She studied the cigarette and glanced up at Franklin.

"You know, if God did away with men and cigarettes, the world wouldn't be half bad. Present company excepted, of course."

"Throw in women, and that'd take care of the other half," said Franklin. "Present company excepted. Of course."

"Let me guess. Your clown name's Happy. Lucky? Jolly Jack?" Gladys pulled the small bowl of goldfish closer and tossed a cracker into her mouth.

"Just Franklin," he said, taking another drag.

"Lousy name for a clown."

"Goes with being a lousy clown."

They smoked in silence for a moment.

"So. Where do you think you went wrong? With—Lucy, was it?"

"Good question. Where do I think I went wrong." He took another drag. "Where do I think I went wrong. How much time you got?"

"Let's hear it. You know what misery loves."

"Company," offered Red.

"Bigger losers!" Gladys laughed and slapped the bar top again.

"Plain and simple? Had to be fifth grade. With Jeannie Krebbs. Cute blonde one desk over from mine."

"Whoa! Fifth grade? If we're going back that far, we'll need more goldfish." Gladys pushed the bowl back toward Red.

Red obliged her, re-filling the bowl.

"I reached the crossroads early," said Franklin.

"Crossroads?"

"You know. Where Puberty Street joins Sexual Inadequacy Road, becomes the Insecurity Expressway, bypasses Dignityville, heads straight into Self-Disgust City. Aren't any street signs to warn you when you're coming up on it, but you can't miss it."

chapter two

LIKE SO MANY OTHER MEMORIES stuffed into Franklin's noodle, what he remembered happening might not be factual. What he remembered feeling was clear as yesterday. Brood on anything long enough and it wears ruts in the soul, feeding the excuses and the certainties that overtake reality.

Fifth Grade.

Franklin sat in class, beaming adoration at Jeannie Krebbs sitting one row over and one desk back, basking in her ignorance of his worship. She and her best friend Amanda Dunston were far more concerned about sneaking whispers across to each other. Everyone else watched the clock, school almost done for the day.

Miss Minchin had finished plowing the aisles, handing back marked-up homework pages. She sat at her desk in the rear of the classroom.

Franklin flicked a glance to either side, then opened his notebook and flipped to the back. He worked on the sketch he'd started, idling away the last few minutes of the day.

He inked in a fleet of airplanes bombing a two-story house with red, kissy lips. He'd marked with a bulls-eye the street number on the door of the house.

Franklin busied himself drawing a face in the upstairs window of the house. Getting the hair just right, he didn't hear Miss Minchin come up behind him.

Her puffy hand snatched up the notebook from under his pen. She wedged the notebook in the crook of her arm and did a slow sashay toward the front of the class. She studied the drawing, *hm-hm-hmming* as she went.

She stopped at the front of the row and cocked her head first one way then another way, studying the sketch.

"Mm-mm-mm," she hummed behind clenched lips, shaking her head. She looked out over the class. "There sure are a lot of drippy wet kisses here, aren't there, Franklin." Miss Minchin smiled. Less a smile and more of a restrained grimace as she struggled to keep herself from gnawing off his head. "Who's the lucky girl?"

Franklin wasn't seeing Miss Minchin. The heat radiating off his burning red cheeks distorted his view. Miss Minchin now looked like a chubby cheese sculpture in a shimmering pool of water.

Miss Minchin scanned the classroom, her eye lighting on each of the girls in turn.

Franklin's guts tightened, sending an urgent electrochemical memo up his spine to signal for a toilet break. Miss Minchin, portly seer into the souls of little boys, all sweet reason and scorn, was about to pull back the curtain on Franklin's secret crush. In that same moment, she managed to heave open a window inside of Franklin, letting him see himself as everyone else saw him.

Standing outside of himself, he watches his transformation into Clown Boy. His hair, face, and eyes blooms into the primary colors of a circus clown in front of the other kids, in front of Jeannie Krebbs.

Miss Minchin sashayed back down the aisle and stopped next to Franklin.

Miss Minchin leaned down, folding herself in half to reach his eye level.

"You want to tell us, Franklin? Or should we figure it out for ourselves?"

Still hunched over, Miss Minchin twisted to scan the classroom again. The girls winced as Miss Minchin's sizzling gaze landed and lingered on each of them.

Franklin was sure none of the girls in the room knew he existed before this moment. But every one of them sat up, primed for a communal barf at the thought of his nerdy clown lips invading their personal air space.

Miss Minchin stared down at his drawing and placed her finger under the number he'd written on the house. She squinted, tapping and thinking.

A smile of enormous satisfaction brightened her face. She straightened up.

"Class? Do we objectify our neighbor?" Miss Minchin continues to stare down at Franklin.

"No, Miss Minchin," the class sing-songs back, well-drilled.

Franklin, wearing the false nose, scarum wig, and painted face of Clown Boy, class buffoon, ratchets down in his seat, his big red nose resting on the desk.

"Class? Do we act out our sexual fantasies on our neighbor?" Miss Minchin sprouts, shedding her kindly teacher husk and grows, towering over Franklin.

"No, Miss Minchin," the class sing-songs back.

Franklin ratchets down to the white arches of his fake eyebrows just above his desk.

"Class? Do we use puberty as an excuse to ogle our neighbor?" Miss Minchin, now enormous and hulking, cracks the acoustical tiles of the ceiling overhead, debris raining down.

"No, Miss Minchin," the class sing-songs back.

Franklin ratchets down to his white pate with its bright blue fringe.

"Do you think," Miss Minchin, her voice becoming an electro-baritone, her face entirely crimson, swoops down on Franklin, "Miss Krebbs will appreciate having her house bombed with all those nasty, germ-ridden kisses of yours? Hmmm? Do you?"

"Oooh, iiiiiiick!" the class shouts.

Jeannie throws herself sideways, pretending a violent upchuck in the aisle.

The class explodes with laughter. Tucker Finn hops up to give Jeannie emergency blasts of cootie repellent, everyone else joining in, with *wooshing* squirts from their imaginary aerosols.

The bell rings. Franklin slides out of his chair. He crawls for the door, passing under a cascade of spitwads, crumpled up paper balls, and rubber erasers.

It's not exactly the way it happened. It *is* how the whole experience wedged itself into Franklin's braincells. Facts don't matter when emotion gets to write the history.

Like the way Franklin remembered his walk home from school the same day, passing right by Jeannie and her posse before he'd realized she was there. The girls clutched their notebooks close, protecting their new bosoms from Clown Boy.

Jeannie's disgust curdled Franklin's hormones, his ardent desire being no match for his budding insecurity. Franklin kept on walking, his eyes on the ground, watching the tops of his clown shoes, not trusting his oversized feet to find solid ground beneath him.

Until he reached a pair of sneakers blocking his path. He looked up, finding himself inside a ring of playground thugs.

The biggest kid stood directly in front of Franklin, his crossed forearms at Franklin's nose level. He could read where Jeannie Krebbs had inked her name across the big kid's ulna in her recognizable flourishing, girlish script. Franklin had at one time thought it important enough to memorize her handwriting in case she slipped him an unsigned note. Instead, she'd turned it into a faded schoolyard tattoo on the big kid's arm.

"Hey! Pucker face! You think you can kiss my girl?" The big kid pushed his fingertips into Franklin's chest.

Franklin looked over toward the circle of girls and fixed his eye on Jeannie. By a nod, a word, a gesture, she could prevent the mauling about to land on him.

Franklin stared at Jeannie, willing her to make eye contact with him.

Wasn't helpless, unrequited love worth some small, altruistic gesture in return from her? Like calling off her dog-boy? Blow a whistle? Rattle a supper dish? Take him to the vet? Something? Anything?

Or she could twist her face up and make gagging sounds, squinting her eyes at the sight of his face. Like she was doing now.

Franklin couldn't see any way this would turn out well for him. His choices seemed limited to crying 'uncle,' eating grass, or explaining to his mom how he managed to lose teeth in a completely random, freak-of-nature, totally unavoidable act-of-God kind of accident.

The odds were impossible, any outcome in Franklin's favor extremely doubtful. Wouldn't the hero, the *true* hero, show his defiance with some devastating joke in the face of all this danger?

Franklin braced himself. "Your girl?" he asked. "I didn't see the leash!"

The big kid twisted his head, eyeballing Franklin.

"You saying my girl's a dog?" The big kid shoved Franklin. "Pucker face."

Behind him, Jeannie's mouth dropped open, the shock rising all the way up from her toes, causing her to *relevé* to the tippy-top of her indignation.

"If the flea collar fits." Franklin shrugged, giving the big kid a sad smile of sympathy.

Franklin's eyes tracked upward watching the arc of the big kid's fist hauled back, cocked. Franklin screwed his face closed.

The resounding smack rocks him backward, dislodging his red rubber nose as it snaps to catch up to his face, his blue wig tumbling skyward. Jeannie and her posse flinched at the crunching impact.

All right, wounded memory sketched in the wig and nose, but it felt better thinking how bad his classmates surely must feel, seeing the big kid slug a harmless clown half his size.

The look on Jeannie's face wasn't remorse. No, more like glee. The look of smug satisfaction that comes over a girl when her dullard of a boyfriend avenges the besmirching of her honor.

Laid out, Franklin watches as the imaginary blue wig tumbles back to earth, landing on his face.

Franklin squeaked out a loud, defiant laugh for them to chew on as they walked away. Amazingly defiant. If it hadn't been swallowed up by their own loud, derisive laughter.

◆ ◆ ◆

Franklin stirred the bare ice with his gloved finger.

"Sarcasm is the match you light to dispel the flatulence of hope." Franklin licked the wet from his fingertip, took up the glass and sucked down the last drops. "Pretty much a straight line from there to the special hell called adolescence." Franklin caught Red's eye and pointed into the empty glass.

"You're still blaming some grade school bully for your girl problems? Way past time to let it go."

"Hard to do in this particular case. He was my brother. Is my brother. Still. Despite repeated efforts to disown him. He had a growth spurt in third grade that lasted through college. Although to be fair, his intellect never did catch up to his size. I got all the brains in the family. There's that going for me."

"Your brother?"

"Buster. Turned out Jeannie had a special fondness for goons. Not just any goons, mind you. Good-looking, self-confident, well-muscled, older goons," said Franklin. "Buster shows up a lot in this story. And not in a good way."

chapter three

OKAY, THERE WAS A CHANCE—the slimmest chance—Franklin gave Buster too much credit for all the relationship trouble dogging him where women were concerned. He said as much to Gladys.

"But," said Franklin, "and it's a big but—it sure feels like the common variable in every one of my—" he stopped, "—whatchacallems. Not relationships, since they never get that far." Franklin thought a moment. "Romantic misfires," he said, satisfied. "The common variable in every one of my romantic misfires is Buster. Just think about it a minute. Why's a guy with so much going for him, hang around me, being a clown? Can you unravel that for me?"

"Can't help you," said Gladys, "I don't know this Buster fella."

"Then let me introduce you." Franklin held up his hand, a pair of eyes and lips already inked onto his glove, a fist puppet he liked to keep handy. "Hey, beautiful," said Franklin in his squeaky clown-voice. "You must not come here very often if you're sitting next to Frankie-boy. He's kind of a saggy-pants when it comes to women. I stay close to pick up the pieces for him. Get it? Pick up the pieces? *Wah-wah-wah*," laughed the fist puppet.

Gladys gave Franklin a one-eyed squint. "No offense, but this Buster guy of yours may have a point."

"I'm out of practice talking to women. Every time I try, Buster turns up right in the middle of it."

"Now it's *you* trying to pick *me* up?"

"If I am, he'll magically appear. Poof. Puff of smoke and there he'll be. It's like he's got radar." Franklin looked around the bar. "I must not be trying to pick you up. No Buster."

"All right. Remind me to be flattered if you should ever try for real. Never had two clowns at once, trying to buy me drinks."

Franklin took a drag on his cigarette. "Or, it could be his search is over. The grip he had on Lucy when I left them there alone, would have thrilled a boa constrictor."

"Wait. You left your brother alone with some stranger you think's a clown killer?"

"Killer of clowns," Franklin corrected her again.

"Anything happens, you'd be an accomplice. Wouldn't you? You don't feel just the least little bit guilty about it?"

"Like you said, you don't know Buster."

♦ ♦ ♦

Early on, Franklin knew that Buster hung around for the girls, not the clowning.

"Piece of cake," said Buster when he told Franklin he wanted to give it a try.

Franklin was glad to have Buster clowning along with him. It got laughs. Buster being the bully and blowhard whiteface character was a natural fit for him. Not that Buster thought of himself as a bully and blowhard. He thought of himself as a laugh riot. That made it funny. A joke on Buster he'd never get. Franklin liked how that worked.

When it came to girls? Not so much.

"We played a lot of years with Buster bouncing me off walls or stuffing me in bags, boxes, and barrels. He loved those gags best. And going around bare-chested," Franklin said to Gladys. "Buster always managed to remove his shirt when there were girls in the audience. Showing off because he could. Like Hercules in clown-face."

"Must've picked up a lot of women that way. I mean, if he's as good looking as you say."

"Nah. You can put a jerk in a clown suit, but you can't take the jerk out of the clown suit." Franklin pondered what he'd just said. "Not sure that came out right. It always seems to make sense when I think it."

"I get the picture."

Buster favored any function where women gathered in large, unsupervised numbers. Buster said it made for better odds they would both score. But having Buster in the game usually meant neither of them put any points on the board.

Like the sorority party where the sisters managed to lock the housemother in the basement for a long weekend.

Doing the bare-chested clowns was Buster's idea. Franklin and Buster made themselves up as a couple of failed male strippers in large, black plastic pompadours. Buster got to show off, being the buffed and browned body in clown-face and a tiny black bowtie. Tight, spandex clown pants let him parade his hard glutes. Franklin, a skinny whippet with rainbow suspenders to hold up super-sized pants, made for a natural stooge.

Buster floated through the crush of sisters, mugging for their pictures and squeezing their butt cheeks.

Across the room, Franklin twisted balloons into poodles.

"Drinks on the clown!" called out a tall, brunette sister, dashing a half-cup full of beer at Franklin.

The other girls showered him with anything and everything liquid near at hand. One spikey-haired blonde struggled to her feet, barking back at her sisters, calling for a cease fire. She smiled at Franklin and held out her cup to him.

"Drink's on *me*." She winked at him.

Franklin smiled back, "Thanks. You know, I have a drinking problem. Since I was a kid." He took the cup and put it under his nose. He tipped it up, stretching his nostrils. The beer trickled down his cheeks, a liquid Fu Manchu. He stopped. "I thought about quitting, but I need the laughs."

The spikey-haired blonde laughed and ran her thumb down Franklin's flimsy physique.

"Do it again! Do it again!" the rest of them bayed.

Spikey put up a finger. "I'll be back," she said and went to the make-shift bar across the room. She picked up two plastic cups of vodka, filled to the brim. She started back through the jostling crowd, holding the cups out in front of her.

"Of course," Franklin said to Gladys, "Buster had his ways of cutting me out of the competition. Like telling women I had a gruesome medical condition. He used that one a lot."

Buster popped into Spikey's view, weaving like he'd barely avoided a drenching from her.

"Whoa! Pull over there, missy," said Buster.

Spikey bent and twisted herself, regaining her equilibrium and steadying the drinks.

"You're doing two drinks in a one-drink zone. Let me have those before you hurt yourself." Buster reached for the cups.

"It's for the other clown." Spikey pulled the cups out of Buster's reach.

"*I'm* the other clown."

"For the nice one."

"We're twins. Our own mother can't tell us apart."

"One of you's been putting his hand down everyone's shorts," she said, then flinched. "Those hands."

"Public service. Checking for wedgies. Some people never recover from the trauma. Ask any psych major. You a psych major?"

"No. And no wedgies." She swung her rear end out of his reach. "Up. Up where I can see them."

Buster flashed his hands. She smiled an 'I-thought-so' at Buster, moving past him.

"That's not alcoholic, is it?" he called after her. "Might aggravate his condition."

She stopped. "What condition?"

Buster grimaced. "It's creepy talking about another guy's body parts."

"Okay." She turned back to elbowing her way through the crowd.

Buster slipped around in front of her. "But since you asked, it rhymes with Venus. Not very interesting unless you're a med student. You a med student?"

Spikey stepped around him. "No."

Buster dodged around in front of her again. "But the Hippocratic Oath requires every citizen over eighteen to report unsafe medical conditions. I could be arrested if I didn't at least mention it."

Spikey dodged left then right then left again, Buster side-stepping, apologizing even as he made himself as much of an obstruction as possible.

"I can't seem to get out of your way," said Buster, laughing. "That's got to mean something, cosmically speaking, right? How about you and me sitting this one out. Too fast for me. You're a dancer, right? I mean, you move like a dancer."

Spikey sighed. "Okay. What condition?"

"Only if you really want to know." Buster rolled his eyes, took a deep breath, and smiled a sad, hard smile at her.

Across the room, Franklin worked to shake off his beer bath. He waggled his foot to drain the beer running down into his pant legs. Through the crowd, Franklin saw Spikey and Buster together. It looked to Franklin like Buster was showing her how to make a martini, demonstrating the best way to get the last olive out of a very skinny jar. Buster waved his hands and screwed his face into a look of utter agony.

"Never fails," Franklin said to Gladys. "Whatever Buster told them, it left women wondering why I wasn't in a hospital somewhere, in isolation, or intensive care, or preserved in a jar of formaldehyde."

Franklin would find out about it when he called to ask the girl out. One or two tried to be kind, understanding. Like the Catholic girl who said she'd lit a candle for Franklin. But she couldn't possibly go out with him because of his—*you know.* She hoped he understood.

From across the room, Franklin could see Spikey's face melt into disbelief. Buster started bouncing and spinning, pitched ice down his pants, and did a tongue-lolling dog-pant of relief. Staring at him, Spikey knocked back the drink in her right hand.

No, Buster wasn't showing Spikey how to make an exquisitely dry martini. That was clear enough.

"That's when you call the paramedics," said Buster. "Happens every time. How about you and me go somewhere and get you out of my wet things."

"Unh-unh." Spikey slugged down the drink in her left hand. "Something like that's got to be genetic."

"Don't worry. He's adopted."

"You said you were twins."

"That's why mom adopted him. We look so much alike."

Weaving, Spikey stared at the empty cups still held out, steadied, in her hands. "I need into some place up which I can chuck. I'm schwoozy."

"You're an English major." Buster took the empty cups from her. "I knew I'd guess it."

Buster held out the cups to a passing sister. "Here. Take these for me, would you? Sister fidelis!" The passing sister curled her lip and kept moving.

Buster shrugged, dropped the cups, and grabbed Spikey by the elbow.

Franklin worked his way through the crowd, looking for Spikey. Seeing no sign of her or Buster, Franklin put two and two together and came up with a five-star rat named Buster. Again.

Franklin moved through the house, listening at doors until he reached a closet just off the kitchen. From behind the door came the distinct sound of a woman straining to vomit. Which meant Buster had to be nearby.

Franklin eased the door open. Buster had Spikey bent over, head down in the slop sink of the janitor's closet. She braced herself, one hand gripping the faucet, the other gripping the edge of the sink. Buster, helping her puke, worked her like a used-up tube of toothpaste, inching her blouse up to her armpits.

"Could you give us some privacy. She's about to show me her meal plan." Buster turned to see who had come in behind them. "Oh, hey, Frankie-boy."

"What're you doing? We're supposed to be working. Out here."

"Just helping some totally random female properly dispose of her recycled vodka. You know what an environmental hazard that stuff can be."

Buster's eye caught something behind Franklin. He grabbed Franklin by the shoulders, moving him a step to the right.

"Stand there."

Confused, Franklin let Buster shift him. His confusion vanished with the crack of leather on his unsuspecting butt cheek that sent him leaping and spinning.

"Yeeeoooowwwwww!"

Franklin found himself nose to nose with the house mother, looking surprisingly unrestrained. Only a few loose strips of duct tape still dangled from her hair and arms. She held up a black leather riding crop at eye level.

"Hey, we've got some serious regurgitation going on in there," said Buster from over Franklin's shoulder. "Sorry, Frankie-boy. She was on us before I could warn you."

Behind them, Spikey gave out with another bubbling barf.

The house mother caught Franklin another sharp crack on the leg with her wand of pain.

"Yeow! Wha'dja hit me again for?"

"Frankie-boy, you're the one standing between mamma bear and her cub," said Buster. "Don't you ever watch Naked Nature in the Raw? Very educational."

Her eyes glowed a molten red. She raised the crop again, but Franklin ducked under and dived through the crowd gathered around to watch. He collided with Buster, who'd managed to get ahead of Franklin, steam-rollering his way toward the door.

"Gotta go!" shouted Buster, making a path through the crush of girls. His hands still managed to find just the right spots on bosom, glute, and thigh as he went. Amazing accuracy even in retreat.

The sisters made a lane for the house mother, giving her room to catch Franklin on the backside with another stinging whack.

"Ow! Get out of the way, Buster. That smarts!"

"She's way good with that thing, isn't she," Buster shouted back at Franklin.

The sisters cheered, pain being funny, and men in pain being twice as funny.

The front door banged open. Buster leaped from the porch, clearing all the steps at a dead run.

The front door banged open again and Franklin followed, making the same leap. He hit the lawn, tumbling once, bounding back onto his feet, and dashed for their mini-van.

Buster, already behind the wheel, executed a weaving K-turn to get the vehicle pointed toward open road. Franklin danced to line up on the passenger-side door, the window cranked down. Timing his lunge, Franklin dived through the open window. His pants caught on the handle, hanging him up midway inside the van. The door swung open and shut, Franklin flailing, as Buster rocketed into the night.

Franklin pulled himself through, twisting to get upright, flopping into the seat. He chuffed, frustrated, the night whipping by, the air blowing in on him.

"She kind of liked me, you know."

"Who?" asked Buster.

"The girl you had throwing up in the slop sink."

"All those babes, you're fixated on the one puking in the sink? That's so like you. Pick out the only girl in the entire place who is physically incapable of talking to you, then tell yourself you've got a chance with her. Frankie-boy, the last thing on her mind was doing it with some guy in half a clown suit."

"I wasn't talking about sex. Looked like you were doing your best to get her shirt off."

"Hey! I was making sure she didn't get anything on it. Vodka stains are the worst. Boy, try to help and right away you think I'm putting the moves on your girl. Who was not actually your girl. I didn't hear you call dibs."

"I didn't say she was my girl. I said she seemed kind of interested in me. Kind of."

"Come on. A woman goes off to puke after talking to you. That means she's interested? You keep thinking that way, Frankie-boy. Just leaves more for me."

They drove on into the night.

◆ ◆ ◆

"About that time I started wondering how long I'd have to hold Buster's head down in the cotton candy machine to smother him in spun sugar," Franklin said to Gladys, "and could I make it look like an accident."

"Sounds like quite the Casanova."

"You'd think. He should be so lucky. And get out of my way."

◆ ◆ ◆

Working one company picnic, Franklin and Buster battled each other with seltzer bottles, bouquets of exploding flowers, and buckets of confetti. Each round ending with Franklin on the ground and Buster doing a victory lap giving him a chance to preen for the crowd and scan for girls.

Later, packing up, Franklin noticed Buster fixing his patented double eye-lock on a girl in a blue tank top. Buster kept dropping props on the ground, missing the carpetbag, unable to break off his gaze. He watched her as she headed for the parking lot disappearing among the cars.

"Back in a minute." Buster left Franklin to finish packing up.

Franklin started to call after him but spotted a big blonde lingering nearby.

She smiled. Franklin smiled back.

"Take your time," Franklin called after Buster.

The big blonde, probably as shy as Franklin, waited until Buster was gone. She came over to where Franklin stood closing the carpet bag.

"Hi," she said.

"Hi back," he said.

He patted the bags, smoothing the lumps, not sure what to do or say next.

"Hey, you hungry? Bet you work up an appetite getting bounced around like that."

"Always."

"You want to go somewhere?"

"Sure. I have to wait for Buster to bring the van around so I can ditch this stuff first."

"I'll bring us something. Stay right there." She left the picnic area and crossed the street to the burger joint.

Us. Nice sound to it.

Buster stood by the door of the burger joint. When she came out, she had the bag of burgers and drinks in both hands. Buster collided with her, mashing his pecs and abs against her and giving her his usual full-frontal encounter. He held onto her as if steadying her, rubbing her back and forth across himself, helping her keep her balance.

"Whoa! I got you!"

"Oh, jeez, I'm sorry. I wasn't looking." She pulled away.

"No worries." Buster slapped his gut. "Can't hurt these babies. You're in great shape yourself."

She snorted at Buster's come-on. Still, she checked herself in the shop window. "Really? I just started working out."

"No kidding? Where?"

"Just around the corner."

"*Double* no kidding! Me, too."

"I ever see you there?"

"When do you work out?"

"Weekends."

"Well, there you go," said Buster. "Weeknights for me and the old elliptical trainer."

"I should get these to your friend."

"Oh, sure. But, you know, I thought I saw him with someone."

"That was me."

"Sure, sure. Could be I need glasses. You look a lot different up close. See you round? At the gym?"

She didn't say, but she winced a little smile and hurried across the street back to the picnic area.

She'd reached the picnic table at the same moment a big guy came up to the table where Franklin waited. Blue Tank Top Girl followed close behind.

"You a doctor? You a doctor?" Big Guy shouted at Franklin.

"Nah," said Franklin in his squeaky clown voice. "But if you bend over and say 'ah,' I might remember why I quit med school."

"Some guy puts his hand down my wife's blouse, he better be a doctor."

"That's the clown," Blue Tank Top Girl shouted. "Hit him, Curt!"

Big Guy caught Franklin with a quick, hard jab square in the face, rocking Franklin's head backward.

"Hey! That wasn't me!" Franklin honked through his mashed snoot.

"It was one of you perverts," screeched Blue Tank Top Girl.

"You can pass it on for me." The Big Guy straightened his shirt, grabbed Blue Tank Top Girl by the hand, and marched away from the picnic area.

Franklin held his nose between his index fingers, checking for damage. Buster with the roving digits got Franklin socked again. Gotta wear different costumes.

Squinting through the pain, Franklin saw the big blonde standing, watching.

"Gag we're working on. Timing needs work." Franklin straightened his rubber nose, his eyes watering. "Funny, hunh?"

"Funny." The big blonde poured the cold soda down Franklin's pants, followed by the hot fries. Franklin sucked in a mighty wind and let loose with a warbling *woo-woo.* He danced to put as much distance as he could between himself and his own, fry-filled pants.

Franklin waddled to the parking lot. Buster pulled up next to him.

"Where'd you disappear to?" Franklin threw the bags into the back.

"Had to put gas in the old buggy. Somebody didn't fill it up like they're supposed to." Buster arched his eyebrow at Franklin.

"That's your job."

"I didn't say it was you, did I? A little defensive, aren't we?" said Buster. "What happened to you?"

"I'm sure you can guess."

"Hmmm. Punched in the face by a guy saying you put your hand down his wife's blouse, and then had a soda dumped into your happy place."

Franklin flopped back in the seat, pulling his hat over his face.

"Did I get it right?"

"You left out the hot fries."

Buster sucked in hard, a sympathetic wince.

"Of course, you wouldn't know anything about that, would you?"

"Lucky guess. Hey, sorry about the blonde. You two looked like you were hitting it off."

Franklin lifted his hat. "You saw us?"

"Not really your type. She's a workout monster."

"How would you know?"

"Ran into her getting burgers."

Franklin groaned. And so everything was explained.

"I get why you zoomed off after the girl in the blue tank top. I get it. But the blonde? Come on. She's totally unlike the women you're always drooling over."

"Maybe I like playing the field. You think of that?"

"Stop trying to put your balls through my goal posts."

Buster laughed. "You are such a virgin." He gunned the engine and they headed down the road.

♦ ♦ ♦

"You and my brother have a lot in common," Franklin said to Gladys, rolling an ice cube around in his mouth.

"We do?"

"You both are the reason Lucy ended up in my bedroom in the first place."

chapter four

APPROACHING THE EXPRESSWAY, Franklin relied on the down-slope of the on-ramp to give his car enough speed to merge with traffic.

Buster hated Franklin's car, and never missed a chance to let people know. He called it the Car-With-No-Name, of no known make or model, its emblems and markings stripped off for the chrome. Buster told everyone how Franklin stapled it together out of beer cans and pie tins during auto shop class back in high school.

For a while, Franklin denied it. But people could see for themselves. The door handles looked like pull-tabs.

Franklin's car was the perfect car for him—small and beat-up. He'd bought it used, painted it himself, and nursed it back to tolerable automotive health. It ran and that was all Franklin could expect for the money he'd spent.

With gentle chest bumps against the steering wheel, Franklin managed to reach the minimum legal speed limit. If he could keep it up, he wouldn't have to put on his flashers declaring his vehicle a moving obstruction. He eased the car left, avoiding a delivery van bearing down on him.

Franklin mugged and smiled at the other drivers. Already dressed in his clown get-up, Franklin tried doing his hapless clown shtick. Sometimes it won him a little sympathy on a highway full of cars and trucks crowding and whizzing around him.

Not working today, that's for sure. Bunch of cutthroats out here. No time for a clown behind the wheel this morning.

Franklin's head swiveled as he watched for traffic coming up behind him as his lane came to an end up ahead. He saw that he was bearing down on a stalled vehicle parked on the shoulder, its hood raised. Puttering along well below highway speed, he could easily make out the figure of a woman in vehicular distress.

She leaned against the car, shaking what looked to be her cell phone. The old jar-a-little-juice-loose-for-one-last-call trick. Franklin often used that one himself.

He took his foot off the accelerator. The car immediately slowed, its metal mass useless in maintaining any meaningful forward momentum. He steered onto the shoulder, the gravel crunching.

"Don't let her be cute, don't let her be cute, don't let her be cute." Franklin kept his eyes fixed on the rear-view mirror, watching her. Coming to a stop, he shifted into reverse and backed up.

The sound of tires on gravel and the whine of the gears made the woman turn. She smiled, gave a wiggle of relief and spread her hands wide.

His car rolled to a stop. Franklin squeezed his face tight. "She's cute." He bunged his head against the steering wheel. Too late to drive off. That would make him a prize-winning clunk.

Franklin shifted the gear into park and got out. "Need help?" He gave a great big smile right back at her.

The driver's face stretched wide, fright taking over from delight.

No mistaking that look. Still standing next to his car, Franklin gave the woman his best I'm-a-really-safe-clown smile and his jauntiest wave.

Panicked, she started screaming and jumped back into her car. She locked the doors, raised the windows, then flashed her headlights and honked the horn, the clarion call of Doomsday.

Franklin edged closer to her car, feeling the eyes of every passing driver rake across him as they zipped by. He hunched and twisted his body, so she could appreciate how harmless he was.

"It looks like you could use some help." Franklin nodded, smiling, holding his empty hands up so she could see them. "I could look at the engine for you."

She'd flung herself to the other side of the car as far away from him as she could, pressing herself hard against the door.

This was useless. He moved around to the other side. He'd say he was leaving but he would call someone for her.

She flung herself back across the seats. She held out an ice scraper, ready to impale him with it if he managed to get inside her car.

Franklin backed toward his own car, keeping his hands where she could see them.

He'd nearly reached his car when a highway patrol cruiser, its lights flashing, pulled up behind the disabled vehicle.

The trooper, a short female in mirrored sunglasses, bunned hair, and a crisp, flat-brimmed olive drab cover, stepped out of the cruiser.

"Ma'am! Trooper Lady! Officer!" Franklin called out. "Glad you're here. As you can see, this poor, fear-crazed lady is—"

"Stand away from the car, sir," said the trooper.

"It's all right, officer, I'm leaving anyway." Trying to salvage some sliver of dignity, he added, "Always happy to let the professionals do their job." He hoped the trooper could hear him over the fear-crazed lady's shrieking.

"Stay there, sir." She rested her hand on the butt of her service weapon.

"I could see she was stuck so I stopped to help—"

The trooper raised a finger to silence him.

"—then she started—"

She cocked her head.

Franklin's over-active imagination filled in what would happen next. The Trooper Lady raises her sunglasses. Laser beams lance out of her eyes, melting Franklin where he stands, nothing but his shoes left smoking by the side of the road. Fear-Crazed Lady dances a jig around the smoldering ash pile.

Trooper Lady touched her sunglasses and Franklin froze. She adjusted them on her nose. But didn't raise them and eyeball him to death. Franklin deflated, relieved.

Trooper Lady approached the car and leaned down, tapping on the glass so Fear-Crazed Lady could see her.

Fear-Crazed Lady lowered her window a bare crack.

"Make him stop smiling! He's evil!"

Franklin frowned as hard as he could, hoping to neutralize the painted smile glowing, radioactive, on his face.

"I'll radio for help. While I do, get out your license and registration for me." Trooper Lady thumbed the button on the mic hooked at her shoulder. She reported the mile marker number and the disabled car's condition.

"Make him stop looking at me," shrieked Fear-Crazed Lady.

Trooper Lady interrupted herself and looked back at Franklin. "Sir?"

Franklin slapped his arms against his sides, but he turned around.

"He's going to get away if you don't arrest him!"

"Let's get you on your way first. A tow truck's coming."

"So, can I go now?" asked Franklin, his back still to the two women.

"Let's have a look at your license and registration, too, while we wait."

"No good deed—" said Franklin as he got back in his car and pulled the registration from the glove box. He had to reach deep into the pocket of his jumpsuit to pull out his wallet for his driver's license. He handed both to the Trooper Lady.

"Why the get-up?" Trooper Lady scanned his papers.

"I'm a clown." Franklin hoped his skin had the tensile strength to keep the exasperation and sarcasm from tearing through his face.

Trooper Lady squeezed down hard on a snicker.

"I *work* as a clown. It's my job. For which I get paid."

"Won't you disappoint all those kiddies, stopping when you see a woman alone? In a disabled car?"

"No."

"I'm going to run these. In the meantime, you got anything that says you're a clown?"

"They don't issue us a license."

"Maybe they should."

Franklin pointed to his face. "One-of-a-kind make-up?"

"Anyone can paint their face."

"I make balloon animals, juggle, ride a unicycle."

"How about making a few balloon animals?"

"I'll get my stuff." Franklin waggled his keys as he edged past the trooper who gave no ground. He turned the key in the trunk lock and gave a yank on the deck lid.

Nothing.

He yanked again.

Still nothing.

He smiled at Trooper Lady, held the key to his lips and breathed a long, wet breath on it. He polished the key against his chest and re-inserted it. He twisted it back and forth in the lock, jerking at the handle. He stopped, took a deep, deep breath, brought his palms together and closed his eyes, visualizing.

The deck lid *will* pop open, flowers *will* spray everywhere, a beautiful girl *will* rise up—no! No girl! Just the deck lid wide open and a satisfied expression on his face as he presents all the paraphernalia of his profession to the scoffing Trooper Lady.

Franklin placed his hands on the handle and the deck lid with the care of a surgeon and then—*yankedy-yankedy-yankedy-yankedy-yaaaaaaaaaaank*—straining with the pathetic agglomeration of muscles he called a physique, finally collapsing onto the deck lid, his chest heaving air.

"The balloons are in here. Honest." Spent, Franklin rested his forehead on the unforgiving metal of his incredibly disloyal transportation. "Because I can hear them. Laughing at me."

"Juggle a few balls?"

Franklin pointed. "They're in here."

"Ride your unicycle?"

"In here." Franklin still pointed, still forehead-down on the deck lid.

"I see. Anything else that might prove you're a clown?"

How about the way I'm making a complete ass of myself, solely for your benefit? Should be credential enough. Instead, Franklin reared up. "I could do some of my bits for you. Would that help?"

"Maybe. You work kiddie parties?"

He looked inside his car for anything, anything at all he could use. Finding nothing, Franklin straightened up and shrugged. "Everything's in the trunk."

"Of course it is. Turn around and put your hands behind your back."

"Aw, come on. I got a job at the mall."

"With all your stuff in the trunk, which you can't open. Turn around."

"I'd improvise. I'd use the stuff I'd find there. I'm a professional!" he said, doing a jerky gut-dance.

She stopped, her handcuffs dangling. "Okay. Let's see how funny you are."

"The way you're looking at me doesn't make it easy. Kids are usually glad to see me."

Her impenetrable shades sat on top of a serious scowl. She jangled the handcuffs.

"But, okay. Ummm." Franklin's mind went blank.

She jangled the handcuffs again.

"Okayokayokay! Frat parties! Nobody's ever glad to see a clown at frat parties. I can do that. Conventions and frat parties. Here's what I do for the finish. Kills 'em every time. By which I don't mean actually kill. It's a show business metaphor and not a Freudian slip that could be construed as a confession or anything, for which my rights have not been read. Not that I'm acting guilty or anything."

Trooper Lady shifted from one foot to the other, her gaze remained iron-hard behind her shades. If Franklin had to guess.

"Ho-kay." Franklin grabbed the soda cup from the floor of his car, popped off the lid and sloshed the leftover liquid, grateful for the weeks of trash he'd allowed to accumulate.

"I probably shouldn't be here with you guys. Look at all the free booze! I have a drinking problem, you know. Since I was a kid."

Franklin hooked the rim of the cup under his nose, missing his mouth completely, tilted the cup, his tongue lapping at the air as the soda streamed down the sides of his face. He stopped. "I've thought about quitting but I need the laughs. Good night, you've been great. If you're not going to finish your liquor, don't spit in the glass. I'm drinking clean-up." He held out the soda straw. "And then I hold up a giant cocktail sip stick. Big enough to suck up a family of gerbils. If you could picture it." Franklin waved the soda straw.

Trooper Lady gave Franklin a long, cold stare, then snorted, putting a knuckle to her nose, hiding the choked-off laugh.

"'Don't spit in the glass, I'm drinking clean up,'" said Trooper Lady. "I have to use that sometime."

Franklin eased into a smile, relieved.

"Turn around and put your hands behind you."

"What!"

"She's not coming out of the car unless she thinks you're restrained." She snapped the cuffs on Franklin.

"I could get in my car and drive off. I'd be gone like a bullet," said Franklin. "Not over the speed limit. Like a bullet from a very slow gun?"

"And have her think you're waiting down the road to clown-jack her when I'm gone? I want her well on her way before I let you go."

"Forgive my asking, and with all due respect to your-self, your uniform, and the entire personhood of law en-forcement professionals across this great land," said Franklin, "but is that legal?"

"Look at her. You see how scared she is."

What Franklin sees is a caged-up Rottweiler, all teeth and slobber, barking and throwing itself at the glass, ready to bite a bloody chunk out of the clown-faced chew toy.

"It won't kill you to be the hero for a few minutes. Or is that locked in your trunk, too?"

Franklin sighed and let the trooper walk him back to her cruiser, past Fear-Crazed Lady in the car. Of course, now she laughed. Her lips peeled back in a hateful grin, and she jabbed her pointed fingers at him, doing a victory-over-clowns butt dance.

One very happy Rottweiler.

The tow truck rolled past them as Trooper Lady guided Franklin into the back seat of the cruiser.

The minutes ticked off while she wrote up the incident and the tow truck guy hooked up the disabled vehicle.

The tow truck guy tapped on the window of the disa-bled car, telling Fear-Crazed Lady she had to get out so he could lift it. She slunk from the car, keeping the ice scraper aimed at Franklin still locked in the back of the cruiser. She scuttled to the cab of the tow truck, felt around behind her-self for the door handle, her eyes fixed dead on Franklin. Finally getting a good hold, she yanked the door open and jumped into the tow truck cab, locking the doors.

Tow truck guy had to rap on the cab window for her to let him get in.

"Get in, get in, get in!" Fear-Crazed Lady shouted at the tow truck guy, pulling him by his jacket into the cab.

Trooper Lady went around to the side of the tow truck and said something to the two of them. She stepped back and waved them onto the highway, watching as they pulled away.

When the tow truck and car had dwindled from sight, the trooper let Franklin out of the cruiser, helping him from the back seat. She turned him around and unlocked the cuffs.

"That wasn't so hard, was it? Your good deed for the day."

"Thank you, officer." Franklin kept his natural born sarcasm in check. He could still make it to the mall if he avoided aggravating law enforcement any further.

He started to step past her, but she reached out, fingertips rigid, pressed to his chest, stopping him.

She took off her cover, gave a shake of her head as if letting her hair loose which remained hard-bunned at the base of her neck. She looked him up and down, a tiny slip of tongue wetting her lip.

"What?" Franklin's every muscle fiber alert for nerves tuning up to flash the fight, flee, or flatulate signal down his spinal column.

"You know what you could do for me that'd really make my day complete?"

"What?" Franklin's nervous system screeched a U-turn, his libido shoving everything out of the way, rolling up its sleeves. He relaxed enough to let himself see and admire her compact figure and bulky bosom. "Trooper Lady? Uh. Trooper Sunshine?" he read from the nameplate pinned to her chest. "Really? Sunshine?" Franklin stood ready to forgive the universe for his run-in with the long arm, firm breasts, and cute butt of the law. With a name like hers, it had to be a sign, right?

"Tell your brother, Buster, if it had been him sitting there and not you, I'd have let that driver use my taser on him."

She put her cover back on, straightened it, and leaned in close to Franklin. "Have a nice day, citizen."

She got back into the cruiser and drove off, spinning just enough tire to throw gravel over his shoes as he stood there, all alone.

◆ ◆ ◆

"See," Franklin said to Gladys, as he squinted against the smoke of his cigarette. "I told you Buster shows up all the time and not in a good way. Even when Buster's not there? He's there."

◆ ◆ ◆

Franklin pulled into the parking lot at the mall. He got out and slammed the door, angry at Buster and whatever he'd done or not done to Trooper Lady. Sunshine. Trooper Sunshine. He wanted to remember her name so he could rub it in Buster's face.

Franklin went around to the trunk and stood ready to do battle with the deck lid again.

He didn't have to. The deck lid popped open. He sighed, dropping over. He straightened up and took out his flower-print carpetbag of props. He slammed the deck lid and turned to run for the mall. The deck lid squeaked all the way open. Franklin put down his carpetbag and slammed the deck lid down again. And again. And again. And again. And again. It refused to catch. He eased it down, listening for the click of the latch. He leaped up and landed his whole weight, butt first on the deck lid. If force didn't work, maybe surprise would fool the lock into latching. He slid off. It squeaked open.

Franklin shook his head hard, his cheeks warbling in frustration. He grabbed his carpetbag of clown goodies, leaving the deck lid wide open. If someone passing by has a crying need for a bald spare tire, a scissor jack, or a unicycle, take them, he said out loud to the parking lot gods. He dashed for the mall's main entrance.

Franklin bolted through the door of the entryway. He ran, following the balloons and the photocopied clown signs pasted up, pointing shoppers toward the shoe store.

A young brunette in jeans and a lavender Henley shirt reached out, catching Franklin by the sleeve. She had her other hand resting on the head of a small child gripping her leg.

"My son's kind of afraid of clowns," she said, working to lever the child off her leg and out where Franklin could see him. "See, Earnest," she said to the boy, "he's not so scary."

Earnest gripped his mother hard at the knee, his face buried into her thigh, only a part of one eye free to examine the hideous beast in front of him.

"Could you, y'know, show him you're harmless? It'd really help me out. I'm a single mom, and the Funny Farmhouse day care near where I work has all these big wooden clowns in the front yard. He won't go in." She winced a sorry-to-ask smile at Franklin, as much a plea as a question. "Please? It'd help me out. A lot."

From further down the arcade, Franklin could hear the tinny calliope music at the shoe store. In front of him, so much cuteness in one smiling, needy package and him late for his gig.

No time for anything fancy. He dropped his carpetbag, turned around, offered his backside, inviting her to kick him. She gave him a half-serious boot in the pants that sent Franklin soaring through the air, diving into a tumble, and rolling out flat, sprawled on the tile.

Earnest inched his face out and gave a half smile. Franklin gathered himself, planted his hands on either side of his head and did a kick-up back onto his feet. He stumbled forward and into a tubby security lady in a vermillion jacket. Still bent over, he looped her arm around his waist and kicked out as if being squeezed. Then he put both her hands around his neck, faking a stranglehold as he waggled his head, his tongue lolling out, bouncing around, helpless as a rag doll. Then he held her arm up in victory, adding the rasping cheers of a mighty crowd, applauding the security lady's victory, getting the rest of the shoppers to join in.

Earnest, his fingers still in his mouth, gave out with a huffy laugh, a chesty bark of victory over the unsavory creature in clown white his mom had so thoroughly bested for him.

"Thank you," the brunette mouthed at Franklin, her face wreathed in adoration. The pucker of her lips would haunt a pushover like Franklin a good, long time. He fixed her face, curly bobbed hair, and fulsome figure in his mind so he could pick her out of the crowd later. He dashed down the arcade.

"Was that Lucy?" Gladys asked Franklin.

"No, but she shows up later," Franklin said to Gladys.

Franklin reached the store where a crowd of grandmoms and kidlings were already gathered around the entrance, waiting. Franklin slid to a stop, the manager stepping in front of him.

"You're late."

"Stopped to help a lady with her car," said Franklin, huffing. He left out the parts about the screaming, the police, and threat of recreational tasering.

"I'm paying for a clown, not a superhero." The manager waved his hand at Franklin by way of introduction to the crowd.

Franklin stepped past the manager to face the collection of grandmoms frowning at the wait and the kids starting to bounce and dance.

Franklin dropped the carpetbag and wiped his brow with a great big sweep of his hand, grimaced at the handful of sweat. He made to wipe it on a nearby kid who *icked* and *ooohed*, shrinking away. Instead, Franklin wiped his hands on the manager and blew out a breath. He gathered himself, then inhaled so long and hard it bent him backward. His face puffed up as he prepared to blast them with a wide-open hello, which came out in a high squeak. He opened his mouth and sprayed his throat with an atomizer and tried again. "HAAAAA-Lo-ho-HO-ho-HO-ho-HO!" he blasted out until he doubled over, out of breath. He inhaled again, inflating himself back to full size and gave them a frog-mouthed smile of relief.

"Everybody know what day it is?" shouted Franklin.

The kids, drilled by years in rows of classroom seats, all raised their hands. Franklin pointed at the smallest kid in front.

"I don't know?" answered the small kid.

"It's shoesday!" Franklin bounced and flapped, dancing in a circle, stirring up the kids who were more than ready to go crazy.

"Wait, wait, wait!" Franklin leaned over the crowd of kids, sniffing a long, hard pull of air, making an awful face at some stench his nose detected. He wrestled a large bug sprayer out of his carpetbag. He aimed it at their feet and pumped the handle as he blew a string of raspberries fart-fart-farting over their shoes.

"Now we're ready!"

The kids let out with another wave of crazy.

"Great," said the manager. "You're going to turn that mad mob loose on my store?"

"Hey! You're paying for a clown, not a superhero." Franklin gave out with a *hi-yoh-oh* and dived through the crowd, leading the screaming pack into the store.

Franklin acted as traffic cop, aiming kids at the sales clerks. He'd pull a long face when they showed off their high tops and sneakers with the blinking lights. Instead, he whipped out wooden shoes and swim fins, doing a sell job on the grandmoms, sweet-talking them into a test walk around the store.

Franklin pulled out baby booties for big kids, fisherman's waders for little kids, and clown shoes for the grandmoms.

For one girl in a princess tee-shirt, he knelt and presented a glass slipper. She flung her arms around his neck, hugging the air out of him and offered to marry him when she grew up.

Franklin fainted over smelly socks. He counted toes and came up short. He showed kids how to wear the metal foot-sizers as improvised skis for a little carpet skating. He gave kiddie rides on the clerk's fitting stools, pushing them all over the store.

Posing for pictures, Franklin knelt with short kids, sat with large kids, and hid under the chair with shy kids. For the grandmoms, he dusted his butt, ready to plant his bottom in their laps, getting a swat and a shove-off instead.

Until Gladys showed up.

She plopped herself down and pulled Franklin onto her lap. She threw her arms around him and called out to anyone listening, "Take a picture! Take a picture!"

"You just happened to be shoe shopping?" Franklin asked Gladys.

"I saw the signs, followed the balloons, heard the circus music. You clowns do something to me," Gladys said to Franklin.

There in the store, still sitting on her lap, Franklin tensed up. He played the lap gag to be so uninviting he didn't usually get any takers.

Franklin let Gladys hug him, her scratchy cheek to his, giving her the best of his gleeful, wide-eyed surprise.

"I'm not wearing any underwear," she whispered, hot and breathy, into his ear.

His head followed his eyes around to see the person giving his ear the breathy lip-massage. No mistaking that look. They've all got it. Clown junkie!

Back in the dark of the bar, Gladys snorted, embarrassed. "I really was, by the way. Just so you know."

"Was what?"

"Wearing underwear. I like to say I'm not. Sometimes I'll get lucky with one of you clowns."

Sitting on Gladys's lap there in the shoe store, Franklin could feel all eyes in the place fixed on him. It's the worst of the bad dreams in his eclectic collection of performance-related nightmares. The biggie. He's lap dancing in some seedy bar for a bunch of female clown junkies. All he's wearing is a spangled pair of saggy boxers, his clown head, ruff, and the big shoes. Clown junkies all around him whoop and whistle, stuffing dollar bills down his boxers, calling out, "take it off, take it off for momma!" And they don't mean the wig and nose, nosirree. He rips the big red ruff from his neck, spins it around his head, and flings it at the women. Now they're schooling sharks feeding in a frenzy as Franklin climbs the stripper pole to escape. Climbing and sliding, climbing and sliding, teeth snapping below him.

His imagination pixelated back to reality in the shoe store, with Gladys's hands locked around his waist. Franklin planted a great big, smacky kiss on Gladys's cheek, unlocked her hands and stood up. He gave her a gallant patting of the air, urging her to keep her seat. He drew him-self up and—dashed for the door.

A half-second later, every kid in the place dashed after him.

"How'd you get the kids to chase me?" Franklin asked Gladys.

"Offered ten bucks to the one who caught you."

"Ah."

The kids ran through the mall, a boiling herd of highly motivated clowndogs.

"Cost me the gig," Franklin said to Gladys. "And the manager made me pay to get my stuff back. Told me it was his basic storage fee."

"Sorry. I see a clown, I go a little nuts. No hard feelings?"

"None," said Franklin. "When I see a clown junkie, I go a little nuts. No hard feelings?"

"None."

Outside the shoe store, it was hard to miss Franklin's bouncing flounce of blue hair weaving through the shoppers. Gladys shouted directions to the kids in hot pursuit of Franklin and the prize money.

She saw Franklin pivot for the toy store, elbowing his way through the mall walkers and stroller moms.

"Figured it'd be easy to lose them in there," Franklin said to Gladys.

"They were playing for ten whole dollars," Gladys said to Franklin.

Gladys headed out of the mall, circled around, planted herself in front of the street-side exit to the toy store. She stood, arms wide, ready to corral Franklin as he came through.

The door whisked open, letting a straggle of kids through to the outside. But no Franklin.

She cupped her hands and put her face to the window, trying to see through the displays back into the store. She charged off through the store, leading the kids along.

"I was impressed," Gladys said to Franklin. "Not many clowns can outrun a pack of kids. They make the best bloodhounds. How'd you give them the slip?"

In the display window, a hand-standing clown folded over, back down onto his feet. He took the sand bucket off his head. It was Franklin.

"Trade secret," Franklin said to Gladys. "You never know when a trick like that'll come in handy again."

Gladys studied him through the cigarette haze, gave him a one-shoulder shrug. She said, "Anyway, you were saying how me and Buster were responsible for you meeting the clown killer."

"Killer of clowns."

chapter five

FRANKLIN STAYED BENT OVER in a hard stoop, waddling between the cars in the parking lot. Every few yards he dropped to a knee, peeking over the hoods of the cars, watching for Gladys.

Back outside, Gladys roamed along the walkways girdling the mall. She shaded her eyes against the sunny sky and scanned the vast parking lot for tell-tale flashes of goofy blues or outrageous reds. Anything that might give away Franklin's hiding place.

As Franklin watched, Gladys tensed up, her eyes locked on something. She could not have spotted him from that far away. Could she? From all the way across the parking lot? Gladys sprinted off the walkway, into traffic, into the path of an oncoming SUV.

What Franklin sees is gruesome and emotionally satisfying. Gladys bounces up over the hood of the SUV, shatters the windshield, passes through the vehicle, and bursts out the back glass. She slides down the tailgate, her skin squeaking along the metal as she oozes to the ground, landing with a plop. People converge on her, telling her to lie still. Insufferable Good Samaritans render first aid to her, wind her up in bandages, strap her into a neck brace, buckle her onto a back board. They cart her off to a hospital where she'll receive the very best of care and live to a ripe old age.

Of course, that's not what happened, and Franklin felt bad for feeling good about seeing it that way. Honest. He did. Even though Gladys kept on coming, having taken only a moment to eyeball the driver to a screeching halt. She slapped the hood of the SUV with both hands to punctuate her point.

Still stooped over, Franklin scuttled away.

His knees ached from duck-walking for what felt like a hundred eighty-two miles around the parking lot. What in hell good's a place this size? Franklin had to stop. He flattened himself out on the asphalt, worming himself under a van, watching through the tires for any legs that might be in hot pursuit.

Seeing nothing, Franklin squirmed back out from under the van, coming nose to toes with a pair of big black brogans. He rolled his head up, squinting into the bright sky overhead. A security guard stood over him.

Franklin tapped the tire while keeping his eyes fixed on the guard. Franklin put his ear to the tire, listening. He got to his feet and pulled out his invisible tire pump, inflating the suspect rubber donut with a dozen or so hefty mouth squirts for sound effects. Franklin tapped it again, satisfied he'd saved the day, giving the guard a thumbs-up. The guard shook his head and kept on moving.

Franklin eased himself upright and scanned the parking lot. Seeing nothing of the shock-haired clown junkie, Franklin blew out a deep breath of relief and shivered at the close call.

Franklin took the long way around the mall, walking back to his car.

He hated cutting the gig short. But once a clown junkie hijacks the crowd, a working clown is little more than an inflated punching bag.

The sun baked the asphalt. The heat had him streaming sweat from under his wig. He moved along the perimeter of the parking lots, keeping the acres of vehicles between himself and Gladys in case she was still on the hunt.

He reached his car, the trunk still wide open. Franklin took hold of the deck lid and eased it down until he heard the latch snap. He held the deck lid down for a moment, stroking it.

"Good boy." Franklin lifted his hands. Relieved, he moved around to the driver's side. He fished his keys out of his pocket and bent down to sight in on the keyhole.

From no more than a half-dozen cars away Franklin heard a woman's voice calling out, "Hey! Hey, clown!"

Please let there be two identical clowns in the same parking lot. And neither one of them me.

Franklin stayed hunched over. But the huffing and scraping of shopping bags on car metal closed in on him. No such luck. Franklin, out of breath and out of energy, didn't have the gas to run anymore.

Still hunched over, hand on the key in the lock, Franklin peeked under his arm. Not the shock-haired clown junkie from the shoe store. The opposite of the clown junkie. A fetching shopper in cork-heeled wedgies, spandex pants, and a flowered shirt belted at the waist. Her shopping bags outsized her, loading her down.

"You're the clown from the mall!" she said, a great relief in her voice.

"You're the big-spender from K-Mart!" Franklin said back.

"They towed my car. Can you believe it? I was inside a minute, tops, and they towed me." The cute shopper shook her head, eyes fixed on Franklin, her shoulders drooped, inviting him to share in her disbelief. "Could you give me a lift?"

Franklin interlaced his fingers, stretching and flexing his hands, squatting down, making a stirrup for her. "When I say *allez oop*, you *oop*."

"Oh. Oh, ha, ha. Right. *Allez oop*. Ha. No, could you give me a *ride*?" she asked, adding, "In your car."

Franklin put a hand to his ear, listening at the window. A high squeaky voice seemed to come from behind the glass, "Let us out, let us out!" Franklin straightened up. "Sorry. They took a vote. No more room. You know how it is with these clown cars. Stuffed to the door handles."

"I got lost at the circus once and a clown rescued me. You're like—superheroes to me." She gave Franklin the most winsome, pathetic, needy smile he'd ever seen on the face of any woman of any age anywhere. How could he refuse when she goes to all that trouble, just for him? She added just the barest apologetic squeeze of cleavage and a peek of silver lace brassiere, in case he'd missed it.

Where were his ancestors in the dim dawn days of humankind when women were learning life hacks like this to get around his defenses? Was it too much to ask for a little something extra in his DNA? Something to call on for protection against all that winsome appeal standing in front of him?

Why couldn't he take charge of his mouth? Why couldn't he be the bad boy for once? Why couldn't he say 'no' and make it stick?

Go on. Try it. His brain sends the word to his mouth even as his lips, cheeks, and tongue conspire to resist. He forces it out. The 'no' leaves his mouth in a long slow-motion wave of sound.

A radiant shield materializes around her, deflecting the waves back at Franklin to pound his head like a boxer's speed bag.

That's why.

Franklin grips his head to stop the vibration and regain his hold on reality.

It's got to be some kind of unlicensed, tactical under-garmentry that women can buy from hidden boutiques, tucked away in malls across the country.

Her hands were still full of shopping bags. Franklin swallowed the sad sigh of inevitability and came around to the passenger side. He unlocked the door, offering her the seat with a spin of his wrist and a courtly flourish.

She slid in, pulling her bags in onto her lap. Franklin closed the door, did a little hip-twisting chivalry dance, and skipped around the front of the car to the driver's side.

Franklin slipped in behind the wheel. The cute shopper had scrunched herself up beside him. Her fragrance sent fingers of desire up his nostrils into his brain.

The courteous thing to do would be to ask her name. He was a performer, used to the pressure. He could come up with something totally natural and friendly, couldn't he? Something funny like, 'in case we have an accident and they need to identify our tangled corpses—no!' What idiot starts a life-long romance with a line like that?

Franklin would.

Truth was, if he started he may not know where to stop. 'What's your name? Do you like me better with or without the clown face? How would your parents feel about having a clown for a son-in-law?'

Or he keeps it simple, like, 'What's your name?' and she turns into a craggy-faced, long-haul trucker in barrettes and bangs, with a 'What's it to ya, ya perv?'

So, okay, no names. Too much of a commitment. But he needed to say something. There was an attractive woman sitting alone in his car.

"Now you can tell everyone you've gone out with a real clown," said Franklin, slipping the key into the ignition.

"I have dated some real clowns," she said, laughing. "Not a *real*, real clown. But I'll bet you're loads of fun."

Oh, if only, thought Franklin, becoming a bystander in the battle between his under-fed libido and his over-protective imagination.

Here comes the usual screech of psycho circus music as his imagination takes over, plumbing the depths of her tolerance for his shortcomings with The Test.

The world inside his car shuts out the reality around the two of them as it stretches and skews.

Franklin leans in, tender, holding out a can of peanut brittle he always keeps handy for these chance romantic encounters. "I am," he says, "When I get to do—" a twist of the lid, "—this!" Paper snakes spring up and maybe she shrieks in surprise, maybe she doesn't. If she's The One, she'll absolutely yodel with glee.

"And when I get to do this," says Franklin, blasting a spray of seltzer down her blouse, and maybe she woofs at the cold, her eyes bright with shock. And longing.

"And this," he says, smacking her with a cream pie.

Franklin studies her, watching for her reaction, watching for the hint of delight, the flicker of something that says he's finally found the soul mate meant just for him.

She fingers the shaving cream from her eyes, giving him a look of utter pity.

"You think I can't see what's wrong with you?" she'll say, rubbing her face clean, blowing the shaving cream from her mouth, pushing back her hair. "Poisoned by rejection and a lifetime of mistreatment at the hands of women?" If the stars align and the fates allow, and God is keeping office hours that day, she grabs Franklin's face between her hands. "Let me be the one to make it all up to you," she'll say, then latch her mouth onto his face. She'll lock her lips onto his with a lip-smacking, moaning, monster kiss. She'll smear him with the shaving cream, leaving crimson pucker marks all over his face.

Kissing and breathing, she'll say, "That's for Jeannie Krebbs!" Kissing and breathing. "That's for Amanda in high school." Kissing and breathing. "That's for Denise in college." Kissing and breathing. "Did I leave anybody out?" she'll ask.

"Um. Sheryl? Works the drive-through at the Swif-Tee Burger Barn?" Franklin might suggest, having recently added Sheryl to the list of colossal romantic mis-fires.

"Right, how could I have forgotten her, with her torn fishnets and tongue stud!" she'll say, planting another big kiss on Franklin.

The music in his head faded, the world righted and straightened itself out. Which left Franklin watching the cute shopper. No, not watching. Gazing, really. No, not gazing. Staring. Franklin's slack-faced, saucer-eyed look of longing capable of creeping out the strongest woman.

Franklin shook his head to unlock his eyeballs.

"Rudy, my boyfriend, would crap kittens, me going out with a clown," said the cute shopper. "No offense."

"Of course not." Franklin gave a hollow knock on his noggin. "Nut'in' up here but elephant poop."

Franklin smiled at her and turned the key. The starter gave out with a grinding *whirr.* Franklin released the key and smiled at the cute shopper again, turning the key harder. The starter continued its grinding *whirr*. Franklin smiled at the cute shopper. She smiled back. Franklin turned the key again. Nothing but the grinding *whirr*. Franklin twisted harder and harder on the key. The starter kept grinding and grinding and grinding and grinding and grinding until he'd used up the last, solitary spark of a charge left in the battery.

"The old out-of-gas routine works best somewhere dark and deserted, Frankie-boy." Another clown leaned in at the window on the passenger side.

Franklin gripped the steering wheel, staring straight ahead. "We'll be fine, thanks, Buster. Don't you have a gig somewhere? Somewhere else? Way way way somewhere else?"

"Did have. Had to finish up for some clown working the shoe store. A real flake, sounds like. Got scared off by a bunch of kids and never came back. I figure he went out for a smoke and got lost. Lucky thing I was already in the mall."

Buster leaned in at the window, his eye on the cute shopper. He doffed his hat and smiled.

"Rookies," he said to her. "What can you do? Too old to spank. Too cute to drown."

"They towed my car."

Franklin, defiant, turned the key, and the starter dredged up one last, pathetic *whirp*, then stopped.

"They'll be back any minute for this one." Buster pointed a thumb at his own souped-up clownmobile idling behind Franklin's car. "Need a lift, I assume? Because it's the only reason an attractive and intelligent young woman would risk a ride in this self-propelled cheese grater." He opened the door, a knight in clown-white, offering his hand to help pull her free of Franklin's car.

Once she could stand upright, the cute shopper shimmied to straighten and smooth her clothes. She reached in for her shopping bags.

"Oh, bag boy," said Buster, "Get those for us, will you? There's an extra fiver if you don't sweat all over everything."

Franklin muscled the bags out of the front seat and loaded them into the van. He grabbed the door frame to climb in the back. Buster stepped in to block the way.

"Sorry. You won't fit," said Buster. He was the only clown Franklin knew who could turn his grease paint smile into an unpleasant scowl.

"There's plenty of room in the back."

"Not," said Buster, speaking slowly so any idiot would get the point, "when you put the seats down. Now, if you'll excuse me. My good deed needs doing." Buster slammed the side door shut. Franklin plucked his arm clear before losing it.

Buster went around and got behind the wheel, tooted the horn, tootling a musical calliope call.

"What am I supposed to do?" Franklin called in at the open window.

"You could practice on a pool toy," Buster shouted back to him. The clownmobile roared off between the cars and out through the parking lot, the tires squealing.

Franklin tore off his wig and threw it to the ground.

"Shi.i.i.i.i.t!" Franklin machine-gunned every extra syllable, jerking himself in a twisting, whipping dance of gyrational frustration.

"Thanks a lot, bozo," shouted the brunette from the mall, standing behind him. Her boy Earnest was wrapped around her leg, his face buried in her thigh. "I convince him there's nothing to be afraid of, that clowns won't hurt him, and there you are, going off just like his father. Asshole!"

Of course, out of the twelve thousand women passing through the mall today, it would have to be her. Franklin watched her storm off, little Earnest in tow.

Franklin sensed a sudden heaviness in the atmosphere and turned around. The shock-haired clown junkie!

He streaked off, his clown shoes squealing, nothing but the smoke of burned rubber left behind.

"Almost had you," Gladys said to Franklin.

"It's all in the shoes," Franklin said to Gladys.

"So, your very own brother hijacks your girl and here you are."

"The girl with all the shopping bags? That wasn't her. I wish it had been. I could have skipped the lousiest week of my life. Then Buster could be sitting here, not me."

At the mall, Franklin reached the metal benches of the bus stop where the bus waited, idling. A line of passengers stood and watched a young woman blocking the doorway. She struggled with her luggage to reach her purse hanging behind her. Her skirt rode up her thigh as she lifted her knee to keep her bags from falling.

It was easy for Franklin to see she was attractive, despite the floppy hat and large sunglasses concealing much of her face.

He was ready to bolt and leave Miss Ready-Made-Heartbreak to wrangle alone for exact change. Until one of three scruffballs in the line of waiting passengers called out, "Almost there!" He elbowed the other two scruffballs with him. They were much more interested in seeing how high her skirt would rise than helping her out.

Franklin screwed up his face, fighting off the heartless whimsy of his imagination working to take over. But he loses.

The spinning flutter of a silent film projector and a tinkling piano fills his head. Franklin the movie hero taps the shoulder of her nearest tormentor. All three scruffballs have transformed into hulking brutes. Franklin treats each bruiser to a spinning wind-up and solid uppercut, knocking them all into a sprawling heap. The dancing stars of unconsciousness circle their heads.

The mystery babe flings her arms around Franklin, his amazing muscles visible through the skin-tight clown jumper. He lifts her and her luggage, carrying her onto the bus. He catches only for a moment, then squeezes through with a loud cork-pop, and the tinkle of change dropping into the fare box. The mystery babe puckers up and plants a wet smacker on him. Franklin's vision irises out as his fantasy evaporates.

"Here, let me help," said Franklin, pushing his voice down half an octave. "I juggle for a living." He took hold of the nearest bag.

"When I have balls, I'll call you," said the mystery babe, her wallet nearly out of her purse.

"Oooooh!" The three little thuglings nodded at each other, impressed.

The mystery babe turned and found herself nose-to-red-rubber-nose with a clown. She shrieked, yanking the bag out of Franklin's hands and knocking him flat. The bag's contents went flying everywhere.

"*That* was Lucy," Franklin said to Gladys. "I didn't actually know her name until a few hours ago."

"Oh," Gladys said to Franklin.

Lucy dipped low, gathering up her scattered things.

The scruffiest of the three thuglings snatched up a pair of her panties, letting them unfold and flap in the breeze as he held them out to her.

"Nice," he said, while he toed her wallet far enough away for the short thugling to grab it.

She pulled the panties from his hand, stuffing them back in her bag. She looked inside her purse.

"Where's my wallet?" she growled, looking up at the crowd of passengers.

All three thuglings pointed at the handy clown.

She turned to an old guy, leaning on his cane

"You any good with that cane, Pop?"

He whipped it up, at the ready.

"Watch my bags." Lucy stalked toward Franklin, who'd made it back onto his feet.

The geezer gave the cane a deft, two-handed spin, getting himself ninja-ready.

Lucy homed in on Franklin, who'd already relaxed his face into his default harmless-clown mode for defense.

"Gimme back my wallet!" Lucy's hands locked open, fingers spread.

"Fight! Fight!" shouted the thuglings.

Franklin's imagination made sure he could hear her talons unsheathe with a metallic *zzzhing*. Doing his best harmless-clown schtick didn't mean much right now.

Franklin looked to the bus and its passengers for sanctuary. What he saw was an eager audience hanging out the windows, the driver stepping down for a better look. Every single passenger, young and old, held out their smartphones, aimed at Franklin. Don't want to miss an actual disemboweling, no sirree. This'll be too good not to share.

The adrenalin hit Franklin's feet and he was gone, flying, all the way down the street, Lucy right behind him.

"Hell hath no fury," Franklin said to Gladys, "like a woman you can outrun."

Traffic lights favored Franklin as he ran. He kept going until he reached a quiet side street of tree-shaded residences. He dodged between two parked cars and up onto the sidewalk. He ran along the fenced-in front yards, hopping the first low fence he found.

Franklin shot toward the narrow space between the house and the fence, slamming into a locked backyard gate.

He could hear the clacketing of Lucy's footfalls and her huffed breaths getting closer.

Franklin scrambled up and over the gate, the sharp palings tearing a pom-pom off his costume. Diving down on the other side, he tumbled, flipped over and scrambled to his feet. He put his eye to the space between the wooden boards of the gate. He saw Lucy come to a stop on the sidewalk in front of the house. She listened. She tilted her head up, her nose in the air like she could sniff for his scent.

Great. Just great. What was it about him? Why did he always manage to piss off the most feral of the fairer sex? Could someone answer that? Please?

Lucy cast her eye along the high fences in front of the other houses. She turned and stepped through the front gate of the same low fence Franklin had jumped.

Oh, boy. This one's good. He backed away from the gate, turning to look for a way out.

The yard was filled with kids. He'd fallen into a birthday party. Worse, a birthday party with no clown.

The kids inhaled as one, ready to shout their glee.

Franklin did the biggest, most impassioned and silent *hush* he'd ever mimed in his life. It took both hands to contain the unexpurgated neutron explosion of happy about to burst.

Lucy reached the backyard gate, rattling it, finding it locked. She went up on her tiptoes, trying to see over. She spotted the torn pom-pom still wedged between the palings at the top.

She hitched her skirt up to her waist and got a foothold in the cyclone fencing separating the houses. She pulled herself up and over the gate, dropping to the ground.

The yard was still filled with kids, still frozen, a birthday party waxworks.

Lucy stalked through the crowd, her eyes roving for anything to prove a clown had been there.

Nothing. She picked out the pony-tailed birthday girl wearing the rhinestone birthday tiara.

Lucy leaned in to her, eyeball-to-eyeball, her hands braced on her thighs.

"Did a clown run through here?"

"You think a clown'd get through all of us?" asked the birthday girl.

Neither of them blinked.

"They will steal your soul," said Lucy.

She straightened up and looked around at the crowd of kids, still unmoving. She stalked back to the gate, flailed at the latch, furious, slamming it behind her.

The birthday girl signaled. Two kids ran to the gate, checking to make sure she had gone. They gave a thumbs-up. Three kids standing near a tree untied a rope, lowering Franklin out of the branches. He thumped onto the ground, breathing hard.

The expectant horde closed in on him.

"What's this going to cost me?" asked Franklin, imagining how an ever-expanding river of children would stream into the back yard once word got out.

◆ ◆ ◆

Franklin rolled ash off his cigarette.

"Kids can smell a clown and free ice cream over a mile away," said Franklin. "True fact."

"So where'd Lucy go?" asked Gladys.

"To find the burrows where clowns hide at night."

chapter six

Back at the Big Top, there weren't quite as many clowns when the phone rang.

Red picked up. "Big Top. Yeah, we got clowns. You know his name? Lady, they're all wearing big shoes, baggy pants, and a fake smile. Okay, okay, slow down. Yeah? Where?" Red made notes on the pad by the phone. "All right, listen up," he said, hanging up the phone and turning to the crowding clowns. "I got a surprise birthday party for a bunch of cowgirls out at the fairgrounds."

Rib Eye, a character clown in bushy red sideburns and a tiny cowboy hat, red union suit, vest, and chaps, grabbed for the note.

"That's for me!" Rib Eye yodeled his glee.

"Anybody seen Franklin?" asked Red, holding the note away from Rib Eye.

"Those girls're looking for a real bucking bronc, not a cayuse off a kiddie carousel." Rib Eye snatched the note, calling out, "Hi-yo, Silverfish! Away!" as he galloped out the door.

◆ ◆ ◆

Franklin decided against returning to the Big Top. Instead, he'd made the long walk back to his place. The sky was darker and the air much cooler when Franklin reached home. He trudged up two flights of stairs to his front door, overlooking a dismal side street.

Franklin let himself in. The place was ramshackle, done up in Early Carnival Chaos. Buster sat in the big chair, behind a magazine.

"What happened to Miss Pool Toy?" asked Franklin, surprised to see Buster back already.

Buster lowered the paper, his face scrubbed clean of his make-up. He gave Franklin the stink-eye, made all the worse by a radiant shiner of a bruise, purpling the skin around his eye.

"Oooh. You need some painkillers for that?"

"Of course, you idiot."

"Good," said Franklin. "You left me stuck, you know that, right?"

A knock at the front door interrupted him.

Buster didn't move. "You're closer and I'm recuperating."

Franklin went to the door since it was clear Buster meant to wallow in self-pity the rest of the night. "I couldn't get the car started, so I went to catch the bus. Ran into some crazy female who nearly—and speaking of crazy females, what's this about you and some state trooper? Officer Sunshine?" Franklin opened the door. "Yes?"

Lucy stood framed in the doorway, her hands on her hips.

Franklin slammed the door, leaning against it.

"Do we know a first-class exterminator?"

More pounding on the door, way harder this time.

"Is somebody there or not?" Buster came up behind Franklin to peep through the spy hole. He elbowed Franklin out of the way, scrambling to yank the door open, holding it wide for Lucy.

"I was just this very minute telling Franklin, my houseboy, how we desperately needed—whatever it is you're selling."

"You're the clown at the bus stop." Lucy reached around Buster, knotting a handful of Franklin's costume in her fist.

"We all look alike to you civilians." Franklin pulled himself free of Lucy's grasp.

Lucy held out the pom-pom torn from his costume. "Looks like you're missing one of these, doesn't it?"

Franklin grabbed it away from her. "They don't grow back. You cost me eighty-five bucks in ice cream."

"Where's my wallet!"

"Come on in," said Buster. "I'll hold him down so you can search him. Then you can search me. You're welcome to whatever you find."

"Do I look like I'd take some perfect stranger's wallet?" Franklin held onto Buster, using him as a shield.

"You're the one with the fake face."

"She's got you there, Frankie-boy," said Buster. He elbowed Franklin aside, "May I interject here and say, you are the most perfect stranger I've ever met."

"All right, all right." Franklin pulled out the polka-dot snap purse he used for carrying cash. "How much did you have in your wallet?"

"Seventeen hundred dollars and sixty-two cents," said Lucy, leaning in to check out the contents of his purse.

"No way!" Franklin yanked his purse back.

"You'd rather have me call the cops?"

"Buster, loan me seventeen hundred dollars."

"And sixty-two cents," added Lucy.

"Not gonna do it, Frankie-boy. You'd hurt yourself with that much money."

"I loan you money all the time."

"You'll do something stupid with it."

"I'm going to give it to her so she'll leave."

"My point exactly." Buster hadn't taken his eyes off Lucy, who'd edged as far away as she could and still intimidate Franklin.

"You don't give me back my wallet, I'm calling the police. I mean it."

"Say—let's you and me snuggle on the couch until it turns up."

Lucy ignored Buster and took a swing at Franklin. "You don't think I won't?"

Down on the street, a police cruiser rolled to a stop.

Buster and Franklin looked at the cruiser, then at her, then at each other.

"I never saw her lips move," said Franklin.

"Me either. And I've been watching the whole time," said Buster.

Lucy frowned. She looked behind her.

A portly police officer, wearing a red nose, fringed wig and clownish face paint got out of the cruiser. He crossed the street and climbed the stairs toward Lucy and the boys.

Lucy zigged past Buster and zagged past Franklin, through the door, disappearing into the apartment behind them.

Buster hid behind Franklin.

"If he's asking about Miss Pool Toy, it was some other clown," said Buster. "Do I still smell like pepper spray?" Then he called out, "Officer Joe! Little early for Founders' Day, don'tcha think?"

"Founders' Day?" Gladys asked Franklin.

"Founders' Day," Franklin said to Gladys. "Big deal around here. Everyone dresses up like clowns. Long story. Officer Joe's a good egg. Goes all out."

"Explains a lot. I thought I'd wandered into a parallel universe," Gladys said to Franklin.

"Hey, guys. Got some bad news," said Officer Joe, climbing the last few steps. "They found Blinkers out at the Hudson Hotel. Buried up to his nose in cement."

Buster sighed, sounding relieved, before adding, "I mean—really?"

"Accident?" asked Franklin.

"Doesn't look like it. Red got a call earlier to send a clown. Chief thinks it's some kind of grudge between a couple of you 'pie-faced troublemakers.' His words. You know how he is. Got out of hand. Me? I'm thinking it's the work of a drifter, maybe. We're not all that far from the city. But you know how he feels about clowns. I'm keeping my eye out for strangers."

Officer Joe hitched up his gun belt and headed back down the stairs. "Sorry I had to be the one to tell you. You be careful. Let us know if you come across any suspicious characters."

"Officer Joe?" Franklin called out.

He stopped on the stairs. "Yes?"

"I—" Franklin started, "—*aaaayyyyyiiiii!*" he finished.

"My feelings exactly," said Buster. "We'll be careful."

Franklin rubbed his buttocks, feeling them inflame with blood from Buster's pinch.

Buster waved at Officer Joe as he got back in the cruiser and drove off.

◆ ◆ ◆

Gladys put down her glass and said to Franklin, "So this girl, the Baggy Pants Slasher, ends up hiding out with a couple of clowns. That's a slick move."

"Like a fox among the rubber chickens," said Red.

"I guess if you're afraid of clowns, slicing them up into bloody bits would be one way to solve your bozophobia."

"I didn't say she was afraid of clowns. I said she hated clowns."

"Same difference."

"*Au contraire, mon chéri.* She wasn't the least bit afraid of clowns. She hated clowns."

"Mad dogs have hydrophobia, right? What makes 'em so mad? It's the water, right? Hydro? Water? Help me out here, Red."

"Anybody hates clowns has got to be a hunnert percent mental." Red wiped away any further debate with a sweep of his hands.

"Like the way somebody hates spiders. Nails on a chalkboard. Squeaky Styrofoam ice chests," said Gladys.

"I hate that one." Red shivered.

"If it's not bozophobia, what is it when you hate clowns?" asked Gladys.

"Simple mathematics." Red rested his hands on the bar. "Bozo equals clown, right? Phobia equals fear, right? Add it up for yourself, whaddya got? Bozophobia. Fear of clowns."

◆ ◆ ◆

"What'd you do that for?" Franklin rubbed his butt cheek.

"You'd call the cops on somebody who just might turn out to be the girl of my dreams? All because a couple of clowns can't get along?"

"Officer Joe said it could be someone from out of town."

"Come on, you know clowns around here don't get along."

"Since when?"

"We're brothers, and we barely tolerate each other."

"Hey! You saw her all of two minutes. She chased me for nearly a mile."

"Because you stole her wallet."

"I didn't steal her wallet!"

"Women looking that good don't have any reason to lie."

"Fine. You go in and find out how harmless she is." Franklin gestured toward the front door of their apartment, wide open and uninviting.

"You know I'm a terrible judge of women." Buster shoved Franklin toward the door that had become a portal to something sinister. "You're smaller and harder to hit." Buster pushed Franklin again.

Buster outweighed him by a good fifty pounds, so Franklin decided he might as well go in first. He stepped through the doorway and reached into the umbrella stand for something weapon-like. He pulled out an industrial grade soup ladle.

"That's perfect if she's allergic to gravy."

"You should have let me say something to Joe."

"Have I ever been right about any woman? She may be perfectly harmless as well as perfectly gorgeous."

Franklin stopped and looked back at Buster. "I've never found that to be true about any of them." He crept into the living room with Buster crouched behind him. He did a hundred-and-eighty-degree sweep of the room, his ladle thrust out before him.

Nothing.

Franklin moved toward the kitchen, his ladle at the ready. He took a deep breath and leaped into the middle of the room.

"Ha!" Franklin pivoted first to one side, then the other, ladle out.

Nothing.

They edged up to Buster's bedroom.

"On three," whispered Franklin. He counted to three and barged into Buster's room.

Nothing.

He looked back at Buster still hiding behind the door frame. "'On three' means you come in with me."

"Sorry, thought you meant three o'clock. My watch stopped." Buster shook his wrist and listened. "Don't keep looking at me! She could be waiting to jump you."

Franklin pushed past Buster, who slipped in behind Franklin to avoid any surprise assault. Franklin stopped.

"She might come up behind us," hissed Franklin.

Buster whipped around in front of Franklin, watching back over Franklin's shoulder.

"Or straight ahead."

He whipped around behind Franklin.

"Maybe the side."

Buster straightened up.

"You're doing that on purpose." Buster turned and pressed his back against Franklin and grabbed him by the waist. "You watch the front, I'll watch from behind." They turtled along to Franklin's bedroom.

They sidled up to Franklin's bedroom door. Again, with a silent count down, they burst into Franklin's room, Franklin holding Buster by the sleeve, dragging him along.

Lucy had tucked herself under the bed, lying on her side, only her backside visible, still poking out.

"That," Buster whispered into Franklin's ear, "is not the face of a killer."

She pulled her protruding backside all the way under the dangling covers.

"It's the other end I'm worried about," Franklin whispered back.

"Come on. I've seen some sinister rear ends in my time. I don't see anything the least bit sinister about hers."

A barrage of pillows came out of nowhere, driving them from the bedroom, the door slamming and locking behind them.

Buster grabbed a chair and wedged it under the door handle. "There. Happy? That oughta keep her awhile."

The door opened inward and the chair fell backward into the room. Lucy threw out a scraggly clown doll.

"Hey! My mother gave me that!" said Franklin.

"We've been meaning to throw it out!" said Buster, smiling.

Lucy kicked the chair out of the way, slamming and locking the door again.

Buster picked up the chair and leaned it against the door but didn't say anything this time.

"If she's so harmless, let her hide in *your* room." Franklin went to grab the door handle.

"Okay, okay, wait!" said Buster. "I will. But let her calm down first. Jeez, Frankie-boy, calm down. You scared the beejeezus out of her."

"Me?"

"Give her a minute. Okay? Be a sport."

Franklin wasn't so much giving in on Buster's say-so. He was hearing himself, and how he must sound to the attractive female on the other side of the door. The attractive—maybe-cold-blooded-killer—female.

"Hey," she called out from the other side of the door. "You out there." Franklin pushed past Buster, leaning his head close to the door.

"What?" he barked.

"Not you. The nice one."

Buster lit up and pushed Franklin away from the door.

"I'm here," said Buster.

"Is that you?" she asked.

"The genuine, hundred per cent true me."

"You have a nice voice. Kind of sexy, but in a nice, safe, non-threatening way, you know?"

"I hear that a lot."

Franklin rolled his eyes. Oh, brother.

"I'll bet you're a real gentleman under all those muscles and good looks," she said.

Buster leaned his cheek against the door and drew little hearts on the wood panel with his finger tip. "You know, I've been told I'm just like your teddy bear."

"Bears are scary," she said, alarm in her voice. "I like unicorns. Unicorns are nice."

Oh, brother and a half. Franklin would like to barf all over Buster's shoes.

"Unicorns. A barnyard full of them," said Buster. "You can come out now. I'll protect you from the nasty old clown."

Buster reached out a finger to Franklin before he could explode all over the two of them.

"Is it okay if I stay in here tonight?"

"No way," hissed Franklin, but Buster raised the finger again.

"What do you expect," Buster hissed back at Franklin. "You stole her wallet. She needs a place to stay."

"I keep telling you, I didn't steal her wallet."

"Well, some clown did. And it would be a nice gesture if we make it up to her. For the brotherhood of clowns."

"Let one of them find her a place to stay."

"All I had in the world was in that wallet," she said.

Buster scowled at Franklin, who scowled back, wounded.

"Would—" said Buster, "—would you like me to come in and keep you company?"

"No," she said. "No, that's okay. But there is one thing I'd like you to do for me."

"Anything. Anything at all."

"Would you keep watch for me? Stay right there? The other one makes me nervous."

"I'll be here the whole night. I won't move a muscle." Buster gave Franklin the whole eyebrow treatment, loaded with warning.

Buster righted the chair and seated himself, back to the door, his arms folded. The faithful watchdog. Ready to stand guard the whole night against any sort of mayhem Franklin might try.

"You know, I always had more confidence in your self-preservation mechanism," said Franklin.

"Oh, it's obvious, isn't it? She's just the type of killer who uses ninja throwing pillows on her victims." Buster held up one of her deadly projectiles. "You think maybe it's her nesting instinct kicking in right after she got a look at me? She could be settling in, and it's her way of showing she's got a thing for me. You think of that?"

"She locked herself in *my* room."

"But she called *me* the nice one. Face it, hot babes have given you hives since fifth grade. That's what this is about, isn't it?"

"No. What's obvious is she's new in town. Blinkers gets it. She chases me here—"

"You'd throw away my future bliss on a coincidence like that?"

"All right. But if you wake up dead, don't come running to me."

Buster, like always, had gone rock solid knucklehead on yet another female. There'd be no talking reason to him. Not with his gonads pressing so hard on his brain. Franklin rapped on the closed door with the ladle.

"Hey! You in there," Franklin shouted through the door at her. "Throw out my pajamas, too."

Franklin listened at the door, catching the sound of a window sliding open.

"Glad to oblige," she said from behind the closed door.

"Not outside!"

Franklin burned a look at Buster as he slouched out the door to rescue his pajamas.

Out behind the apartment complex, Franklin waded through the bushes until he stood under the open window of his bedroom. A homemade rope of sheets and pajamas dangled from the window above. The hedge was crushed flat where a body had landed. She was gone. Even better, it was too dark to see which way she might have gone if Buster took it into his head to chase after her.

Franklin rested his hands on his thighs, doubled over with relief. "Good riddance!" he said. "Really," he added. Because he wasn't sure he meant it the first time.

A dark car, no headlights, rolled along the alleyway behind the apartment complex. It eased to a stop near Franklin. A shadowy figure cranked down the window.

"Lose something?" asked the figure in the car, a hissing whisper.

"Nothing I'm sorry to see go."

The figure cranked the window up and the car rolled on by.

When Franklin returned to the apartment he saw Buster kneeling by Franklin's bedroom door, his mouth at the keyhole.

"I never said this to a girl before," said Buster, "but I'd face the meanest clerk in the mini mart just to buy you feminine hygiene products." Buster frowned and looked up at Franklin.

"What? I'm trying to have an intimate conversation here. Do you mind?"

"She's gone."

"She's not gone."

"She climbed out the window. She's gone."

"You would say anything to have her to yourself. You are so transparent." Buster turned back to the keyhole. "Don't pay any attention to him, girl-of-my-dreams. I'm right here all night." Buster stood up, keeping himself between Franklin and the door of his dreams.

"You would do anything to keep us from being happy."

"She came looking for me," said Franklin.

"So, it's lucky for her she found me. I'm the heat-seeking missile with a warhead of love. Ka-*BOOM!* You're a floating mine all alone in the ocean, hoping a ship'll pass by close enough for you to go off, like—" Buster scrunched up his face, tiny, European, "*büme!*"

"You see the way she looked at us?" Could Buster be that dense? For real?

"I've seen the way she looks at *you,*" said Buster. "At me, the way she looks, I can feel the heat, the *el-ragerino* of passion just itching to blow. You may want to stand back so you don't get singed."

"Weren't you listening to what Officer Joe said?"

"Right. You pull the old Steal-The-Hot-Babe's-Wallet-So-She'll-Notice-You trick, then blame her when she gets mad and calls the cops on you."

"Would you let that go? I did not steal her wallet. I'm talking about Blinkers."

"In all the years I've known you, that's got to be the lamest excuse for avoiding women I've ever heard."

"I'm sure she hid under my bed because she's on the lam for not separating her recyclables."

"She does too recycle. She loves polar bears. Eats her vegetables. Wouldn't harm a steak."

"And you know this because—?"

"We talked. A lot."

"When?"

"While you were outside. I was able to get her to open up about herself. You are completely wrong about her."

"You're an idiot."

"And you're jealous. Behind this door is perfection in a pedicure, and you can't change my mind." Buster leaned his ear against the door again.

Franklin stood with his mouth open, but the hurricane of words he wanted to unleash on Buster failed to line up in coherent thoughts. All he could do was shrug. "Go ahead. I'll leave you two love birds alone." He leaned toward the door. "Goodnight, Miss What's-Your-Name." He listened at the door for a moment, then covered his mouth.

"Don't get snot on the door handle, my sweet," came a high squeaky voice.

"Franklin!" shouted Buster, yanking his head away. "You left the helium on in your room again." Buster put his mouth to the key hole again. "Don't inhale. There's plenty of air out here."

Franklin chose the knitted throw with its figure of a clown on a ball. He shook it out and settled into one of the two club chairs. A very unsatisfactory bed. He snuggled under the throw, his extremities dangling. The victory over Buster and Who-Cares-What-Her-Name-Is would be a night of discomfort.

◆ ◆ ◆

The fairgrounds didn't seem all that lively to Rib Eye as he stepped down from his pick-up. He tried the doors along the big exhibition hall. Nothing seemed open.

In the distance, he spotted a colorful string of flashing lights.

"Saddle me up, and call me Trigger!" yodeled Rib Eye, galloping toward the lights.

He'd reached a metal shed draped in Christmas lights taped around a hand-lettered sign reading, "Dressing Room—Cowgirls Only!!!"

Rib Eye checked for anyone watching. He opened the door, stepping inside.

It was dark. He felt along the wall beside the door for a light switch. The door swung shut behind him.

Outside, a gloved hand closed a hasp and snapped a padlock through the eye, locking Rib Eye inside.

Rib Eye rattled the handle, then put his shoulder to the door. It wouldn't give. He pulled out a match and struck it, looking for a handle of some kind.

A humongous bull snort sounded behind him.

He turned to find himself chin-to-muzzle with the biggest, angriest damn bull he'd ever seen, its nostrils flaring and hoof pawing at the floor.

The aluminum siding of the shed rocked as the bull slammed Rib Eye around inside, his face and body slamming against the walls and stamping his form in the metal siding. A snort and a yodel as a face bloomed in the front wall. A snort and a yodel as a butt bloomed in the back wall. A snort and a yodel as a torso bloomed in the side wall.

Outside, gloved hands lit the end of a fuse that flared and sparked. Flame sizzled along the cord and over the ground toward the shed, disappearing under the door.

Then silence, not even the hiss of the burning fuse.

The shed went up in a bright ball of flame, a concussive explosion ratting metal and glass all around, prime rib and flank steaks flying.

Rib Eye's scorched hat spiraled back down to earth, smoking where it had landed.

chapter seven

THE SMELL OF FRESH COFFEE steaming somewhere close by roused Franklin. The aroma drew him out of the chair where he'd hunkered through the night, wearing a pair of gumboots for mittens covering his vitals.

Nose still a-twitch, Franklin tumbled onto the floor, cramped and aching, tangled in his blanket. It took a moment for him to figure out why he'd gone to sleep in the chair. He remembered the lunatic female, and jumped up, searching himself for wounds. Relieved there weren't any, he remembered the rope of sheets out the window and Buster convinced she was still in the bedroom.

Relieved she was gone, he shook off the dregs of sleep, and padded to the kitchen to witness what had to be a major miracle. Buster up before Franklin and making coffee for the two of them with his very own hands.

It wasn't Buster.

Lucy stood at the sink pouring coffee, unaware of him standing in the doorway behind her.

Her backside looked so safe and abnormally normal standing there. Nothing like the dangerous frontside from which he'd barely escaped at the bus stop. An unhealthy infatuation had taken hold of him and overwhelmed his instinct to run screaming from such a chimera. He shook his head to rattle the unwholesome idea already taking root.

Nothing but disappointment or madness waited at the end of that shady lane.

"I'm surprised." Franklin scanned for anything sharp, heavy, or poisonous she might have within easy reach.

"Surprised I'd leave without my money?" Lucy put the carafe back in the coffeemaker, not looking at Franklin.

Surprised I didn't wake up dead, is what Franklin wanted to say. Amazing, since she had all night to finish off him and Buster both. Instead, he said, "Surprised you got back in without waking Buster. He has radar for females in motion." A thought struck him. "Excuse me, I have to go check and see if Buster's still breathing."

"I'm sure he's fine."

"It'd be an improvement. He's never been fine."

Franklin put his head out the kitchen door and saw Buster still asleep in the hallway. He'd slid off the chair, his back arched, head thrown back on the seat, his arms and legs splayed out.

"He looks—unconscious."

Lucy's eyes shifted away as she sipped her coffee. "I'm sure he'll be up and around, back to his old self in no time."

"How did you get back in?" Franklin considered himself a light sleeper and worried how she could have gotten by him.

"Same way I got out. It helped that you left the window open." Lucy finally looked at Franklin and gave out with a bark of disgust. "You ever take that face off?"

He touched his cheek and looked at the white on his fingertips. He checked his reflection in the polished steel of the toaster.

"We had unexpected company last night."

"That face of yours gives me the creeps."

"Good to know it's working."

"You can take it off now."

"I think I'll wait." Franklin wasn't about to give up his handy-dandy bozophobe repellant if it kept him out of claw's reach.

Lucy turned her back to him once more, steadying her mug of coffee between her finger tips to sip.

"I smell you made coffee." Franklin took the carafe from the coffeemaker, hoping she'd turn around again.

"It took some work getting the measurements right."

Franklin tipped the pot to his mug. A single drip hung on the spout. He shook it into his mug.

"I was able to make a half cup. I don't need coffee and a clown working my nerves at the same time."

"They had me decaffeinated as a baby." Franklin sipped, savoring the drop, smacking his lips. "Aaahhhh! Nothing like a good cuppa joe to start the day."

"I have to find a job in this doormat you call a town because of you."

"You can't stay in my room."

"Cough up some cash and I'm out of here."

"Why didn't you tell Officer Joe? At least in jail, I'd get a bunk to sleep on."

"What's the point making waves?"

"He might've let you drink my blood."

"You don't look like there's enough in you for me to enjoy."

A hit, a palpable hit, leaving him no swift reply of equal devastation. He needed coffee. If the only way to get any coffee was for her to find a job, then, "By all means, let me help you find a job."

Franklin left and came back with a newspaper still in its plastic bag.

"How quaint."

"It's the neighbor's. The least I could do for you is steal their paper so you can be on your way."

"You don't have a computer I can use?"

"Yes, I have a computer. That you can use? No."

"What about Buster?"

"You have anything to barter? Anything he's desperate to have and you weren't saving for marriage?"

At least she's having to think about it. She kept her eye fixed on him, a little twitch of her cheek, suggesting some deep thought. Like calculating the number of trash bags she'd need to use for their body parts.

"Give me the newspaper."

Her choosing to use the newspaper instead of bartering for Buster's computer relieved Franklin. He didn't want to think why. He held out the paper and she yanked it from his hand.

Buster came into the kitchen, his arms full of clothing.

"Good morning, good morning. Great day!" Buster pressed the pile against Franklin, forcing him to catch them before they hit the floor.

"Wait. What're you doing with all my stuff?"

"I needed some place to put all *her* stuff." Buster nodded toward Lucy.

"You went through my bag?" Lucy dodged around them and flew to the bedroom, slamming the door.

"Helping you unpack. I want you to feel at home. Forever," said Buster, following after her.

"She's not staying," said Franklin, following Buster.

"Yes, she is. You stole her wallet."

"I refuse to dignify that delusion with a denial."

"Well, I didn't take it. She says a clown took it. Here she is and here you are. Need I say more?"

"How about, 'Sure, Franklin, I'll loan you seventeen hundred dollars.' She does not want to stay here."

"Frankie-boy, this is why you're such a dud with women. You know nothing about them." Buster wagged his head, chuffing a laugh. "If my name was on the lease, I'd give her your room and you could sleep in your car." Buster went back to the kitchen.

"It doesn't matter. She's not going to stay," said Franklin, still following Buster.

Buster pulled the pot from the coffee maker and tipped it into a mug.

"Of course she is. She must've been dreaming about me the whole night," said Buster. "The sheets were all twisted up and thrown everywhere." Buster shook the pot. "Thanks for drinking all the coffee. Did you at least leave her some? Next time, make enough for all three of us."

Franklin bit off another useless remark and stormed out of the kitchen. He went to his bedroom but the door was still shut. He took hold of the knob. He should just burst in. It was his room. His name was the only one on the lease. Buster didn't even pay his own share of the rent on time.

Lucy opened the door a crack, pulling the knob out of his hand. She showed one angry eye fixed on Franklin.

"It'll be like a game," she said through clenched teeth. "Figuring out where he put all my clothes." She slammed the door.

Buster came out of the kitchen and planted himself by the bedroom door. "You can ask me. I'm ready to wait on you hand and foot. Hip and thigh. Tooth and nail. Name a body part. I can handle them all." Then he said to Franklin, "I think she's getting used to me. Most women hate it when I go through their clothes for souvenirs."

Franklin picked the paper up off the floor where Lucy had dropped it. He flipped through the pages to keep his mind off the thought of her in his room, leaving her scent everywhere.

"Ah!" Franklin folded back a page of the paper. "Here's a cheery item." He read, "'Blinkers the Clown was found dead in wet concrete at the new Hudson Hotel pool.'"

Buster wasn't listening. That was clear enough. How could he? Buster's entire neural network is running sexual fantasies in high-definition. Not a single synapse left for self-preservation.

Franklin leaned down to read at Buster's ear. "'The killer remains at large.'"

"Ix-nay," said Buster, "with a capital 'Ix.' I'm listening to her heart beat."

Franklin straightened up, still reading. "'The funeral is Saturday.'" He stopped and let the paper flop at the fold. "We can send a nice arrangement of patio furniture instead of flowers."

"Why don't you run on along, Frankie-boy. I plan on spending the day growing on her." He shivered in delight.

Lucy opened the door again.

"Sound like tons of fun."

That's what she said, but Franklin caught her brief, fierce and flaring glare as she sized up the target that was the back of Buster's head.

"Ooo-kay," said Franklin, as if he hadn't seen, and hadn't had a wonderful flicker of inspiration. "You two go right ahead and have a nice life. What's left of it. For one of you."

"You could get lost, you know," said Lucy, but Franklin could see her face turn into a clash of dismay and anger aimed at him.

Franklin leaned in, smiling. "He'll grow on you." Franklin saw a single flicker of panic behind those deep, amazing, hazel eyes. "You think I'm kidding. He's impervious to every kind of weed killer. I've tried. Don't waste your money. Not that I want to give you any ideas that'll be used against me later in a court of law."

The dismay had vanished. She crooked her finger at him through the crack in the door. Franklin leaned in close. Lucy snagged Franklin by the nostrils.

"You got me into this, you get me out."

Franklin winced at the amount of pain a pair of female fingernails could inflict on the insides of his tender snoot.

"I don't think clearly with your fingers deviating my septum," said Franklin, his eyes squinted shut.

"You don't need your nose to think."

"It's all connected."

"You want it all to stay connected, get me out of here."

Buster dangled a pair of Lucy's undies between them.

"I've always wondered—do girls fold their panties crotch in or crotch out?"

"The fun's in finding out for yourself." Lucy gave him a huge wink.

Buster's face melted in ecstasy. So easily played.

Lucy turned her laser gaze back on Franklin.

Buster finally noticed Franklin's predicament. "That looks painful."

• • •

Buster's clownmobile pulled into the gravel parking lot in front of the Big Top Tavern.

Buster shut off the engine. Lucy sat in the front seat and Franklin sat in the back, two cotton swabs stuck up his nose.

"Has the bleeding stopped?" Franklin tried to see for himself in the rearview mirror.

"Get her a job at the Big Top!" said Buster. "I was thinking the exact same thing just before Franklin said it. If I weren't so tall, it would've come out faster."

Lucy slipped out of the clownmobile, pulled down the brim of her floppy hat, and slid her sunglasses on. She headed across the parking lot toward the tavern entrance.

"Come on. She's hiding something," said Franklin.

Lucy passed a clowned-up Peterbilt tractor belonging to Big Rig, a red-neck character clown. An air-horn blast blew her skirt up, giving the boys a stunning vista of skin and lace.

"And what a lousy job she's doing," said Buster, as Lucy whirled around, slapping down her skirt.

Franklin started after Lucy, but Buster caught him by the arm.

"I was saving this for a special occasion. But now's as good a time as any." Buster handed Franklin a hand-drawn, crudely colored real estate flyer. The picture was of a smiling house, its windows sprouting a woman's legs on one side and a clown's legs on the other.

In big red letters across the top, the message read, 'Looking for a Place of Your Own?'

"Where'd you get this?"

"Found it on my windshield this morning. Naturally, I thought of you."

"I'm not the one who needs to find a place of his own."

"But look what comes with it. Read what it says here." Buster pointed to the smaller blue letters at the bottom below the smiling house. It read, 'Free massage with every appointment. Ask for Lady Fingers. Call now!'

"And I don't need a massage from some woman I've never met."

"That's why you make the appointment."

"You're the one who throws himself at every strange woman that comes along," said Franklin, shoving the flyer back at Buster.

"Not anymore. You won't catch me doing something so creepy like that ever again. No matter how good they might look. Now she's here," said Buster, nodding toward Lucy, "I'll never be this desperate again."

"I have a place to live. Yours is looking iffy. And, I don't need a free massage."

Buster folded up the flyer and put it back in his pocket. "Fine. Don't say I never tried to give you anything."

Lucy had nearly reached the entrance of the Big Top. Buster hurried to catch up with her.

Franklin watched as Buster took her elbow, escorting her the rest of the way. She smiled at him. No flinching or growling as far as Franklin could see.

Up inside the Peterbilt cab, Big Rig laughed and waved his cap at Franklin. He pulled the cord over his head and sounded his wolf-whistle horn.

Franklin did a quick trot to catch up with the two of them as Buster ushered Lucy inside.

The place was full of clowns. Franklin came in behind Buster and Lucy just as Dougie sprang up in front of Lucy's face. He wore whiteface with dagger eye accents, a black smile reaching to his ears, crowned with a mane of orange hair.

Lucy squeaked and whirled away from Buster, right into Franklin, an accidental half-embrace. It lasted only a moment before she flinched out of his arms and steeled herself for the ordeal, her face hardening.

As she stepped away, shoving Dougie from her path, she eased through the crowd and made her way to the bar.

Franklin remained frozen, his arms still out, holding the air where she'd been. He'd been reduced to memory foam holding onto the phantom feeling of the now empty embrace.

"Whadja bring us, Buster? A clown junkie?" shouted Biscuits, a fat character clown made up as a moon-cheeked baker.

The clowns shoved in close, trilling blow-outs in Lucy's face.

"Settle down! Settle down!" said Buster. "She's with me."

Franklin grabbed a plastic clown-topper of yarn hair and a red nose from the stack by the door and held it out to Lucy. "Better put this on. It'll make you an honorary clown."

"That's a good way to lose a couple of fingers—right up to your neck," she said.

Stubby, a skinny auguste, called out, "Guys! Guys! Is that any way to welcome a friend of Buster's to the Big Top?"

The rest of the clowns, their shoulders sagging with a deep chagrin, moaned, "No, of course not. Shame on us."

"Show some respect. Let's have a little etiquette if you please," said Skinny. "And you know what that means?"

"Blanket toss!" all the clowns shouted back and cleared away the tables and chairs.

Franklin took a seat at the bar. Red slid a bar napkin in front of him.

"You're not joining in?" asked Red.

"Nah. This won't end well."

Behind Franklin, all was in chaos.

"Red? What's a cure for bozophobia?" asked Franklin.

A clown dashed past, a shoe bouncing off his skull.

"Anybody we know?"

Another clown flashed by covered in foam, Lucy right behind, hosing him down with a fire extinguisher.

"No one from around here."

"I always wanted to try the Epsom Salts and bubble bath cure," said Red. "Fill a tub with warm water, Epsom Salts, and bubble bath. Get 'em all relaxed. Then—hold 'em under 'til they stop kicking."

A bevy of clowns flashed past pursued by Lucy with hedge clippers, *snick, snick, snicking* away at their vitals.

"Why?"

"In case it comes up." Franklin looked back at all the mayhem. "Never mind. Too much of a long shot."

The front door opened. A flash of daylight sliced through the dark. Chaos took a break while everyone turned to look at the new newcomer filling the doorway.

A portly guy, the newcomer wore a rumpled brown suit and straggly tie, topped off with a clown-hair cap and rubber nose. A few dashes of odd colored paint made up a clown face under his horn-rimmed glasses and three-day stubble of whiskers.

He squeezed through the crowd of clowns, planting his big keister on a barstool.

Lucy put down the hedge clippers and grabbed up a clown-topper, slapping it onto her head. She edged toward the shadows.

The rumpled guy raised a finger to signal for a drink. He had on white, three-fingered cartoon gloves.

The rest of the clowns circled around him.

"New in town?" asked Skinny.

"Just another one of you clowns," said the rumpled newcomer.

"You know what that means, of course," said Fricka-Frack, a beefy whiteface.

"Blanket toss!" they all shouted.

They had better luck getting the rumpled guy into the blanket. They took hold of the blanket edges and lugged him to the middle of the floor. They gave a mighty heave— and collapsed under the weight, herniating everyone, slamming the rumpled guy to the floor.

"If they want this tradition to catch on," said Red, "they'll have to do it right at least once."

The clowns scrambled to their feet, grabbed hold of the blanket again. "All together!"

"All right! All right! I'm working undercover." The rumpled guy rolled off the blanket. "My aching back."

"As a clown?"

"Private eye." He gave them only a quick flash of his badge. Skinny grabbed it away from him.

"Dick Lisker? Department store security?" Skinny gave Lisker a cold hard stare. "You know what that means?"

"Blanket toss!" the clowns shouted with renewed glee.

"Waitwaitwait!" Lisker shouted over them. "You heard about Blinkers, right? How they found him in wet cement, right? But did you hear about Rib Eye? Last night?"

The clowns moved in closer around him.

Franklin saw Lucy's face crumple up with fear and surprise.

"I didn't think so," said Lisker.

"When last night?" Franklin still watched Lucy.

"Late. Midnight. Maybe one a.m. Nothing left of him but his hat. It can only mean one thing." He looked around at the clowns fixed on him. "The Baggy Pants Slasher's in town."

The clowns exploded in terror, running in circles, screaming and shouting, grabbing each other, pulling their hair.

"The Baggy Pants Slasher?" the cry went up. "Here? Why? When? How long?"

Red reached across the bar and grabbed Lisker by his tie, pulling him up eyeball-to-eyeball.

"What in hell's a Baggy Pants Slasher?"

The clowns froze in mid-panic. A very good question.

"Come on. You're clowns. You don't know? Don't you get news out here in the sticks?"

From inside his jacket, Lisker yanked a tattered old map marked with dead clown faces in blood red ink.

"Look!" Lisker pointed to the map. "Every X is a dead clown. Now the Slasher's here. I've been on the trail half way across the country, since Bakersfield."

"Why here?" asked Red, the other clowns nodding at the fresh doom so unnaturally settled on their little town.

"I'm guessing for that." Lisker pointed at the poster plastered on the wall. 'Clowns! Clowns! Clowns!' the headlines screamed. 'Chumleyville Founders Day Circus Scramble Charity Golf Tournament' said the sub-headlines quietly and with more dignity.

"To play golf for charity?"

"Less than three days this place'll be crawling with clowns. Every one of you'll be a target."

Franklin could see Lucy shudder.

"Your lives won't be worth an Adolf." Lisker finger-pistoled two shots at Red. "But the Slasher finally slipped up. There's nowhere to hide in a town this size." Lisker blew smoke from his fingertip, spun, and holstered the imaginary side-arm.

"Why'n'cha point the Slasher out," asked Red, "and the police can grab him."

"Nobody's ever seen the Slasher's mug and lived to tell about it. Just a clown face and gloves. Then—lights out!" Lisker grabbed at them, the clowns flinching backward.

Clowns started checking each other's face and gloves.

"I'm watching every taxi, bus, and train for the face that doesn't fit in. The stranger trying to avoid attention, or who suddenly leaves town. That's when I strike." Lisker barked out a yappy dog bark. "A bulldog."

"Uh, that's more like a Shitzu or a maybe a Chihuahua," said Fricka-Frack.

"Not a Chihuahua," said Skinny. "Maybe a Jack Russell terrier."

"Yeah, more like that," said Freckles.

"All right! All right! All right!" Lisker swept his hands back and forth over the heads of the clowns still crowded around him.

Lisker folded up his map and stashed it inside his jacket. "Last night. Two a.m. I saw a girl. By herself. At the bus station. A little bit suspicious, if you ask me."

"What was she doing?"

"Waiting for a bus."

"Lot of people take the bus," said Red.

"At two in the morning? I'd bet a month's pay it's the mystery chick I've been following since Reno. Lemme tell ya, she ain't no Avon Lady."

"What's she look like?" asked Franklin.

"Like her." Lisker zeroed in on Lucy. He leaned toward Franklin. "What's that girl's name?"

"No clue," said Franklin.

Buster whimpered. The clowns edged away from Lucy.

"Phyllithh," lisped Lucy. "P.H.Y. Double L. Ethh. Ethh."

"Phyllithh, of course," said Buster, "I'm surprised you had to ask. Everybody knows Phyllithh, right? Right, guys?"

No one said anything, watching her.

"See? She's one of the regulars."

"Wait a minute," Gladys said to Franklin, "You said her name was Lucy."

"Something she pulled out of the air, I guess. I didn't know her real name until much later," Franklin said to Gladys.

"You look exactly like her." Lisker moved closer to Lucy, backing her up against the wall.

Buster had stopped breathing.

Lisker straightened up, chuffing his disappointment. He turned to the clowns who hovered out of range. "Except for the red hair. And her nose wasn't so big. And she didn't have a lisp."

Buster's eyes rolled back in his head as he let out all the air pent up in his shivering body.

"I'll know her when I see her again." Lisker turned back to Lucy. "Are you sure I haven't seen you somewhere before? Maybe another bus station?"

"She was in bed all night," said Franklin.

"Oh, ho, ho, ho, ho! Was she now? And did you keep your eyes open the whole time?"

"Oh, yuck!" Buster swatted away the unappetizing mental image.

"She snores. Kept me up the whole night."

"It'thh twue. I have my dad'thh noethhe." She gave the plastic honker a squeeze, adding a beep of her own.

"What's he using to keep his glasses up? Hmmm?" Lisker swooped in closer to Lucy. "Answer me that, Miz Smarty-Britches."

"If my little brother says she snores, she snores." Buster turned to Lucy. "I for one love a woman who can rattle the windows when she snores. Helps me sleep."

"Okay, okay. For now. But I'm watching. My eyes are everywhere." He V-fingered his eyes then V-fingered Lucy, making sure she understood he was locked in on her. Then traced down her figure. Then back up. Then stopped. Then did a little, excited finger dance.

Lucy slapped his hand away.

Lisker kept his eyes locked on Lucy, holding his wounded fingers, and said to the other clowns, "It could be anybody behind the clown face and gloves." Lisker backed up to the window facing out onto the alley and turned, taking hold of the sash to lift it.

"I'm—a—caaaaaaat." Lisker strained against the sash which gave way with a slam, rattling the panes, slamming his fingers. He shoved them in his mouth, squinting hard against the pain. Shaking his hands, his voice reedy and strained, he said, "The Slasher won't hear me when I pounce." He squeezed through the narrow opening, lost his grip, and fell into the alley with a long, resounding crash of trashcans. Then silence.

The clowns eased up to the window and peered out.

"Don't look! Don't look!" Lisker shouted up at them. "Pretend you don't see me." He paused. "Meeooooow!"

chapter eight

It was late, and the Big Top nearly empty. Red stood at the register, cashing out for the night. Big Rig sat at the bar draining the last of his beer. Buster and Franklin, at a table by the window, nursed the last swallows of their drinks. Red turned off the neon signs in the windows. Lucy counted out her tips.

She emptied the pockets of her apron onto the bar, finding very little in the way of negotiable currency. Mostly an assortment of play money, buttons, and funny badges.

"Yeah. I'll be on my way in no time."

"Money's never much good here." Red slipped Lucy an extra couple of twenties. "It's the prestige. Being able to say you worked the Big Top."

Franklin watched her and Red. There's a joke she'll never get.

Buster leaned across the table at Franklin. "She could be the most exciting thing that's happened to me. Ever."

"Try bungee jumping with strangers," said Franklin. "You don't need a condom."

"Admit it. You had your eyes on her the whole night."

"Just making sure she didn't spit in my beer."

Big Rig put the glass mug on the service rail, slid off the stool. He gave Lucy a goodnight swat and honk of the bulb horn on his belt as he passed behind her.

"If looks could kill," said Franklin, "Big Rig would be a grease stain on the highway by now."

Franklin watched through the window as Big Rig mounted the steps of his truck, pulling himself up to the cab. Franklin envied Big Rig his audacity, and the feel of Lucy's fundament on the palm of his hand. Which was just shameful, of course, just shameful.

Big Rig was still on the step when he picked up a flyer plastered against the windshield.

The flyer had a bikini babe stenciled at the top and a hand-lettered headline below it. 'Free! Free! Free!' it read. 'Fooling and Fueling!! Midnight Gas-Up for Clowns.'

Big Rig smiled. He was, after all, driving a gas hog. And he was a clown. He smiled at himself in the big side mirror.

Back at the bar, Lucy threw off her apron and grabbed up her purse. Franklin's butt flexed, ready to propel him to the door and hold it open for her. The rest of his skeleto-muscular system refused to believe the electrical impulses from his brain were serious. It was finely tuned to Franklin's crippling insecurity with women. It wasn't ready for a risky act of chivalry.

Buster leaped to his feet and held the door for her. Lucy worked up a bit of a half-smile, letting Buster play the *gal-lante*. Franklin's butt relaxed. His nervous system breathed a deep sigh of relief, glad Franklin's near-brush with embarrassing stoogery had passed.

Red came over to the table to pick up the glasses.

"I can get those," said Franklin.

"Thought I saw a little chemistry between you and her when you two first came in."

Easy enough to recall the moment. Frozen, his arms still out and holding the air where she'd been.

"Like disco and nitroglycerin," said Franklin.

"Come on. Looked like—"

Franklin could see himself still standing there, the phantom feeling once more filling up the now empty embrace. All the time he'd been thinking it was—

"Nothing. Nothing at all."

The glaze over Franklin's eyes cleared. He noticed a black sedan in the parking lot of the thrift store, parked just out of the light from the street lamp. Odd, since the thrift store was closed for the night. The sedan looked like the one he'd seen the night Lucy had shinnied out of the apartment.

Franklin could see Lucy climb into Buster's clownmobile and hear the engine start. An alley cat howled.

Franklin jumped to his feet.

"Gotta go." Franklin dashed out the door.

Franklin hopped into his car, twisted the key, grinding the starter. Just grinding.

Buster appeared next to Franklin at the window.

"Should take better care of your car, Frankie-boy." Buster clonked something down on the roof. "Things keep coming off in my hand."

Franklin hopped out and found his distributor cap on the roof.

"Don't lose that. It could be important," Buster shouted back, already behind the wheel of the clownmobile. He threw gravel as he fishtailed out of the parking lot onto the street and into the night. With Lucy sitting right next to him.

Big Rig's semi grumbled to life. Franklin ran and jumped onto the running board, hammering on the window.

Big Rig lowered the glass.

"Follow that van!" he shouted in at Big Rig.

"Sorry, Frankie-boy. No hitchhikers." Big Rig bounced the wadded-up flyer off Franklin's forehead. "Got a date with a gas pump." Big Rig gave out with a yodeling trucker's laugh. He closed the window, catching the tips of Franklin's gloves. Franklin pulled loose, his gloves still caught in the window. He hopped off the running board before Big Rig could get the truck in gear and drive off with him still dangling from the side.

Left in yet another swirl of dust and gravel, Franklin bent to pick up the crumpled flyer. Seeing the pin-up and the headline, a very bad idea hit him.

Franklin rolled back the last few minutes, back to Lucy's death ray scowl at Big Rig after he'd swatted her on the caboose. Thick blue lights lance across the bar and shrivel Big Rig in his boots, the crack and sizzle fading as smoke filled the room.

A very, very bad idea hit him.

◆ ◆ ◆

Axle's Gas and Go sat alongside an access road to the on-ramp for Interstate 80. The station was dark, except for one concrete island of pumps. Big Rig's truck pulled into the station. He rolled past the large, hand-painted sign announcing, 'Free Gas for Clowns Here.' A painted arrow pointed to the lit-up pumps.

Big Rig hopped down from his truck and gave a shout, "Hey, hey, Big Rig's here!"

Not another soul in sight.

"Dang." He glanced around the dark station. "You'd think there'd be a line a clowns getting free gas."

Big Rig gave a shrug. "More for me," he said and went to work filling the large, saddle tanks on the Peterbilt.

A gloved hand reached from behind the pump, slipping a hose into the seat of Big Rig's clowned-up Dickies.

Big Rig swelled until he was the shape and buoyancy of a beach ball. He tried to grab for the door handle on his truck, but his costume had fully inflated, all the way to his gloves. He could only swipe at the handle as his feet left the ground.

The gloved hand gave Big Rig a push and sent him bounding across the service area as Franklin's car skidded to a stop at the entrance. He got out of his car. The rotundular form of Big Rig bounced directly at him. Franklin stretched out his arms to corral Big Rig before he bounced into the interstate traffic beyond.

Big Rig landed on Franklin, flattening him, bouncing over the fence and slamming into the night-time traffic. Franklin peeled himself up off the cement and ran after Big Rig. But the globular clown was in a sudden-death round of high velocity vehicular volleyball.

As Big Rig sailed from car hood to car hood, Franklin pulled out his cell phone, then stopped. He didn't want them tracing the call back to him. And maybe her. Phyllis. Whatever her name was.

Instead, he ran for the payphone, sliding, slamming into the booth. He grabbed the handset, punching in 9-1-1.

"I want to report—I want to report—a runaway—beach ball!" Franklin shouted into the phone. "Right. A runaway beach ball—with a clown inside it." He listened for a moment, then hung up.

"Yeah. They'll take that seriously."

Big Rig was already out of sight in the stream of traffic.

Another idea hit Franklin and he bolted for his car, revved it, and putt-putted back onto the interstate toward home.

Franklin drove along the street behind his apartment building, pulling in next to Buster's clownmobile.

The makeshift rope dangled from the back bedroom window again. Franklin tromped the gas pedal and motored off.

At the edge of town, outside the bus station, Lucy sat alone in a pool of light from the building's security lamps. Franklin pulled into the parking lot and stopped in front of her. She wore his favorite sweatshirt, a pair of his pants, and a knit cap pulled down over her ears.

Great. Just great. A favorite sweatshirt he could never wash or wear again if he wanted to keep her smell on it.

He rolled down the window. She kept her head turned away, looking off into the night. He sat looking at her for a long moment. "Aren't you afraid that private eye is watching the bus station?" he asked.

"Not two nights in a row." She continued looking off into the dark.

"Doesn't matter. No buses run after midnight."

Her eyes closed and her head drooped. She twisted around to look up at the posted schedule behind her. The frame was empty. She flopped back against the seat.

Franklin got out and came around to open the door on the passenger side. Lucy sat there for a moment longer and gave out with a long, low, grunting exhale. She let her head drop again, the burden of it pulling her forward off the bench and onto her feet. Bearing the weight of the world, she slouched to the car, throwing up her arms to fend off any help from Franklin. She dumped her bag in the back seat and got in.

Franklin slid in behind the wheel. He twisted the key in the ignition and the engine coughed to life. The headlights came on, throwing a wash of light across the sign board in front of the car. Happy, capering clowns decorated a giant poster for the Founder's Day Golf Tournament.

Lucy cried out, squeezing her eyes shut against the assault springing at her from the darkness.

Franklin pawed at the ignition to kill the engine. The lights went out.

"Sorry," said Franklin, small, trying to watch her without looking at her.

"It startled me is all." Lucy pulled the cap off, slapping it into her lap. "Let's get out of here."

"It's only a picture."

"*You're* not." She stayed silent a long moment. "Sorry. I hate clowns, okay?"

"I guess I don't understand how a fake nose and a little bit of goofy hair sets people off."

"Oh, it is a lot more than that!" Lucy clinched her arms across her chest. "Because of your fake nose and goofy hair? You could machine-gun somebody's mother and everybody would laugh at how funny the clown is."

"I prefer poison lawn darts."

She didn't answer. Just sat shaking her head. "You could have told everyone about me back at the Big Top. Save yourself gas money."

"What's the point of making waves?" Watching her, the way she stared, he marveled how it made her eyes appear to glow in the dark.

"They might've let you drink my blood," she said.

"You don't look like there's enough in you for me to enjoy."

Lucy's smile got the better of her, slipping free for a delicious moment before she grappled her face back to a sullen frown.

"So, I guess I should say thanks for not leaving me to sit there all night?"

"I was out driving around anyway. In the middle of the night. In the scariest part of town."

Lucy latched onto Franklin's mouth, gripping his cheeks and giving him the world's chewiest kiss. The kind of kiss with the power to change a stronger man's political convictions.

Franklin had to open his eyes to see if this was real or if he'd blundered into another of his fanciful and futile hopes. He saw Lisker leaning on the hood, staring in at them.

"Didn't expect me, did you?" said Lisker. "I like to be where you think I'm not."

Lucy unlatched her lips from Franklin. He inhaled with a hiss, air rushing out of a broken airlock lost in deep space. Franklin put his hands on the steering wheel, regaining his breath, dignity, and cynicism. Lucy still twirled a lock of Franklin's bright blue hair in her fingers.

"I'm—I'm showing Phyllis all the places she should avoid late at night now the Slasher's in town." Franklin turned to Lucy. "So, write this one down, too. Avoid dark bus stops." He rolled his lips in his teeth, sucking in the taste of her, while she wrote on her hand with an imaginary pen.

"Kinda dangerous," said Lisker. "Who knows what'll happen in all this dark. With a woman you hardly know."

Lucy ran a knuckle along Franklin's cheek. "Yethh. Thhumthing awful."

"Slasher could be anybody. Gains your confidence. Gives you a false sense of security. Then—*WHAMM!* You wind up tomorrow's headline."

Lisker slid off the hood, slapping a hand-drawn wanted poster onto the windshield. A clown face done in black marker. He popped up on the other side of the car.

"It's the last face some clowns ever see. May want to keep that in mind, buddy."

Franklin rolled the window up, Lisker barely saving his fingers. He back away, fading into the night, leaving Franklin and Lucy alone.

"That's twice," said Lucy.

"You're welcome." He was glad she noticed who had been covering for her.

"That he's seen me sneaking out of town."

Then again, maybe she hasn't.

Lucy twisted the rear-view mirror to check her face and wipe the greasepaint from her mouth and chin.

Franklin didn't have the nerve to ask the big question. Seemed safer to ask, "You owe that guy money or something?"

"First morning I'm here, he picks me out at the diner. The one down from the shopping mall."

"Pecker's? Guy doesn't seem smart enough."

"The way I stuck out? I was the only one in the place *not* wearing a clown get-up."

"Oh, right. Founder's Day. It is kind of a big deal around here. Runs the entire week."

"What kind of town makes everyone go around in wigs, those stupid shoes like yours, and their faces all painted up?" She was getting the teensiest bit shrill.

"It's a charity thing. For Founder's Day. Cops give out tickets for not wearing something makes you look like a clown. Stick you in the outdoor jail if they catch you downtown. Kind of funny seeing guys in the cage on the plaza. If they want to get out, they pay a fine and let a bunch of schoolkids paint their faces. Mostly harmless."

"And everyone's okay with that? You know what a nightmare that looks like from the outside? Like I really needed that. Get caught up in your bizarro world with a private eye on my trail."

A few days earlier, Lucy, in her floppy hat and sunglasses, tried losing herself among the sleepy denizens starting their day at Pecker's, with its legendary three-ring breakfast special. She'd slipped in, took a booth at the back, and stayed low behind the oversized vinyl-covered menu.

Lucy should have known right off something was wrong when Gabby the waitress stood next to her table. She had done herself up in wig and hair bow, red heart lips, and a clowned-up waitress uniform with an overstuffed bosom.

"I'd have never gone in the joint if they'd warned me," Lucy said to Franklin.

Gabby put down a paper placemat, a mug, and flatware wrapped in a napkin. She started pouring coffee for Lucy who hid behind the menu.

"What'll you have?"

"Give me a minute." Lucy kept the menu up, covering her face.

"Sure thing." Gabby held out a paper party hat trimmed with a spray of green hair. "You might need this, hon." She left the hat on the table and went back behind the counter. Lucy peeked around the side of the menu. The place looked like a circus had exploded somewhere and all the clowns landed in the diner.

Lisker, wearing the same frazzled wig and the red nose, sat at the counter with Gabby and Officer Joe. The three of them scanned the diner, cataloging the customers.

"Everybody comes through here," said Gabby. "We're a straight shot from the interstate. Next to the motel and down the street from the bus station."

"So. What's this Slasher look like?" Office Joe tapped his coffee spoon on the rim of his mug.

"Never seen the face," said Lisker. "It'll be a stranger in town."

"Got plenty of those out this way." Officer Joe sucked the last of the sweetener stuck to his spoon.

"That's why he thought it might be some drifter," Franklin said to Lucy. "The day he came by to tell us about Blinkers."

"You can tell the out-of-towners," said Gabby, studying the faces in the diner. "They're all wearing the party hats. The locals are way more serious about Founders Day."

"What about the couple from Muncie?" Gabby pointed out the large man and woman chowing down on a pair of lumberjack breakfast specials.

"Slasher works alone."

"The salesman from Ogden?" Gabby pointed out a scrawny guy slurping cereal while he pestered his counter-mate.

"Too loud. Slasher's quiet."

"Maybe he's a she." Officer Joe pointed toward Lucy's booth, but Lucy was already heading for the door. Lisker watched her backside, intrigued.

"No one's ever seen his backside, either."

"I was trying to get on that bus," Lucy said to Franklin, "and give him the slip. You decided to be a hero and stick your big red nose in it."

"Tough luck for you, what happened to those clowns right after you showed up," said Franklin.

"Yeah. Tough luck. That's my life." Franklin could see the irony was lost on Lucy. "Always moving, never one place very long, working odd jobs. Having to wait tables at truck stops and greasy spoon diners. Or working office jobs for guys who pay in cash and don't ask questions if your skirt's short enough."

Franklin sees it. All the guys would look like clowns to Lucy. Clown-headed guys holding her tip out of reach to plant kisses up her arm. Clown-headed guys reaching up under her skirt to pull out a pair of bright red bloomers. All the other clown-headed guys stomping, whistling, and clapping at the antics.

"Then it happens. One of you clowns turn up dead."

Classic *noir* is how Franklin sees it. A dumpster out behind some gas station. Clown shoes sticking out. Inside the dumpster, a clown corpse buried under the banana peels, pie tins, and peanut shells.

Lucy reads the local paper with her coffee, minding her own business. Franklin sees it all the way it looks to her. She sits, staring at a picture in the newspaper of the dead clown's shoes sticking out of the dumpster.

"You all turn into a mob with torches and pitch forks to find whoever it is hates clowns so much."

The whole town is one giant canvas tent turning inside out, deflating as the clowns sally forth to find the plain-faced monster.

"And it's back on the road, off to someplace new."

Franklin sees her alone by the side of the road, shivering, her thumb out to hitch a ride. She gets into some creepy guy's van and disappears down the dark road until the taillights wink out.

"You tried sticking to one place?"

"Clowns keep dying. Everybody asking, 'Who's the stranger?' Always wondering if you've got an alibi for every single second you're awake. God forbid you have blackouts and honestly can't remember every little detail."

"Blackouts?" Franklin's eyes popped wide so hard and fast, she must have heard his eyelids smack into his forehead.

"I hate clowns." Lucy looked over at Franklin. "This the old out-of-gas routine?"

Franklin reached for the key in the ignition, but Lucy put her hand on his, stopping him.

"Do something for me first."

"Ohhhhh-kay," said Franklin when he finally found the breath to make the whole word come out. Write her name in the moon's dust, fetch down a handful of the brightest stars, subdue a whole litter of rabid dragons. Nothing seemed too hard for him at this moment, the way her hand rested on his.

"Get rid of that thing?" She pointed at the flyer of the clown face stuck under the wiper.

He reached out and pulled it off the windshield, balling it up and tossing it on the floor. He twisted the key in the ignition, praying it would start. He had to put some distance between himself and the atmosphere of the place closing in on him. A place made unbearably magical by the moon, the dark, her scent, and the prickling skin of his hand where she'd touched him.

The engine coughed to life, and he aimed the car onto the street.

Back at the apartments, Franklin steered the car under the parking shelter. Lucy hopped out and slung her bags over her shoulder. She turned without a word and headed for the makeshift rope still hanging out the bedroom window.

"That could be very incriminating."

"In case Buster's waiting up for me." Lucy shinnied up the rope with far more skill than Franklin would have imagined. He watched until her khaki'd derriere disappeared over the sill into his bedroom.

Franklin eased open the front door and tiptoed for the bathroom, hooking his foot on something in the dark. He went sprawling, landing flat on his face.

Franklin tore at whatever snagged his feet. He pulled it close to his face to see. Twine. Running from the knob of his bedroom door into Buster's bedroom.

Buster came flying out of his room.

"Hah! I knew you couldn't keep yourself locked away from me," cried Buster. He saw Franklin on the floor. "Oh. Don't waste your time. You can't see anything good under the door. I tried."

Franklin waved Buster in close.

"You're barking up the wrong pair of shins," said Franklin. "She hates clowns."

"She spent all night selling beer to clowns."

"Immersion therapy. Worst case of bozophobia I've ever seen. It'd never work out between you."

Still on the floor, Franklin could see Lucy's toes from under the door. She must be standing close, listening. Franklin lost himself in how those toes summed up the total wonderfulness of the person attached to them.

"Therapy? Like she's got a problem?" asked Buster.

"Right." Franklin tore his eyes away from the sliver of space under the door.

"Like—she's got a mental problem?"

"You could say that."

"Like—a girl would have to be bug-ass crazy to choose me over you?"

"I believe that's the medical term for it." Franklin picked himself up off the floor.

"Which do you think is worse? To have loved and lost, or never loved at all?"

That had to be the weirdest question Buster ever asked.

"You must've thought about it. You're love life's been a total failure since fifth grade. Which is worse?"

"You bringing it up again?"

"If you met the perfect girl, you'd do anything to get her to like you? Right?"

"Alcohol's a tolerable substitute when your charm wears off."

"She's different. She's got what no other girl in my life ever had."

"A working gag reflex?"

"Something to hide." Buster pulled out a scrapbook and started to hand it to Franklin. He changed his mind and held onto it.

"I found it in her luggage. In a secret pocket. Totally by accident."

Franklin glanced at the sliver of space under the door. The toes were gone.

Buster flipped through the pages for Franklin.

The scrapbook was jam-packed with pictures and clippings about the Baggy Pants Slasher. The clipping about Blinkers was on top.

Franklin picked the old newspaper off the floor. He paged through it until he reached the hole where the Blinkers story used to be.

"She needs an alibi, and I need her undivided attention," said Buster. "The way the private eye's poking around, she could be gone tomorrow."

"With any luck."

"Oh, yeah, right. You're just mad there's finally a girl in your bed and you're stuck sleeping out here."

"What'll you do if she turns out to be the Slasher? For real?"

"Come on, you and I both know there's no way she's the Slasher."

"What about that thing?" Franklin pointed at the scrapbook.

"Maybe it's a hobby. Like collecting stamps."

"A gruesome hobby."

"She doesn't strike me as the type to take up knitting."

"I don't know. Seems a natural. Those long, pointy needles?"

"As long as there's a chance the private eye thinks she could be the Slasher, I'd make a great alibi. And—while I have this."

"You can't blackmail someone into liking you."

"Pish. I don't want her to pretend she likes me. I want her to pretend she's *crazy* about me."

"If she's not the Slasher, this won't matter. If she is, you'll wind up with your own page in it."

Buster stroked the scrapbook. "All I want is time for us to grow on each other."

"Watch out she doesn't take pruning shears to your huckleberries first."

Buster re-tied the twine to his toe and stood up. "On the other side of that door is the cure for what ails me. I plan on being sick a long time."

Buster limped back into his bedroom, dignified, twine trailing. He shut the door.

"You've got it down to a fine art."

"Pssst. You out there."

Franklin looked around, realizing it came from inside his bedroom. He leaned his head close to the door.

"The nice one's gone back to bed."

"Not him. You."

"Okay, what?"

"Since I was a kid, I'd pray at bedtime all the clowns in the world would burst into a big ball of fire," Lucy whispered through the door.

"Thanks for the heads up. I'll keep a bucket of sand handy."

"I'm making an exception for you tonight."

Franklin leaned back from the door, puzzled. Then he smiled.

He made his bed in the big chair again. Tonight, it didn't seem as uncomfortable as last night.

chapter nine

Morning again. Franklin came into the kitchen.

Lucy was already up and at the sink again. She hadn't noticed him yet. She'd drained the last bit of her coffee but still held the cup. She stretched up on her tip-toes, straining to see the street behind the apartment building. She kept the curtain close to her face as she spied out the window.

"At it again, I see," he said.

Startled, she whirled around. She flung the empty coffee mug at him. He ducked as the mug sailed past his head and bounced off the wall, *pock-pock-pockiting* around on the floor. Lucy shook and grunted her frustration.

"Don't feel bad," said Franklin. "Years of clowning plus the occasional heckler hones the reflexes to razor sharpness. You'd have beaned a lesser clown."

"Don't you clowns wear bells, or honk, or something?" She shaded her eyes to avoid looking at him. "Can't you look normal?"

"Clown's gotta eat." He picked the cup up off the floor. "Relax. Buster and I will be at the Super City Mall all day." He hefted the cup a few times. "You managed to find the only plastic coffee mug in the place. Someone's looking out for me."

He stepped toward the counter, keeping himself out of Lucy's range as he stretched to set the cup back on the counter. He yanked his hand away and edged backward to the coffeemaker, keeping Lucy in sight the whole time.

"Everything else had clowns painted on it. The cups, the plates, the silverware."

"Mom. She had a thing for clowns. She figured everybody else should, too. She had me sleeping on circus sheets and wearing clown boxers until my senior year."

"High school?" Lucy winced at the picture.

"College." Franklin tipped the coffee pot. A single drip made the perilous drop into his cup. Refusing to let her beat him, Franklin used his finger to wipe the drip out of his cup and popped it into his mouth.

"Ahhhhh. Better than yesterday's. Coffeemaker must like you. I've seen it bite the fingers off strangers who get anywhere near it." He stroked the coffeemaker. "Good boy."

"Make your own coffee."

"So. How'd you get out without waking Buster?"

"Trade secret."

What she'd done was re-rig the cat's cradle contraption Buster had hooked up to the door, then plucked a strand. Buster yanked open the door, ready to begin his new life joined to this strange and wonderful creature with the fake first name and no last name. A steam iron swung in, smacking him in the face, laying him out, unconscious. She stepped over him on her way to the kitchen.

But Lucy didn't tell Franklin any of that.

"I may need it again," she said, leaving him to wonder.

Franklin took a fistful of bills from his clown purse and held them out to Lucy. "It's all I've got. Give us thirty minutes and call a cab or something."

"You're admitting you took my wallet?"

"I'm admitting you deserve a head start."

"I'm going to need every bit of my money you lost to get out of this town. A few bucks and a bus ticket won't cut it."

Buster came in holding his eye, moving his hand to squint at Lucy and Franklin in the kitchen.

"Hey, now they match," said Franklin.

"I've been thinking," Buster said to Franklin, but keeping his eyes on Lucy. "Maybe it's time for me to hang up the old nose. I never liked clowns. I mean, have you ever looked at one up close? I've always been on the inside looking out. How do little kids stand it?"

"We've got an all-day gig at the mall today. Founders Day? Remember?"

"Very appropriate. This is the first day of the rest of my life with the girl—I mean, *woman*—of my dreams. You honestly expect me to spoil it by going to work?"

Lucy froze, her eyes locked on Buster.

"Of course not." Franklin gave Lucy a sidelong glance.

Lucy's eyes clicked over onto Franklin.

"So it's just you and me," he said, shrugging at Lucy.

"Wait. What about you and her?"

"She wanted to be a clown for a day. You know, walk-a-mile-in-your-size-fifty-six-shoes kind of thing?"

Lucy twisted her neck so she could glare at Franklin with the volcanic intensity he was learning to know and dread. He fished an extra clown-nose from his pocket and held it out to her.

Buster leaned in at Franklin, whispering, "You said she hated clowns."

The curl in Lucy's lip was more than enough proof if he needed it.

"I told you. Therapy." Franklin leaned in to Buster. "Maybe it's *me* who could be the cure for what ails *her*."

Franklin smiled and sucked a big, airy swig from his empty coffee mug.

Lucy's mouth smiled at Franklin. Her eyes, however, could only be described as a warm, I-will-kill-you-and-eat-your-entrails-sautéed-in-hot-sauce kind of smile.

"No way, Frankie-boy." Buster pivoted and dashed back into his bedroom.

"I will not. Do you have any idea how badly I wanted to spit in your beer?"

"Best way is to lose yourself among all the other clowns. I'll keep Buster busy. You grab a cab, come back here for your stuff. Key's in the mailbox. You give Buster and the private eye the slip. Kill two birds—I didn't mean kill."

"What about my money?"

"I don't have it. Buster's not about to give it to me. Money won't do you much good if the detective figures out you're the one he's been tracking. You're running out of time."

Franklin could see the veins stand out in Lucy's neck, primed for her to go full negatory when Buster came bounding back in.

"Hey! I know! We could have a clown wedding! Clown bridesmaids, squirting flowers, whoopie cushions in the pews."

Lucy, her eyes flashing in a kind of angry surrender, fixed on Franklin. She snatched the clown nose from his hand and twisted it on.

"Brings out the blood red fury of your eyes," said Franklin.

In no time, they were dressed and headed for the street, with Franklin helping Lucy down the stairs. Franklin had Lucy all clowned up, her face painted with triangular eyebrows and a red-and-white frown. She insisted on the frown. She wore a multi-color, checkerboard jumper, red vest, topped off with tinsel hair under a Swiss-cheesed top hat full of random holes. She struggled down the stairs in a pair of Franklin's biggest shoes. He could see that Lucy trying to walk a mile in anyone's clown shoes would be tough going.

"How am I supposed to sneak anywhere in these things?"

"You're a natural. Your own mother wouldn't know you."

"You think this makes up for what happened at the bus stop?"

"Could it?"

"No way."

"Okay then, no. And I didn't take your wallet."

"It's your fault I dropped my bags. Doesn't matter who took it. It's your fault."

Franklin ran her bit of logic through the old neural network. "Can't argue with that." Although he wanted to try.

Buster burst from the apartment, still thrusting his arms through the sleeves of his coat. He pulled the door closed and duck-walked down the steps.

This was the first time Lucy had seen Buster done up in his own clown rig.

"Say something nice," said Franklin.

"I'd like to puke on him," said Lucy.

"The way Buster's feeling right now, he'll figure out a way to make it into a compliment and still blame me for it."

"In that case, I'd rather not waste it."

Buster wore two-toned clown shoes, multi-color baggy pants, a bright oversized red swallow-tail coat with gold buttons, a blue and white striped undershirt, fake collar and big, butterfly bowtie. He'd painted his face with oversized eyebrows, an oversized mouth turned up at the corners, which could be flexed into a sleazy leer with the twitch of a cheek muscle. He wore a long red nose, a mop of orange hair parted on the side and topped off by a battered blue derby with a tulip in the hatband.

Franklin reached to open the car door for Lucy, but Buster hip-checked Franklin out of the way. With a flourish, Buster pulled open the door.

Lisker yowled, throwing his hands out, startling the three of them and himself. He brushed an old clamshell container of stale fast food off his lap. He hooked his arms on the door and roof of the car, struggling to extricate himself from Franklin's vehicle. Very much like a baby yak working itself free of the birth canal.

"You could help, y'know," said Lisker.

"Makes you stronger if I don't," said Franklin.

With a grunt, Lisker popped free. "Thanks a lot, buddy."

"Anytime—buddy," said Franklin. "Why are you sleeping in my car?"

"I never sleep." Lisker brushed himself off and straightened his clothes. "I'm on a stake-out." He yawned, rubbed his face and fixed his clown wig and nose back into place.

"For what?"

"Catch the Slasher using your car. Saw some pretty odd tire tracks out where Big Rig nearly got it."

"My tires don't have any tread left on them."

"Exactly. Coincidence? I don't think so."

"I go out there for gas all the time."

Lisker circled Lucy, studying her closely but talking to Franklin. "What about last night? You need any gas last night?"

Lisker stopped and straightened up, his head cocked, still studying Lucy. He shook his finger at her. "That face."

Lisker clinched up his own face as if working hard to pull something stuck between the dried-up lobes of his brain.

"You haven't heard, have you?" Lisker went on. "They found Big Rig out on the highway early this morning. Lucky for him, he landed on somebody soft. Maybe saved his life."

"Lucky," said Franklin.

"Lucky for Big Rig. Lucky for the rest of you clowns."

"How's it lucky for the rest of us?"

"Slasher's getting careless. Maybe soft-hearted even. You know what happens when Slashers go soft?"

"They're easier to peel?"

Lisker pivoted, swooping in close on Lucy. "That clown face. Those clown gloves. Are you the girl from last night? At the bus stop? Phyllithh?"

"This is someone completely different. Phyllis is long gone. Never did get her last name." Franklin pushed Lucy behind himself.

Lisker's mouth popped open. "I only closed my eyes for a minute!" He scrambled, tumbled, pirouetted, then recovered and dived into his own car, driving off, fish-tailing all the way.

Lucy exhaled, pure relief.

"The fake face comes in handy, doesn't it?"

"You are a real pal. You had me thinking the whole clown thing was so you could horn in on my girl."

Franklin and Lucy turned around to look at Buster as he closed the hood of Franklin's car.

"But—in case you do get any ideas about horning in on my girl." Buster handed Franklin the distributor cap. With a gallant sweep of his arm, Buster invited Lucy into his clownmobile.

Lucy hesitated.

"You want to be stuck here when the private eye comes back?" Buster asked her.

The twist in Lucy's neck as she looked from Buster to Franklin made it easy for him to see she didn't like either option. But she got in with Buster.

Franklin could only watch them drive off.

◆ ◆ ◆

"She never looked back or anything," Franklin said to Gladys. He took a puff of his cigarette. He studied Gladys a long moment. "You seem like a needy person, given to meaningless relationships in search of a manageable intimacy."

Gladys's mouth hung open for a moment. "Damn." She took a drag on her own cigarette. "It shows?"

"I mention it because I want to ask—what do you look for in a guy?"

"Right now?"

"Like what's-his-name. Whoever it was stood you up?"

"It's still early."

"Early keeps getting later and later. What do you look for?"

"Something sharp. All the way up to the handle." Gladys sipped her drink, sucked hard on an ice cube, and crunched it.

◆ ◆ ◆

Sitting in the front seat next to Buster, Lucy *had* looked back, which Buster saw. He gunned the accelerator, putting a lot of quick distance between Lucy and Franklin. Lucy watched Franklin diminish into a red and blue speck.

"What a pest." Buster checked the mirror.

"He must've been in Franklin's car half the night, waiting for us."

"Not him. Frankie-boy."

"He's—okay, I guess. If he wasn't a clown."

"But would he lie under oath for you? I don't think so. Candy? Jewelry? Doesn't mean a thing. Perjury? Come's straight from the heart."

"Jail time would sure put a crimp in your style."

"It'll take more than jail time to keep you and me apart. It'll take a coma or a full-body cast."

"I like the sound of that. Do you have a preference?"

"Doesn't matter. Suffering for love is my middle name."

"Fair enough." Lucy settled back in the seat.

Buster smiled and did his fanny dance, swaying and bouncing.

The clownmobile motored onward.

chapter ten

At the shopping mall, a giant, noisy parking lot carnival was going full tilt. The place swarmed with shoppers, visitors, strolling entertainers, and scores of kids. Everyone dressed up, playing clown for a day.

A temporary midway of charity bazaar booths offering games of skill and chance lined the walkways.

A ring of hay bales encircling a carousel of padded steel pipes and bridled ponies made up the Enchanted Pony Ride. The enchantment consisted of colorful unicorn horns attached to the browbands of the ponies' headstalls.

At a propane fire pit, Wilderness Girls, in khaki skirts and camo vests, toasted marshmallows and sold campfire cuisine.

At Seafood Sam's booth, a large, decorated display tank held Goliath, billed as the biggest lobster in the tri-state area.

Three Wilderness Girls hung over the side of Goliath's tank. They waved a stick across the water, enticing the monster lobster to grab it. Out of the murky water, a giant, lightning quick claw snapped the stick, splashing the Wilderness Girls. Soaked and left holding the stub of a stick, the girls squealed until Seafood Sam chased them away from the tank.

Buster's clownmobile rolled up to the edge of the crowds. Lucy slipped out and flinched up against the side of the vehicle as a passel of shoppers all done up as clowns swarmed by. She dashed around to the rear of the clownmobile. Buster was already there waiting for her.

"So, you feeling a little more spiritually connected to me?"

Lucy pivoted and fast-walked around to the front of the vehicle. Buster was right there waiting for her.

"You're getting pretty fast in those." He pointed at her feet.

Lucy pivoted—right into Franklin who had been standing behind her.

"All right, all right." Buster pushed Franklin's arms away from Lucy. "How'd you get here?"

What Franklin said was, "Trade secret."

What Franklin did was a little more desperate.

As the van pulled away and left Franklin standing there back at the apartments, he burst into a dead run in the opposite direction. He achieved cartoon velocity in less than half-a-second. A personal best, if he'd thought to clock himself.

Commandeering rides as he went, Franklin perched on the handlebars of the paperboy's bike, doubled up with a skateboarder, straddled a mom's baby jogger, and finished up on the roof rack of a Volkswagen. It stopped just short of Buster's clownmobile, dumping Franklin onto the asphalt. Franklin had barely enough time to spring up behind Lucy, ready for her to collide with him. It gave him another moment of full frontal contact to savor the rest of his life.

The crowd of kids gathered around Buster's clownmobile grew with the spectacular arrival of the lanky, blue-haired clown.

Franklin said to Lucy, "Why aren't you gone?"

"I'm having trouble achieving escape velocity from Buster, the human glue-stick here."

Franklin turned to the crowd of youngsters.

"Hey, kids! You know what Mister Dippy's got in those great big pockets of his? Free candy bars! Get them before he gets away!"

The kids dived for Buster's pants.

"Whoa! Get out of there, ya pickpockets!" shouted Buster, overwhelmed by the snaking hands of swarming candy bandits reaching deep into his pockets all the way down to his socks.

"Quick!" Franklin waved to get Buster's attention as he struggled under the weight of a dozen sweet-seeking missiles. "Head for the stage! It's your only hope!"

Buster high-stepped it for the safety of the mini-stage, slapping at the grabby-handed kids.

Franklin turned to Lucy. "Get lost. The only things Buster keeps in his pockets are holes."

Lucy hesitated only a moment. Franklin thought she might even say thank you. Instead, she turned and ducked away, disappearing through the crowd.

Franklin joined Buster on the mini-stage set among the charity booths of the midway. He dropped his giant carpetbag of props with a clunk. Buster stuffed the linings of his turned-out pockets back in, then swiveled his pants to straighten them.

Franklin dived head first into the carpetbag, digging out juggling clubs, flipping them over his shoulder. As Franklin flipped each club, Buster snatched it mid-flight until he had all four of the clubs spinning in the air. He finished with a flourish, the clubs fanned out in his hands.

As Buster paraded around, soaking up the applause, Franklin went searching for the clubs he'd pulled from his bag. When he didn't find them, Franklin turned to the kids, mouth stretched wide and arms outspread. He circled the stage, asking where, oh, where in the world his clubs had gone.

Buster, once more juggling clubs, bounced a club off the back of Franklin's head.

Glaring at Buster, Franklin rubbed his head, hitched up his pants, and picked up the club, ready to bean him back. Buster flipped another club at him, and another, until they were juggling the clubs together, circling, Buster keeping an irate Franklin at bay.

Away from the stage, with everyone else fixed on Buster and Franklin, Lucy eased backward through the crowd, letting people fill in the gap she'd left.

The backside of the crowd thinned, clearing the way for Lucy to skedaddle. She tip-toed past a large, blue metal thrift store container piled up with donations of discarded clothing and housewares.

Before she could get her feet free and fly, a metal hinge creaked. The face of Lisker peeked out of the container.

"Leaving town?" he asked. "A little birdie told me you might be the mystery girl I'm looking for."

Lucy threw a box of underwear at him and fled back through the crowd.

Up on stage, Buster tripped over a dirty spot and ordered Franklin to clean it up. Franklin frowned and did his slope-shouldered march over to the carpetbag. Pouting, he pulled out a bucket and a mop with a telescoping handle. Franklin scowled at Buster. He went to work cleaning the whole stage. Running the mop under Buster, Franklin forced him backward around the stage. Buster took hold of Franklin, still mopping furiously, and pointed him in the opposite direction. Once Buster's back was turned, Franklin took aim with the mop. He raised it up over his shoulder, ready for a home-run swing at Buster's head when suddenly Buster turned around.

Franklin jackknifed himself into an innocent mop stroke—over the shoulder, down to the floor, up over the shoulder, back to the floor. Just a clown mopping a floor. Nothing to see. Franklin waved at him to turn around and ignore what he was doing behind Buster's back.

Buster turned his back again, then whipped around. But Franklin ignored him and kept mopping, faster and faster, his mop a pumping piston. Franklin backed into Buster, catching him in the gut with the mop handle in rapid fire strokes.

Buster, winded, staggered around the stage, recovering his breath. Franklin held his heart and pulled his mouth into a great big, sorrowful frown, making a great show of regret, even as he threw a secret laugh of victory at the audience.

Buster put an arm around Franklin and lifted his hat, tousled his hair, placed his hat on the ground and tromped it flat. He peeled it up off the ground and placed it with great care back on Franklin's head.

Lucy swam through the crush of people along the midway and straight into a heavy-set woman. Lisker, now wearing a dress and curly wig, watched her from behind a magazine he'd rigged up with eye holes.

Lisker lowered his magazine. "Aren't we in an awful hurry to get out of town?"

"Just one of the clowns," said Lucy with a slapstickity laugh and clap of her hands.

"That's not what the little birdie told me."

Lucy fled back the way she came, elbowing her way through. She jinked and dodged between people still milling around the stage and among the booths.

By this time, a local rock band had taken over the stage, pounding away for the crowd. Franklin and Buster moved along the midway, doing their walkaround gags.

Lucy found a gap in the crowd and paused, breathing hard, her hands on her knees. She gave a quick glance behind herself and dashed right into the back of a tall, fat farmer with his straw hat pushed low on his head. The farmer lifted his hat. It was Lisker facing her, wearing his overalls backward.

"Okay, okay. Who's this little bird?" Lucy huffed to catch her breath.

Lisker pointed across the midway.

Buster gave out with a big smile, using both hands to make moose antlers at her.

"Cheep-cheep!" Buster warbled at them, doing a little leap and a click of his heels.

Lucy backed into a gaggle of kids who swarmed her, plucking at her costume and tugging at her arms.

"Heyheyhey! I'm not a clown!" she shouted at them, prying their arms from her legs.

"I knew it!" Lisker grabbed her wrist.

"He's the clown!" She pointed at Lisker.

The kids looked at Lisker and gave out with a collective "Ewwwww!"

"What a mopey old face," said one of the kids, his own face pinched up at the sight.

"Hey. You know the best way to fix a sad face like his?" Lucy shouted at them.

"What?" they shouted back.

"What?" Lisker asked as well, surrounded by a pack of eager kids who looked primed and ready for some serious mayhem.

"Tickle bombs!" Lucy radiated waggle-fingers at Lisker.

Kids are always up for a game of torment-the-grouch. Especially if a bona fide clown says it's okay. The kids flew at the sad old clown, reaching to get through the denim overalls and body fat.

Lisker burst into a dead run, showing some smooth moves for a lumpy kind of guy.

Lucy scampered in the opposite direction.

Reaching the bus stop, Lucy dropped onto a bench next to three grannies in face paint and yellow derbies. She kept glancing backward.

She sensed a presence and whipped around. The grannies were gone, leaving Buster sitting on the bench beside her. He sucked on a lollipop like he hadn't a care in the world.

"How long do you plan on keeping this up?" she asked.

"Until I run out of tattle-tales." Buster fanned a handful of lollipops. Kids pounced on them from everywhere. Buster sauntered off, leaving the kids sucking lollipops and watching Lucy.

Lucy, her eyes turned into smoldering slits, watched him go.

"Hey!" One of those lollipop lickers tugged on Lucy's sleeve. "Aren'tcha supposed to be funny? Tell a joke or something."

"You hear the one about the stupid clown they had to take away in an ambulance?" asked Lucy, watching the back of Buster's head.

"No!" shouted the kids, primed for a great personal injury joke.

"Neither did he." Lucy continued to watch Buster's melon-soft head in the distance.

The kids checked with each other to make sure they were all thinking the same thing—this was one unfunny clown.

◆ ◆ ◆

Franklin and Buster were still working the midway, roaming among the charity booths. Kids clustered around them, turning into a forest of arms stretched out for instant tattoos that Franklin drew with color markers. Buster, standing next to Franklin, tied balloon animals for the little kids, and suggestive figures for girls willing to show him a driver's license proving they were over eighteen.

A flaming marshmallow flew past, plopping on the ground at Buster's feet, smoldering down to a charred lump of wet goo.

Buster, twisting a long balloon into a bulging pink knot, frowned as he locked eyes with the kid sucking on one of the lollipops. The kid pointed across the midway. Buster held another balloon to his lips. With a long and mighty puff he inflated it, weaving as he blew so he could catch a quick look behind himself.

Across the way, Lucy stood with the Wilderness Girls at their fire pit. She turned to hide her face and the stick she'd been holding.

Buster tied off the balloon into a rose bud with an engorged stem, as he did a *do-si-do* around Franklin, swapping places with him as he handed out the balloon figure.

At the fire pit, Lucy had turned away to light more marshmallows. She didn't see Buster make the switch.

"How about we make it two dollars a bulls-eye?" Lucy said to the Wilderness Girls gathered around.

Sticky, flaming marshmallows arched over the midway and machine-gunned Franklin's britches with amazing accuracy.

Lucy looked around to check out their handiwork and tally up their reward.

"Oops." Lucy handed the girls the stick and lost herself in the crowd.

Franklin sniffed, smelling something sweet, maybe a little something acrid mixed in.

"Is that you?" Franklin asked Buster.

Buster leaned back to check the seat of Franklin's pants, now in flames licking up the back of Franklin's costume.

"Nope. It's you." Buster kept twisting another biologically accurate appendage that could pass for a deformed jalapeño.

The pain finally reached through Franklin's underwear.

"Whoa-ho-ho-ho!" he yodeled, bounding through the crowd, leaping butt-first into Goliath's tank, the steam hissing and dying away.

Franklin's face sagged into an ecstatic smile of relief.

Ka-SNAP!

"Yeoooow!"

Franklin launched himself off the edge of the tank, Goliath dangling from his britches, holding a good-sized chunk of Franklin's glutes in its claw.

The kids swarmed to watch the swinging, dancing, leaping fight to the death between Franklin's buttocks and Goliath's claws. Franklin twisted and torqued himself trying to dislodge the beast. Franklin grabbed the shovel away from the guy scooping pony poop at the riding ring. With great, wide swings, Franklin whacked himself on the fundament, trying to bop his crustaceous attacker insensible.

What ingenuity, everyone would say later. What flexibility! What comic timing! The crowd flowed with Franklin, giving him room for this titanic battle of the species. A truly and seriously crowd-pleasing performance. Too bad Franklin was in no position to enjoy any of it.

The battle over, Franklin sat on a big, cushy pillow behind the stage, stripped down to his union suit, a red, sleeveless number. He patched the scorched and shredded bottom on his britches. Across the way, under a newly hand-lettered sign, a sour-faced Seafood Sam served up a hasty batch of lobster fritters.

Franklin, making a virtue of necessity, stitched two enormous band-aids across the seat of his costume, hiding the burn holes and claw gashes.

When he'd finished, he and Buster went back out to do more of their walkaround gags, filtering through the crowd still milling along the midway.

From out of the crowd, Buster felt a tug at his jacket. He looked down to find a little girl rubbing her eye and pointing to a large Mylar balloon snagged on the mall entrance marquee high above them. A ladder leaned, oh so conveniently, against the marquee. The rope wrapped around the bottom rung, a tad too obvious.

Buster slid a glance at another of the kids sucking on one of his lollipop bribes. The kid pointed back through the parking lot.

Lucy, hunkered down, peered over the hood of a car.

Buster looked up the ladder, shook his head at the crowd gathered round and called out, "Is there a fireman in the house?"

"Come on," shouted the crowd, ready for him to get on with the show.

The little girl twisted her fists in her eyes, boo-hooing for all she was worth.

Buster whistled for Franklin and pointed to the balloon at the top of the ladder. Franklin took one look at the height and shook his head. He didn't want any part of it.

Buster stretched his face into the biggest frown his cheeks could achieve as he pointed at the little girl and clutched his heart, wringing it for sympathy, circling inside the crowd.

"Come on!" they shouted again. "Be a hero!"

"Hee-ro. Hee-ro," they chanted as Buster circled again, whipping them up.

Buster called for a vote. Who did they want to see go up the ladder? Frowning and shaking his head, Buster pointed to himself, squeezed his flabby arms and showed off his wobbly knees. The crowd booed.

Buster pointed to Franklin, holding his costume by the shoulders, faking some mighty impressive brawn on the skinny clown. The crowd cheered long and hard.

Franklin looked at the little girl who beamed a grateful smile at him, hands clasped under her chin. He looked at the smiling crowd eager for the payoff.

Franklin tested the bottom rung of the ladder and looked up. The top rung looked miniscule, vanishing into the clouds. But the crowd was keen, and an audience is an audience. Unable to resist being the hero, Franklin started up the ladder, a rickety, wobbly climb.

Halfway up, the ladder began bucking under Franklin's heavy steps. He clamped on until it stopped. He started up again, inch-worming toward the top. Almost there, Franklin missed a rung, putting his foot through. He pulled his leg back out and slipped off the other side. Panicked and dan gling underneath, Franklin bicycled his legs, desperate to get a toehold on the rung again. He managed to get a foot through and swung his leg, hooking the side to work his way back around onto the ladder. Counting how many rungs he had left to go, he was convinced there were vul- tures waiting for him. But the crowd, little matchstick heads way down below, seemed so happy, looking up at him. He kept climbing.

Holding onto the other end of the rope, the Wilderness Girls followed a big, bearded guy in boots and ball cap, who climbed into the cab of a pickup truck. The girls scrambled to knot the rope around the truck's bumper as Lucy huddled with them.

Back on the ladder, Franklin had reached the top and grabbed the balloon string.

"Ta da!" crowed Franklin.

The audience cheered as Buster took the bows down below.

The truck's taillights went on, scattering the Wilderness girls. The truck backed into the lane, turned, and headed for the exit, the rope going taut with a thrum. Lucy looked back toward the marquee and saw Franklin at the top of the ladder.

"Oops." Lucy winced, clapping her hand over her eyes.

A moment later, the ladder clanged by, dragged by the pickup, as Lucy peeked between her fingers to where Franklin had been perched.

Franklin clung to the canvas banner hung on the marquee. With a slow, agonizing rip, it tore free of its grommets and swung Franklin cement-ward. Franklin clinched his eyes shut against the coming impact.

Morbid curiosity got the better of Franklin. He had to peek at his certain doom. He wished he hadn't. Vehicles bore down on him as he whipped between them, brushing bumpers, then swung back up into the air. At the top of the arc, the rope stretched taut and whip-snapped, propelling him into a slow, rag-doll tumble over the parking lot.

Franklin landed in a lady's shopping cart. The cart broke away from her and started rolling downhill, faster and faster.

Stuck backward, Franklin rocketed down through the parking lot. Unable to see the horrific danger waiting, he raced for the mall's busiest entrance. He zipped through the intersection, against the light, horns honking, and tires screeching as cars slid to a stop.

The shopping cart carrying Franklin raced toward the parking lot opposite the mall, on the other side of the intersection. It threaded through the slicing traffic, bounced up over the curb, and slammed into the retaining wall opposite. Franklin, thrown from the basket, went flying, hard-stopped against the back-end of a delivery van.

He slid down until his belt caught on the door handle, leaving him hung up, swaying.

The delivery van door swung open, slamming Franklin against the truck body. The delivery guy peeked out, looking around for the source of the big noise against the side of his van. Not seeing Franklin, he pulled the door closed. The van drove off, Franklin still hanging, upside down, from the handle.

chapter eleven

IT WAS ALREADY DARK OUTSIDE when the door of the Big Top Tavern blew open. Franklin, shredded, windblown, and tire-tracked from crotch-to-forehead, stood in the doorway. He made for the nearest stool and planted himself on it.

"Gimme a wedgie." Franklin's voice was as graveled as the roadbeds over which he'd been dragged.

Red set up three rocks glasses, one with a jigger of bourbon, one with a jigger of scotch, and one with a jigger of rum, all neat. He racked the glasses between the triangle of his thumbs and forefingers to slide the triptych of liquor into place in front of Franklin.

Franklin dipped his bar napkin in the first glass and dabbed at the raw spots all over his face.

"Unlucky day?" asked Red.

"Unlucky? Nahhh." Franklin knocked back the rest of the bourbon in the first glass. "Speeding toward the highway, hanging from the back of a truck, falling off just before the on-ramp and all that traffic? You might call that lucky. Missed being run over by, not one, not two, but three long-haul truckers following right behind? You might call that lucky. Being run over by a gorgeous woman on a motorcycle who feels so bad she gives you a ride all the way back into town, and you get to hold her around her perfect waist the whole way? You might call *that* lucky." Franklin took up the second glass. "Not me. But somebody might." He knocked back the second shot, one eye squinted shut against the burn running down his gullet. He blew out hard, licked his lips and set aside the second glass. "Water."

Red set down a glass of water.

"Yeah," said a voice out of the darkness. "Lucky. A lobster in your pants. The old Slasher would've filled the tank with piranha." It was Lisker, nursing his drink and his own wounds at the other end of the bar.

"You sound disappointed," said Franklin.

"Ever hear the one about the trick wading pool at the kids' party in Dubuque? Clown steps in and *woosh*! drops clean out of sight. Slasher used a backhoe. Worked through the night. Neighbors never heard a thing. Clown stepped into a twenty-foot hole filled with water. Right to the bottom. Gone!" Lisker snapped his fingers.

"You want real ingenuity? Try Montana," said Lisker. "This clown used to drive all over the place in a candy-striped school bus. One day, on some back-road in the boonies, way, way out, clown sees a big wooden hand waving on a fence post. He stops. Opens the door. What's he see? Three dozen starving Yorkies, all wearing ruffled collars and red balls on their tails. They're up the steps and inside the bus like a shot." Lisker sipped his drink. "No one could ever figure out how the Slasher managed to round up so many feral Yorkies."

"Sounds like you miss it."

"My personal favorite though, by far, was the tiny car in Arkansas, stuffed full of clowns. You know? Classic stuff. Scooped it up in a skip loader and dumped it into an industrial manure pit. Now every spring torenias and black-eyed susans grow all over the place." Lisker took another slug of his drink.

"The lobster? The shopping cart? The truck? Physical comedy like that doesn't happen by accident. Ouch." Franklin pressed his thumb to the bloody crack in his lip.

"Didn't look like you planned any of it."

"Can I quote you? On my résumé?"

Lisker snorted, clearly unconvinced.

"You know what I'm thinking, pal? I'm thinking today's just a warm-up. The Slasher is getting ready to pull something big. When it happens, I'm gonna be there to slap the cuffs on."

"If you thought the Slasher was behind all that, why didn't you slap the cuffs on then? Save me the road burns."

"For a few practical jokes you could find in the Big Book of Cheap Gags for Boys? Nobody pays a million bucks for the movie rights to the story of how Ace Private Eye Dick Lisker caught the Baggy Pants Class Clown."

"Movie rights?"

"For the book I'm writing. Last chapter. Me and the Slasher. *Mano a mano.* Gonna be big."

Lisker slid off his stool, steadying himself. He pointed at Franklin, sighting along his index finger.

"I feel it in my bones. Because, if the Slasher doesn't break out of this slump soon with something spectacular, it's back to working personal injury claims for me." Lisker tottered toward the door. He stopped, his hand on the door handle, and turned back to Franklin. "In a way, you're doing me a favor."

"I am? How?"

"Fooling yourself, thinking maybe the Slasher's gone soft on you, of all the clowns around here." Lisker shook his head. "Spices up the last chapter with a little romance. Sad sack clown and the beautiful killer? He's wearing a bull's eye like every other clown in this burg. Everybody knows it but him. You might want to keep that in mind next time you go all suck face on some strange broad who just happened to blow into town." Lisker winked, aimed his finger pistol at Franklin again, pulling the trigger and clicking his tongue. He went out the door, disappearing into the night lit by neon and street lamps.

"That's three times." Lucy's voice came out of the dark at the other end of the bar.

"That he nearly caught you?"

"That you covered for me."

"Accidents. I've always been clumsy. People think it's a drinking problem." Franklin hooked the water glass rim under his nose and tipped it up, his tongue lapping at the air as water trickled down the sides of his face. He stopped. "Since I was a kid. I've tried to quit. But I need the laughs."

Franklin listened to the silence at the other end of the bar.

"In the dark, no one can see you smile," he said. "Maybe you heard it before." Franklin took a pull at the third drink, swirled the liquid, washing his teeth with it and threw his head back for a cleansing gargle deep in his gullet. He looked over at Lucy. "Sure-fire way to peg the meter on a breathalyzer test. Officer Joe'd have to throw me in the jug for public intoxication, right? Spend the night in jail? Buster's happy. You're happy. I get some sleep."

Nothing but a chasm of silence in the dark beyond.

"At the bus stop? I didn't take your wallet. I was trying to help."

"You ran. What was I supposed to think?"

"Try this. The idea of letting you go through my pockets seemed a tad suicidal at the time?"

"Not sure what I would have done if I'd caught you."

"Me, either. Reason enough to avoid finding out."

Lucy didn't seem to have anything to say back. They sat there in a silence growing longer.

Finally, Lucy said, "You clowns can't keep your hands or your mouth to yourself."

"It wasn't me kissing you out of the blue the other night."

"The private eye was watching. Didn't mean anything."

"That's okay. I was wearing the wax lips I like to use for kissing that doesn't mean anything. Sorry about the pocket lint."

Still nothing. If Franklin was smart, he'd slip off the stool, race back to the apartment, reclaim his room, and hide under his bed until his romantical delusions evaporated.

But he wasn't smart. So he said, "You know what your problem is?"

"Clowns get to breathe the same air I do?"

"You haven't spent enough time with the right clowns."

Franklin, feeling the pleasant altitude he'd achieved, turned into quite the *gallante*. He slid off his stool, steadying himself with both hands on the bar until he could be sure of his balance. He crossed around to her and offered his arm. She recoiled.

"Cheap therapy. Trust me?"

"Why should I trust you?"

"I'm going to let you drive." Franklin held out his car keys.

She studied him a moment. She slid off her own stool and took the keys from Franklin. She held them in the light, examining them.

If Franklin knew more about women, he might be able to read her look. Was it one of desperation or calculation?

Was he being an idiot? Was he making it easier for her to transport his remains to some secluded spot and dump him?

"Hey? See you tomorrow?" asked Red.

"Yeah. The way my luck's going." She closed the keys in her fist. Lucy seemed to deflate at the thought of another day on the job among the clowns.

Lucy and Franklin made for the door, colliding shoulder-to-shoulder in the doorway. Franklin gave way and made a sweeping gesture for her to go first.

"I don't take freebies from clowns." She waved for him to go first.

They studied each other for a moment. They both made for the door, wedging themselves in the doorway again, shoulder to shoulder.

"I'd have been disappointed if we hadn't done that," said Franklin, spitting out the tumble of her hair covering his face.

Lucy pulled free and launched herself through the door and into the night.

◆ ◆ ◆

The Funny Farmhouse Day Care Center sat in the middle of the block between two residential streets. The front lawn bristled with large wooden clown cut-outs.

Franklin had Lucy by the hand, a marvelous achievement if he'd been sober enough to appreciate it. He led her through the gaily-colored nightmare.

"Didn't I tell you?" Franklin knocked on the wooden cut-outs, pleased at his brainstorm.

Lucy held back.

"Those are a whole new level of creepy." She had a distinct *urp* and growl in her voice, clear signs a drinker's soul-cleansing puke was on its way.

"Creepy?" Franklin couldn't see it.

"The way their eyes follow me around." Lucy shifted to test what she was seeing. "And how their lips curl up." She twisted her lips open, baring her own teeth, mimicking what she saw. "What kind of deviant sticks a bunch of clowns right where kids have to walk?"

Franklin frowned, mouthing the word 'deviant.' He studied the clowns but couldn't see what it was she saw. Lucy kept wincing, turning her face first one way then the other, snapping her teeth together.

"Shit! That one licked his lips." Lucy pulled away from Franklin. "They're all doing it!"

Lucy tripped, sitting down hard. She crab-walked backward until she could flip over, get to her feet, and dash off into the dark.

Franklin watched her disappear. He looked back at the clown cut-outs. Still flat and immobile. He trotted after her.

Lucy collided with a tool shed seeming to have sprung up out of the dark. She clawed at the door until she found the handle. She yanked it open, ripping the lock and hasp right out of the jamb, nearly knocking herself backward when it gave way to her pulling.

"Get rid of them," she shouted, ducking inside the shed, slamming the door shut behind her. "They're *your* friends!"

Franklin eased up to the shed door, careful of what a bottled-up crazy lady with that kind of strength might do to the soft flesh of an inebriated clown. He tugged at the door handle. She'd managed to jam it shut from the inside. He put his ear against the door. No sound.

"Are you okay in there? Hey? You okay?"

A gas motor coughed to life inside the shed.

"I'm fine now," Lucy shouted over the motor's whine.

The shed door swung open. Lucy appeared sporting goggles, work gloves, and a roaring chainsaw.

"Got some therapy of my own." She waved the chainsaw, marching off toward the wooden clowns.

"Uh, wait." Franklin slinked after her. Now the crazy lady was armed.

He caught up to her as she hacked at the cut-out clowns. She swept the chainsaw through the wooden figures, sending splintering heads, arms, and legs flying.

A crazed, berserker lumberjill, she was very good with that thing. He didn't want to think where she got the practice.

Lights in the nearby houses started popping on.

Lucy eviscerated the last wooden clown as a police siren warbled in the distance. The flashing lights of the police cruiser became visible as it came up the street.

"Enough therapy for now," he said. But she was already gone. The goggles, work gloves, and chainsaw lay discarded among the splintered wood. Franklin scuttled into the shadows.

Franklin reached his car and looked around for Lucy. He hunkered down as the patrol car passed by, lights flashing.

His car door opened, nearly clocking him as he squatted beside it. Lucy was inside, her hand over the dome light, covering up the gleam.

"Get in," said Lucy, her teeth clamped down hard on the words.

Franklin crawled into the driver's seat, eased the door closed until the latch clicked. He started the car, the syncopation of the cylinders struggling to catch rattled loud against the night. They creeped away, the darkness swallowing them up.

◆ ◆ ◆

Franklin let the car roll to a stop at the entrance of Kanega's Funtime Village. A weather-beaten amusement park, its big gates were locked, everything shut up for the season.

Franklin got out of the car and went around to open the door for Lucy. She unfolded herself from the front seat and stepped to the ground. She held her hand in front of her, gripping her wrist, nursing a wound.

"Things are made of wood and one of them still takes a bite out of me."

"A few splinters. We can get you fixed up here."

Lucy looked through the cyclone fencing toward the dark and shuttered attractions. The only light came from the security lights overhead on the power poles scattered around.

"No way!" Lucy backed up against the car. "This is where clowns spawn. Underground caves full of clown pods!"

Lucy's fear sucked Franklin in, depositing him at the top of a long, rickety run of stairs down to an unfinished cellar with Lucy next to him. Sure enough, Franklin sees the pods of little clowns hanging upside down from overhead. Their over-sized red noses sniff the scent of Lucy's bloodied hand.

Clown nannies in blood-stained aprons swoop in from behind, elbowing past Franklin. They grab Lucy and carry her down the steps to the pods with shining teeth and snapping clown lips.

Franklin fights to reach Lucy, knocking past armed goons, seltzering them with a convenient soda bottle he's pulled from his big pocket.

When Franklin reaches Lucy, she's thrashing, caught up in the talons of the little clown pods, her clothes torn. He rips at the clown pod hands, freeing her. He's about to scoop Lucy into his arms when she punched his shoulder and said, "Hey! Did I guess right? You come from pods?"

The fantastical escape scene evaporated, leaving Franklin to stare into the darkened amusement park.

"You're standing there like you're having second thoughts about bringing me home to meet your family."

"Mom says she found me in a pile of sawdust at the circus. Buster's the one who came from a pod." Franklin pulled out his keys and opened the padlock, rolling the large gate back a few feet.

"Old man Kanega lets me keep my stuff here. There's a whole circus *schtick* we do when he opens the place up. Summers and all the big holidays when there's a crowd." He stepped through and spread out his arms. "We have the place to ourselves." He pointed to her hand. "We can get you patched up without Buster sticking his nose in. He doesn't like coming in here."

Looking around, Lucy said, "I wonder why the hell not."

"No women to pick up."

"He doesn't bring them here, all dark and lonesome this way?"

"Would you let him?" Franklin shook his head. "Okay, if you weren't bleeding and needed medical attention, would you? No." At least he hoped not. Which he did not say out loud.

The crickets and cicadas made the only noise. A breeze blew through the arcade spotted with pools of light.

Seeing how it must look to her, listening to the sounds around them, the place did seem scary.

Lucy stayed outside the fencing, watching for anything squirming around in the shadows.

"Convenient. Am I just another one of the women you bring here?"

"You don't count." Franklin turned and walked into the park so Lucy couldn't see him wince at his runaway mouth. He heard footsteps, cocked his head slightly, and saw her following him in. Nevertheless, she twisted and turned, alert to anything about to sneak up on her.

They reached the side door to the circus pavilion, a tent-like structure made of sheet metal. He unsnapped another of the locks and led her into the large, open space inside.

Franklin left Lucy standing in the dark by the door.

"You know, the only thing missing is the weird music, just before the pod clowns pop out at me, right?" Lucy said into the darkness.

Nightmarish, throbbing music filled the space.

"Oh, thanks a lot."

It stopped.

"Sorry," Franklin called out from the dark. "Wrong button."

Lights came on around the inside of the tent.

The pavilion was less like a tent and more like a big circular shed. Bleacher seating circled the pavilion, with a front entrance for the audience and a rear entrance for the performers. Ropes and lighting instruments hung from the grid overhead. Rolled-up scenery drops, rugs, and lengths of lumber and pipe filled the rafters above the grid.

Dull blue matting covered the large main floor. Red bumper blocks painted with yellow stars marked out the center ring. Mini-trampolines, bull tubs, ramps, tumbling mats, and chairs in assorted bright colors cluttered the edges of the ring. Stacked up around the rear entrance were racks of costumes and open crates of props and gadgets. Oversized props, like giant baby bottles, safety pins, hammers, and spoons laid around loose.

"Through here." Franklin stood in the doorway of the rear entrance.

Once past the door, Franklin led Lucy through a well-used common area and into a men's locker room. Inside, the space was small, the cement floor and cinderblock walls painted industrial green. The fluorescent strip lights overhead made the place all the more unappealing. The fixtures buzzed with the effort to keep the bulbs lit. Colorful one-sheets for concerts, carnivals, and car races covered the walls. Notes, numbers, and random graffiti filled up the edges of each poster, old or new.

A long countertop ran along one wall under mirrors framed with make-up lights. Lockers were fixed to the opposite wall. One end of the room opened onto shower stalls. The other end led to the toilets, with sinks at either side of the doorway.

"Locker room for the kids working the park. We get to use it for show days," said Franklin.

"Very homey."

Franklin filled a kettle with water and put it on a hot plate, setting it to boil. He took up two mugs, blew the dust out of them and dropped in two tea bags.

"You know, I'd heard somewhere how clown breath could be used as a disinfectant."

"That's just for luck. Boiling water'll kill the germs." Franklin took down a first-aid kit, pulled out chairs for them and sat at the counter.

Obviously, she had to think about it before sitting down. Maybe she felt the need to check for a whoopee cushion.

Franklin opened the first aid kit, took out tweezers, and reached for Lucy's damaged hand. She still held herself by the wrist. Obvious, too, she had to think about surrendering her hand as well.

Franklin went to work pulling splinters out of her hand.

"A chainsaw improves the whole clown experience. I highly recommend it." Lucy studied her wounds as Franklin worked.

"See? You know how to have a good time with clowns."

"Ow!" she barked, yanking her hand free. "You having a good time?"

Franklin hesitated a moment, then reached for her hand, going back to work with the tweezers.

"Should've worn gloves." Franklin concentrated on her hand.

"I did. They were full of holes."

He pulled out a splinter, wiped it off the tweezers, and went back to tweezing.

"You know," said Franklin, fixed on her hand, "I don't even know your real name. Makes me a lousy alibi."

"You don't believe it really is Phyllithh?" She gave him an extra wet blast of the raspberry. He did a big old wipe of his eye for her. She ducked her head. Hiding a smile, maybe? She went back to studying her hand as he tweezed at the splinters.

"You must not think I'm so dangerous, letting me get you alone here."

"When Lisker told us about Rib Eye? The look on your face? Not a dangerous face." Franklin wiped the tweezers on his pant leg. "All done. That didn't hurt so much, did it?" With all the indifference in the world, he asked, "Anything else I can do for you?"

She blew softly at the raw spot on her hand. "You could take off the fake face. I don't know what the real you looks like. In case, like, you know, I need to pick you out of a police lineup."

"Wise old clown once told me, 'never take off your face while the audience is watching.' Words to live by."

"You clowns're all alike. One way or another, we're nothing but an audience to you."

"I have peanuts you can throw if it makes you feel better," said Franklin, but wincing down deep where she couldn't see it.

Perhaps she could feel it, sitting so close to him, because she studied the wound, frowned, and said, "It doesn't look like you got it all." She put her hand, palm up on his knee again.

Franklin chuffed before putting on a pair of spring-eyeball glasses. The eyeballs danced over her hand as he turned it to check the palm and fingers front and back.

"I hate to be the one to tell you this," said Franklin, looking up at her, the eyeballs dangling on his cheeks, "but it's a perfect specimen. May I have it for my collection? You'll never miss it."

She lifted her hand. "Sorry. I'd rather not break up the set. They've been in the family forever."

Franklin took off the glasses and folded them up. "I thought you'd be long gone." It took some effort for him to sound disappointed she was still here.

"Buster and his minions kept ratting me out." Lucy ran her perfect hand through her perfect hair, showing off her perfect forehead and ears. Okay, maybe not *perfect* perfect. But perfect enough for him.

"This town is bad news. The private eye's been on my tail across half the country. I usually manage to ditch him. Until now. I'd have been long gone if—" she stopped herself. Plain enough to Franklin she closed herself off again.

"If you still had your wallet."

"Yeah, well. Nothing to do about it now."

"Why you?"

"Why me, what?"

"What's he got makes him so sure it could be you?"

"I was working a lounge in Reno. A clown convention. One of them got grabby and I poured a pitcher of margaritas down his pants. Got me fired."

"Doesn't sound so bad."

It didn't sound bad to Franklin because he sees Lucy done up as a cocktail waitress. She wears a strapless black satin bustier and a tiny wrap skirt knotted high up on one side. She stands with her hip cocked, a drink tray balanced at shoulder level. He'd love a margarita right now.

"Next morning, same clown turned up as a lawn ornament, spewing water from surgically inserted sprinklers."

"Yeeowch."

"Wired up to the trellis, one hose—" Lucy put up a rigid digit to show him exactly what had been done.

"How about we not. I don't need the details. Ever."

"Best part." Lucy shrugged. For her, maybe. "Anyway, I beat it out of town before the cops came looking for me."

"Why? You didn't have anything to do with it. Did you?"

"I told you. Blackouts! I'm not going to stick around and find out. The private eye happened to be in Reno. That's what he does. Follows clowns, checking any place they gather in large numbers. He connected me to the dead clown and took out after me."

The picture of Lucy the cocktail waitress came back into focus. Franklin's eye travels down where he now sees the bloody knife in her hand. His eye travels further down to her foot, in a black stiletto. Planted on the face of the clown lying dead at her feet. How's a woman able to do that? Work on her feet for eight hours in shoes like those?

"Working in what?" asked Lucy.

Sheesh. He must have said it out loud. The picture of Lucy as a killer cocktail waitress shattered into molecules, dribbling away in every direction.

"It wouldn't take much to turn it into a juicy story," said Franklin. "Homicidal beauty. Harmless clowns. Make for a hot book."

"Yeah, well, I'm thinking it's more like harmless beauty and homicidal clowns."

"Handy." Franklin stared off into the middle distance.

"How's it handy?" She leaned to one side, getting back into his line of sight.

"All Lisker needs is someone to pin it on." Franklin remained lost in the distance.

"What is it?"

Franklin shook himself free of the idea. Although, Lucy in lingerie—he looked at Lucy. "Nothing. Stupid idea."

"What idea?"

"Hey! I'm a clown. I'm full of stupid ideas. Part of the job description." He rubbed his hands on his thighs, breaking the spell.

There was that veil of mistrust over her eyes again. He smiled his well-practiced trust-the-clown smile.

"I have to find some way to throw off that private eye."

"Get married, settle down. Join a book club. Nobody expects that."

"Who've you got in mind?"

"Herman Melville is usually good for a start."

"No. Who am I supposed to marry in all this settling down?"

She's issued the challenge. And if there was a shred of courage anywhere inside his baggy suit, Franklin would say it right out loud. But he couldn't.

"Whom did you have in mind," comes Miss Minchin's voice floating down on him. Franklin is swimming in his clown costume, all of eleven years old again. Miss Minchin looms over him, "Whom did you have in mind, Franklin?"

Her moon-faced grin floats between them and settles over Lucy, a smoky helmet. "Hmmmmm?" Miss Minchin's face pushing toward him, evaporating.

Franklin shivered all the way down to his tail bone, dislodging Miss Minchin from his cranium. "A guy with lots of life insurance?"

Lucy smiled, small, but she seemed willing to let him see it. "Like Buster?"

Punctured, Franklin swallowed his dismay as he glanced away. When he looked back, Lucy's smile was gone.

"That's one idea." A desperately deranged idea, but an idea.

"Some things you can't outrun."

"If you can't outrun it, wear a disguise." Franklin used his fingers to frame his face, still coated in the smeary greasepaint. In case she missed his point.

"Nightmares," said Lucy. "Since I was a kid."

"Ah. You think running in nightmares is hard, try it in clown shoes."

For Lucy, the dream always started with her and two other little girls in matching party dresses. They stand at ringside in a darkened circus tent, only a small wedge of the ring and sawdust floor visible. The rest of the tent, the crowd, the rigging above fades into the murk of the ever-muddy dreamscape.

Three clowns, made up like triplets, approach. They cavort and caper, coming to a wobbling, weaving stop in front of the three little girls.

The first clown opens his costume. A cascade of toys, treats, and fluffy animals showers down on the first little girl. The second clown showers the next little girl with the same deluge of goodies.

Lucy remembers smiling, a resonating glee in her chest. The third clown pulls open his costume. A slobbering, clown-faced demon with razor sharp teeth lunges at her. The stinging wetness of warm goo lashes her cheeks. The glee in her chest becomes a cold, crushing ball of fear, the chill reaching to her toe tips.

Scared awake, little Lucy sits bolt upright in her bed, eyes wide, mouth stretched in a scream.

"There I'd be, screaming my head off." Lucy hunched her shoulders.

"Why clowns? Why not spiders? Or cats? Or, I don't know, why not hideous sports mascots all covered in fur and foam rubber?"

Lucy flicked a glance at Franklin, snorted and looked away.

"Mom loved clowns. I'd tell her my dream and she'd say it was all Dad's fault. He's the one who hated clowns."

"That's a kick in the chromosome. Never heard about it being genetic."

"He had his reasons. Every time I had the dream, Mom would get so mad. At me, mostly. She couldn't take it out on Dad. He was long gone. She'd tell me to go back to sleep. Didn't seem to matter what was waiting for me if I did." Lucy faced Franklin full-on, squint-eyed. Like she had to let the sight of him in drop by drop, to manage the pain of the sensory assault.

Lucy continued hunching her shoulders as if fending off whatever might be driving the nightmares. She said, "Mom loooooooved clowns. Every clown's different, right? Costume? Face? But inside? You're all the same."

Lucy leaned back, shut her eyes, forcing her shoulders down. She twisted her neck to break loose the tension in her muscles, purging her agitation.

How he wanted to work those knots out of her muscles, out of her psyche, out of her life.

She opened her eyes again. "This is the longest I've been in a room alone with a clown in—ever. Has to be a record." She studied him and cocked her head like something new had occurred to her.

"Do you—don't take this the wrong way, okay, like it means anything, but—do you have a girlfriend?"

Oh, what a question, what an opening. What a dark and unwelcoming pit into which he could easily fall. Words had never been his friend. Now they were lurking assassins.

Franklin stood up, pushed in the chair, and gestured for her to follow him.

"More walking?"

He smiled back at her. When in doubt, show, don't tell.

Franklin led Lucy through another door into yet another dark place, lit only by the red glow of the exit sign above. A chair scraped close by. Franklin took her by the shoulders. He could feel her tense up, but she let him sit her down.

He was gone only a moment when the room lit up. The room looked like a misshapen and oddly arranged woman's boudoir. The sound of rain started up.

Lucy flinched at the sight of a dark-haired woman, her back to Lucy, standing in a bathtub. The figure was bare from the waist up, her bathrobe having slipped down low onto her hips.

The figure stood in a bathtub set against a large, thickly draped and valanced window. Lightning flashed and crackled as fake rain pelted the frosted glass.

Lucy sat at a pink, heavily decorated vanity table before a similar window lashed by more fake rain. To one side an oriental changing screen had been draped with stockings and bloomers. On the other side, a full-length mirror distorted Lucy's reflection.

The walls were painted to look like richly flocked red velvet wallpaper.

The ceiling was high, covered in acoustical tile painted black. Electrical conduit and water pipes with sprinkler heads criss-crossed overhead.

On the floor, between Lucy and the figure in the bath tub, ran a single rail curving through the room. It disappeared under the oversized doors at either end of the oddly shaped room.

Franklin appeared again, carrying their cups of tea. He edged over to the dark-haired figure and whispered loudly, "Sorry for dropping in like this, Zelda, but someone asked to meet you." Franklin put the tea on the table and sat down next to Lucy.

"Where are we?"

"Zelda's boudoir. The Freaky Funhouse.

"That's Zelda?" Lucy nodded toward the figure in the bathtub.

"My girlfriend." Franklin gave Lucy a big smile, nodding.

"A funhouse dummy?"

"All right, yes. She's not much for brains or personality, but she is safe. Stable. And totally incapable of falling for a single one of Buster's pick-up lines. No matter how smooth."

"I don't know. He's pretty smooth." She studied Zelda. "Does she ever turn around?"

"Best part of the ride." Franklin hopped up and stood by the tub, slightly back from the figure.

"Boys must love it."

"They do get a surprise." Franklin turned to the figure. "Turn around, Zelda. Don't be rude. She's harmless."

"Ah, no need. She's fine the way she is."

Franklin stepped on a lever by the track. With a screech and wail, Zelda pivoted around, revealing a decayed face and torso. Her dangling entrails shook, and worms wriggled from gaping wounds as Zelda rocked to a stop, her eyes glowing red.

Lucy sat back hard in her chair.

"Your—girlfriend?"

"I haven't met her parents yet, but we've agreed to take it slow, not rush into anything." Franklin released the lever and Zelda rotated away from them. Franklin sat down with Lucy and took up his tea again.

"When you're thirteen, you fall pretty hard."

"With a zombie."

"Ideal woman for a clown."

Franklin is thirteen again, rolling into Zelda's Boudoir, alone in the car.

The car stops. She turns around. She's whole and healthy now. She beckons him to join her in the tub, and he gets out of the car.

"Zelda taught me the only two things I know about women. Great looking outsides. Scary insides."

His favorite ride. Until he rolled in and saw Buster standing in the tub and holding Zelda. While he pretended to make out with her, Buster's buddies hosed Franklin down with foaming fire extinguishers.

"Kanega threw us all out for the rest of the season."

Franklin, watching Lucy watching Zelda, gets tangled up in overlapping fantasies. Now it's Lucy in the tub. A breeze begins to blow. The wind catches her hair as she runs her fingers through the strands. The gauzy silken gown she wears flutters and dances. Her figure, silhouetted under the fabric by the light behind the frosted windows, is dark and winsome.

She turns and looks at Franklin, the clouds tumbling behind her.

"What are you doing?" she asks him.

The gossamer gown vanishes from her body, yanked by an unseen hand. The wind dies away as Franklin stopped blowing the ends of her hair into motion. His lips were still puckered. He looked down at his mouth.

"Whistle practice. I'm not very good at it." He blew a wheezy note. "See? Nothing." He turned away, putting his tea cup to his mouth. His face red, exploded in a cheek-clinching dance of stupidity and embarrassment.

"Why are you helping me? I hate clowns." Lucy had gone back to watching the immobile Zelda.

At least she didn't say she hated *you* clowns. Franklin was going to count that as a victory. Sort of.

"Why?" she asked again.

He shook himself and swam up from the depths of his reverie. "Being a superhero takes lots of practice."

"In a clown suit?"

"Keeps the bad guys guessing. They never suspect the clown. True fact."

"What's your weakness?"

"Don't have one."

"Every superhero has a weakness. Like Wet Washcloth Man? The criminal mastermind who knows exactly how to wipe that smirk off your face?"

"Therein lies the beauty of this disguise. You may think I'm a pushover from the way I look on the outside. But underneath I'm all high-grade rubber and lightning fast reflexes."

"You think I should paint my face, blend in for a while? I bet Buster wouldn't mind."

Emotional alarm bells went off all up and down Franklin's spine. How could she not hear the clacketing of his entire skeletal system vibrating with the noise? So, he stood up.

"Maybe I should get you back. Wouldn't want Buster to send out the dogs looking for you."

He turned off the lights, and led her to the exit door, out through the locker room, and into the night beyond.

He concentrated on locking the door as he asked, "Did Buster make off with any—souvenirs?"

"Like what?"

"In case you didn't notice, there's not much difference between Buster and your average blue jay. He's attracted to all kinds of shiny things that don't belong to him. Sometimes underwear. Sometimes—other things."

"No." She passed by him and headed toward the main gate.

"Just asking." But she was out of range.

Franklin remained standing by the door as his brain ran it all backward, to the point where she said no. Instead, she answers his question.

Her lips part. She puts her hand on his chest, like she's preserving the moment before she speaks. She looks deep in his eyes. She assures him there's a perfectly reasonable explanation for keeping a scrapbook of the Baggy Pants Slasher's crime spree. Then she tells him the perfectly reasonable explanation.

But Franklin's imagination can't fill in the blank. Because his imagination can't conjure anything resembling a reasonable explanation. His imagination moves her mouth, but there's no sound coming out. The only thing he can do is put a finger to her lips, letting her know he doesn't need an explanation. Taking her chin with his thumb and finger, he turns her head toward his, leans down, her lips—

His brain released the fantasy, letting reality snap back into place with a stinging thwack. It left him with the sight of his reflection in the glass of the door. He stands there with his street-smudged glove up, his eyes half-closed, and his mouth in a partial pucker. Seeing himself in so ludicrous a pose sent a chill through him. He shivered hard to shake off the creepy feeling. He rubbed his thumb and fingers together, rolling up the congealed snot of so hopeless a thought into a sticky little ball he flicked away.

It's possible she doesn't know her scrapbook is missing. Maybe. Or she did know and his bringing it up would make her think he didn't believe she was all that innocent. Consider it a bullet dodged. He smacked himself in the head trying to dislodge any more death metaphors rattling around up there.

Franklin ran to catch up with Lucy at the front gate.

◆ ◆ ◆

Back at the apartment, Franklin opened the front door and snapped on the lights. He let Lucy pass by him into the living room.

Buster leaped up from the chair where he'd been hidden from view.

"There you are!"

Lucy gasped and flattened herself against the wall, her teeth clenched as she panted in hard, hissing breaths.

Lucy turned back to Franklin. "My mother gave me a jack-in-the-box once. When that stupid clown jumped out at me, I cut its head off." She stormed past the boys toward the bedroom.

Buster scrambled to follow her. "I turned down the covers and left you a chocolate mint—"

Lucy slammed and locked the bedroom door in Buster's face.

"—on the pillow." Buster checked his nose for damage.

Lucy opened the door and flung out a chocolate-smeared pillow case and slammed the door again.

"Should've put it on a napkin, I guess. I tried licking it up." Buster turned to Franklin. "Must not have gotten it all. My bad!" he shouted through the door at her. He turned on Franklin. "Thanks for worrying me half to death, pal!"

"What've you got to worry about?"

"You go off and have a fatal accident, they might arrest her for it," said Buster, shaking his finger at Franklin. "You do not want that on your conscience."

Franklin studied Buster for a second. "It's good you look so much like Mom. It reminds me we're family."

Franklin popped the head off a clown decanter labeled 'Giggle Juice.' He poured himself a tall glass of warm bourbon and stuck the head back on the bottle. He sat down in the big easy chair, pulled off the huge shoes and dropped them beside the chair.

Buster glanced back at the closed door behind which Lucy had disappeared, before squatting down by the arm of the chair. He whispered hard in Franklin's ear, "All right, you gigolo, where'd you go with the girl of my dreams? I looked everywhere."

Franklin dabbed the spit out of his ear with a twist of his gloved finger.

"Silly me. I thought you'd come looking for me in case I fell off the delivery truck and got run over by an eighteen-wheeler."

"I went by the Big Top to give her a ride home when she got off work. Red told me you two left together."

"You weren't curious what happened to me?"

"I'm supposed to be a mind-reader, too? I don't know what goes on in that head of yours."

"I'm surprised you let her out of your sight in the first place."

"I, uh, figured she needed some alone time."

"Yeah. She mentioned it on the drive over."

"She did?"

"Yeah."

"What'd she say?" asked Buster. "Exactly?"

Buster hadn't planned on telling Franklin what happened after he and the delivery truck disappeared into traffic. How he came up behind Lucy while everyone clapped and whistled for Franklin's death-defying acrobatics.

"Looks like they're headed for the interstate. It'll take him forever to get back," said Buster. "I have to tell you, I'm flattered you went to such trouble getting Franklin out of the way. How about we head back to the apartment for some quality you-and-me time?"

Lucy looked around at Buster's circle of informants sucking on lollipops and watching her. She laced her fingers together, pushing her palms out, cracking her knuckles. She turned to Buster, V-fingered her own eyes, making sure she had everyone's full attention, then, *doink*, poked Buster square in the eyeballs.

"Yeow!!!" Buster grabbed his face and did the rain-of-tears dance. "You said I was the nice one!"

"Now that's funny." Lucy stalked away. The kids danced and skipped along to keep up, calling out to her, "Do it again! Do it again!" as she disappeared.

Franklin considered this and took another sip.

"It's your own fault," Franklin said the Buster.

"My fault!"

"You ratted her out to the private eye."

"I'm watching out for her. She may resent it now, but she'll thank me in the end. What's the gumshoe going to think if she tries skipping town? She's guilty, that's what."

"What if he's setting her up? Guy's planning to make a fortune with the book. He picks out a bozophobe with tons of sex appeal. Waits for the boffo finish. Big bucks for him. Jail for her. You think of that?"

Buster was pacing now. He turned, shaking his finger at Franklin. "Lisker's a pal. He warned me about you."

"About me!"

The way Buster remembered it, he was still hunched over, his hands clapped over his eyes, unable to see which way Lucy had gone.

"Got yourself some girl trouble there, doncha, pal?" Buster's eyeballs were still watery, but he recognized Lisker's voice.

"I had her helping me with a loose eyelash. Doesn't know her own strength." Buster stretched his face, trying to get both eyes working in tandem again.

"You better watch your back with that one, buddy. She's playing you. I saw her plant a big juicy smacker on the scrawny clown."

"Where's he get off thinking I'm scrawny?" Franklin said to Buster, flexing his arm, poking his bicep with a free finger, his glass still in his hand.

"Did you kiss her?"

"No way."

"Good. Her lips deserve better than the rolled-up baloney hanging off your face."

"She kissed me. My lips were totally innocent bystanders. Reminds me. She probably wants her gum back."

"Ow!" Buster flailed, wiping the air in front of him. "I don't need that pucker face of yours stuck in my head!"

"Juicy Fruit."

"You're doing that on purpose!" Buster danced around the room, swiping and sweeping. "I'm doing way more for her than you are."

"Like what?"

"I'm keeping her secret. Zip the lip. Mum's the word. Silent Sam."

"What secret are you keeping?"

"Her scrapbook."

"Where is it now?"

"I'm not telling you."

"You consider giving it back?"

"She wouldn't want it falling into the wrong hands."

"You stop to think how grateful she'd be if you showed her you trusted her? Like you didn't have the slightest shred of a suspicion she could be a serial killer?"

"She's looking at the perfect accessory. Who else would do that for her?"

"Maybe she doesn't want an accessory that clashes with her spring wardrobe."

"You know what I mean."

Buster straightened up and moved toward the door of his own room but stopped.

"Why do they always make me go to such extremes?"

"Women want to know you're good for the mileage." Franklin swirled the bourbon in his glass.

"How much farther do I have to go?"

"When you figure it out, tell me."

But Buster wasn't listening. He turned and left the room, closing the door behind him.

When the door clicked shut, Franklin added, "I'll buy you a one-way ticket." He tipped up his glass and sucked down the last of his bourbon.

chapter twelve

FOUNDERS DAY IN CHUMLEYVILLE has always been a big deal for everyone. It made for a good reason to lay off work, skip school, and dress up like clowns.

It started years ago, around election time, when local jokesters decorated the statue of old Cornelius Chumley, founder and leading citizen, as a clown. It turned into an annual ritual of costumes and petty knavery ever after.

A little past daybreak, across town from Buster and Franklin's apartment, the country club golf course swarmed with clowns and kids. The Founders Day Circus Scramble Charity Golf Tournament was already at a noisy pitch. There'd be no peace in the gallery today. Decorum and good golf etiquette would find itself tossed face first into the water hazard. But, as the club's governors liked to say from the sanctity of their Platinum Club Room away from the chaos, it's for charity.

Cars, vans, and charter buses disgorged an impossible number of clown golfers and clown junkies.

Back at the apartment, Franklin, in his clown get-up and a bag of golf clubs on his shoulder, knocked on his bedroom door where Lucy had taken refuge.

"Big day! All clowns on deck!" Franklin called through the closed door. He jerked his head back to avoid any sharp, skull-piercing objects that might come thrusting through the hollow-core door. He didn't think Lucy could be a serial killer. But he knew plenty of women capable of armed violence when forced to face the morning without a cup of coffee.

No sharp objects cleaved the panel. He put his ear to the door. He heard delicate snoring.

Crap. Even her nasal passages sounded beautiful. He squeezed his eyes shut to avoid thinking about how she looked asleep on his pillow.

From outside, Buster honked his horn, its goofy warble harsh and insistent.

Franklin rushed for the bathroom window. He could see down into the parking area. Buster stood by his van, reaching in through the window to blow the horn. Franklin stood on the toilet seat to lean out the window, waving at Buster to cut it out.

"Get down here, you Benedict Arnold!" Buster shouted up at Franklin.

Franklin waved his arm at Buster again. He wished he could remember semaphore from their scouting days so he could spell out, *shut the hell up!*

As he pulled his head back inside, he caught sight of a tall, aluminum ladder propped against the building. Under his bedroom window. He glanced back to where Buster was standing, worried Buster had seen it, too, and it had him all worked up. But the hedge encircling the parking area was too high. No way Buster could see it from where he stood.

Franklin stepped down off the toilet, his golf bag clattering on his shoulder. Was she pretending to sleep so she could slip out once they were gone? Have another go at ditching the private eye? But why the ladder? Lisker would be sure to keep an eye on a ladder planted out there in plain sight. Unless the ladder was there to keep Lisker watching the back while she somehow slipped out the front.

Franklin would miss her, but he had to smile at the idea of her outfoxing the private eye. It made Franklin sad to picture her on the road again. Hitchhiking, beautiful against a luxuriant, postcard-perfect sunset of rose-tinted clouds.

Franklin hustled out of the apartment, trundling down the stairs, his golf bag knocking against his back.

"Been busy, have you?" Buster stood with his hands on his hips, his head cocked, staring hard at Franklin.

"What?" Franklin gave Buster a big, innocent shrug of his shoulders.

Buster pointed at the tires of his van. All slashed, the vehicle settled onto its rims.

"If you're asking my professional opinion, I'd say you need to put air back in those if you plan on going anywhere. But I'm just guessing. As you constantly remind me, I was never very good in auto shop."

Franklin hefted his golf bag and headed for his car.

"You are going to help me fix this little sabotage of yours."

"I don't think so." Franklin threw his golf clubs in the back seat. "Not mine. I'd have filled your airbags with mash potatoes."

"We'll see about that." Buster marched over to Franklin's car. He unlatched the hood and heaved—nearly herniating himself. Holding his groin, Buster leaned down to see what was going on.

Chained.

"Very clever, Frankie-boy," said Buster, still holding his groin, slapping at the padlock.

"A little preventive maintenance." Franklin smiled, opening the door on the driver's side.

"This so she has to ride with you?"

"Who?"

"You know who."

Lucy didn't need Buster ratting her out to the private eye again. She needed a good, solid head start.

"Oh, her. She decided to sleep back there in the trunk." Franklin gave a nod toward the rear of his car. "*Some*body's heavy breathing through the key hole kept her up all night."

"I was just resting my nose on the handle. It's her own fault. If she wasn't so fragrant, maybe I could get some sleep. But, no, her smell keeps floating out all over the place."

"The way you were inhaling, you might've sucked all the air out of the room." Franklin slid into the driver's seat.

"You going to let her out?"

"Nah. We're working on her claustrophobia today."

Buster gave Franklin a side-long look.

"You'd hate for her to go berserk in a closed room with you, right?"

Buster's face brightened. "Good thinking. I'll ride with you."

Buster pulled his golf bag from his van and threw it in the back seat of Franklin's car.

"You hate my car."

"Like I'd leave you two alone together?" Buster leaned down, putting his mouth close to the trunk. "I want to be there to comfort you when he lets you out."

Franklin inserted the key in the ignition.

"I just hope she doesn't have to spend all day back there," Buster smirked, watching Franklin twist the key.

The engine caught right away, a purring tiger, sounding better than it had in years.

Franklin looked over at Buster.

"Don't look at me."

Across the street, behind one of the hedges, gloved hands held a radio-control joystick. Gloved fingers took hold of the joystick and jammed it forward.

Franklin's car blasted off, slamming them against their seatbacks. The car raced out of the parking bay, tires screeching. Throwing the boys side-to-side, the car steered hard right then hard left, heading for the exit, and zipping up the street.

"You weren't any good in driver's ed either!" shouted Buster.

"It's the car!" Franklin whipped the wheel back and forth, useless.

The gloved hand did a figure-eight with the joystick. The car weaved, spun out, and raced up onto the sidewalk, straight at old lady Cavallo out walking her ancient cat, Sasha.

"Old bat!" Buster held his hat down hard on his head. "Old cat! Oh, crap!"

Buster and Franklin, woo-wooing in terror, covered their eyes, dreading the imminent sound of Mrs. Cavallo bouncing off the hood. She stood fixed in place, adjusting her glasses.

Get out of the way! Don't try to see what's about to flatten you! Franklin couldn't get those words to come out of his mouth, jacked wide open, yodeling in panic.

The gloved hand leaned the joy-stick hard left and the car side-swiped a fire hydrant. A water plume shot skyward as the car rode up on two wheels, skimming past Mrs. Cavallo.

"Sorry, Mrs. Cavallo," Franklin managed to yell as they rocketed by.

The car flopped back down onto four wheels and turned, tires squealing, through a picket fence. Mowing through a well-kept hedge, a fountain of leaves and branches spewed everywhere. The car raced into the driveway and straight at the closed garage door of a nearby split-level house.

The gloved hand centered the joy-stick and released it.

The car screeched to a halt inches short of the door.

The world didn't end in a bone-shattering collision and a hurricane of razor-edged aluminum siding. Buster and Franklin lowered their hands from their eyes. They both let out a sigh of relief measured in megatons.

The gloved hand pulled back on the joy-stick.

The car whined backward across the street, up the driveway opposite, blasting through the garage door in a shower of wood, metal, and glass. A gassy explosion billowed orange and black from inside the garage.

Buster and Franklin staggered out, collapsed on the lawn, scorched and coughing.

"I knew you'd try to get rid of me and keep her all to yourself," said Buster through spasms of coughing. A terrible thought struck him. "She's still in the trunk!"

Buster rushed back into the smoky garage. "Hey! Hey!" Buster shielded his face as he disappeared into the haze. "I'm coming! I'm coming!"

"Buster! Buster! She's not in the trunk! I was kidding!"

Buster came back out holding up a singed shop towel full of holes.

"Nothing left but the clothes off her back. How can you live with yourself?" Buster stroked the rag against his cheek.

Franklin ripped it from him.

"It's a grease rag!" Franklin waved it in Buster's face.

"All she had on was a grease rag?" Buster's faced scrunched up and burst out with a big, teary bawl and great sniffling heaves.

"And I missed it!" he wailed, struggling to get the words out.

Franklin could only wonder what it must say about himself, being downstream of the idiot in his bloodline.

◆ ◆ ◆

Later, the car plunked upside down on a flatbed truck, sat ready to be hauled away. A fire truck, cop cars, and a news van clogged the street.

One of the police officers had Buster walking a white line, touching his nose, and reciting the alphabet backward.

"I wasn't driving," said Buster. But the officer had him hopping from one foot to the other while playing a manic air-guitar riff. Because it was damn funny to watch.

"We're not taking any chances with either of you clowns," said the officer, ducking his head to snicker with his partner.

Another officer took notes as Mrs. Cavallo went through her version of Franklin's runaway vehicle.

Franklin aced his own sobriety test with a little fire-eating and twisting balloons into a dodecahedron. The cops ignored him as he poked around the landscaping. He had no idea what he was looking for, what he hoped to find, or even what he expected to do if he did find it. Assuming he found anything, there were cops and firemen everywhere.

Dropped in the hedge was the Something.

Franklin reached in and pulled out the radio control. He walked back to the car, holding the controller in his scorched, fingerless gloves. He did a quick check, making sure no one was watching him. He twisted the joystick on the controller and the car's steering gear creaked, turning first to the left then to the right.

Buster flopped in the grass next to the car as officers photographed and measured the scene of the accident.

"Okay, if she wasn't in the trunk, what'd you do with her?"

Lisker materialized behind Franklin, grabbing the controller.

"Is this what I hope it is?" Lisker twisted the joystick and the steering gear creaked again.

"It's nothing. Give it back." Franklin reached for the controller.

"Ha-HA! Now this, this is classic Slasher!" Lisker kept the controller out of Franklin's grasp. "I knew keeping my eye on Mystery Girl would pay off."

"She didn't have anything to do with it."

"I saw you guys in the car," said Lisker, talking over Franklin, "and I was thinking, 'it's too much to hope, it's too much to hope.' Then ka-BOOOOOM!" Lisker laughed, still twiddling with the joystick.

"It's a good thing you didn't let her sleep in the trunk." Buster shuddered.

"Why would she be in the trunk?" asked Lisker, still diddling the joystick.

"She wasn't in the trunk." Franklin grabbed for the controller again.

"Okay, what did you do with her?" Buster was on his feet now.

"Nothing. She's still asleep in my room for all I know."

"For all you know? You trying to tell me she slept through all this?" Lisker continued playing keep-away from Franklin. "Oh, she's watching, you soft-hearted sap. The Slasher is always watching."

"She must be asleep," said Buster, "or she'd be out here worried sick about what happened to me."

"She could be a heavy sleeper," said Franklin.

"You could've slipped her a mickey." Buster got to his feet. "He'll stop at nothing to keep the two of us apart," he said to Lisker.

"You think I'd slip her a mickey?" Franklin squared off with Buster, nose-to-nose. "A mickey?" He stopped. "A mickey." Franklin wasn't talking to Buster anymore.

"And not some mouse in boxer shorts, Frankie-boy."

"It'd be a whole lot easier to frame somebody who's un-conscious."

"What are you talking about?"

"Somebody's trying to make it look like she did it."

"Why?" asked Buster.

"She's beautiful and she's handy." Franklin grabbed Buster's lapels, getting up close to Buster. "You keep saying you hope she has something to hide."

"You think I did this?"

"No. You're not that smart."

"Thank you."

"I'm willing to bet a six-pack she's faking," said Lisker. "You check, see if she doesn't have grease under her fingernails. Cops think I'm a cheap crank. This'll wipe the grin off their faces." Lisker turned to where the cops were standing. "Hey! Flatfoot! Flatfeet. One of you. Pay attention here."

◆ ◆ ◆

"So, wait a minute," Gladys said to Franklin. "I thought you said this Lucy character *was* the Slasher.

"I didn't say she was the Slasher. I said she hated clowns. Lisker thought it had to be her, and Buster hoped everyone went on thinking it might be her." Franklin said to Gladys as he crushed out his cigarette. "But watching Lisker got me to thinking. What if it's someone in the back-ground making everyone think it's her? Pulling off those ca-pers. Making like he's tracking the killer. Finds a wigged-out cutie with a bad case of bozophobia, so he decides to frame her for all of it, write a book. Make a million bucks. Has his cake and eats it, too."

"That would make him one very smart cookie, wouldn't it?" Gladys said to Franklin. "A criminal genius, in fact."

"Yeah. I'm coming to that part."

◆ ◆ ◆

Franklin grabbed Buster, whispering close into his ear, "Keep Lisker busy. I've got to find her and warn her. She needs a head-start."

Buster grabbed Franklin and whispered right back, "No, no, no. Don't you see? Jail! They allow conjugal visits, right?"

"That creep is setting her up! He needs a wow finish and a big arrest to sell his book."

"You think he did this?"

"We found him in my car, remember?"

"He doesn't seem very bright," said Buster, watching Lisker show off the controller to the cops. He twiddled the joystick and giggled as the wheels on the car twisted back and forth. He danced a little side-to-side jig.

"It's an act. You think the Slasher just happened to drop a key piece of evidence where we could find it?"

"Hey!" Buster scowled at Franklin, "what'd'ya mean I'm not that smart?"

"Just keep him busy."

"Wait, wait—" Buster sputtered into empty air. Franklin had already gone.

◆ ◆ ◆

"A big mistake," Franklin said to Gladys, "leaving Buster to try and outsmart Lisker."

"That private eye smarter than you figured?" Gladys asked Franklin.

"He only needed to be smarter than Buster. The way it turned out."

.   .   .

The way it turned out, Buster stood on the outside staring in at Franklin behind the bars of a holding cell down at police headquarters.

"What exactly did you tell them!" shouted Franklin, hanging on the bars.

"How far back should I start?"

"How about where you accidentally convinced them I was the Slasher!"

"Yeah, that's a good place. I'll pick it up there." Buster chewed his lips.

.   .   .

It started to go wrong back at the crime scene as soon as Franklin left. Lisker had already turned the controller over to the officers.

"I wish you could've seen it," said Lisker. "Zoom! Whoosh! Bang! I knew all along it had to be her. I can smell a bozophobe."

"But—you need proof," said Buster. "Don't you?"

Lisker jerked a thumb back at the officers. "We've got her doo-hickey."

"That doesn't prove anything."

Lisker whipped out his map.

"It's her. Every single spot there's a dead clown, there's the same gorgeous dame. The same gorgeous dame I spotted at the bus stop. Twice." Lisker admired his own sleuthing.

"But, but, but—" Buster could only motorboat, giving himself time to think of something. In total desperation, he grabbed the map and turned it upside down.

"What if you're reading the map upside down? You think of that?"

Lisker smirked at Buster and looked at his map. A look of horror took over Lisker's face. "You trying to tell me I'm back in Reno?"

"No. He started right here," said Buster, pointing to each X in turn, "then went there first. Then here. Then here. Each trip getting shorter. Until he—"

"Or she—" said Lisker.

"Or *he*—" said Buster.

"—never leaves home," said Lisker, his face glowing with discovery. "Of course! He's even more cunning than I hoped. A fox in clown shoes. And I'm the one who out-foxed him. All this time he's right under your nose."

"Who's under whose nose?"

"Franklin. Your brother!"

"Oh," said Buster. His eyes went wide. "Whoa! No! Do I mean no? Right. No."

"He keeps to himself. No friends. Criminally insecure around women." Lisker canted a chill look at Buster. "Unless you've been covering up for him. Always the accomplice, never the mastermind. That kind of loyalty only gets you an extra ten years in the slammer."

Lisker held up blurry photos of a buttocks-filled back window of the boys' apartment. "I thought at first it was the girl wearing his clothes so she could give me the slip. But I see now that it's him pretending to be dressed up like himself to throw me off. Genius. Pure evil genius. This book's going straight to the top of the bestseller list. Day one."

"That's not—" Buster stopped. Buster would know that tushie anywhere. He'd studied it every waking second since he'd first encountered it. The pants belonged to Franklin. But those awesome cheeks belonged to Lucy, no question. In Franklin's pants.

"My own brother. I'm—shocked! This is genuine surprise on my face!"

"All these years, you never noticed?"

"I—I heard he was adopted."

"You two look an awful lot alike."

"It's why mom adopted him."

◆ ◆ ◆

While *that* disaster unfolded, Franklin stood outside the
apartment door, key in the lock, hoping Lucy was long
gone. If she wasn't, he had no idea what he hoped to find.

He unlocked the door and went in. He tiptoed across
the living room to his bedroom door. He hesitated again.
He turned the handle. It wasn't locked.

He pushed the door open and eased around to see into
the bedroom.

Lucy was still conked out on the bed, her mouth open,
her soft snoring rhythmical and deep.

Franklin coughed. But there was no reaction. He
coughed twice more, hard. Still nothing. He stepped back
from the door. He clomped up to the door, a wake-up
march. Still nothing.

Franklin eased up close to the bed and knelt down. He
lifted her hand and examined each one of her wonderful
fingers for grease.

"You better be a professional manicurist or I'll reach
through your sinus cavity and jerk your brain out by the
root."

Franklin leaped backward. Lucy struggled to sit up, but
she was little more than a self-propelled rag doll. She managed to dump herself into a heap on the floor, tangled up in
the covers.

"Oooohh. My head!" Her eyes popped wide. "Wait. What time is it? Where am I?" She looked up at Franklin standing by the door. "Oh, noooo! Another blackout!"

"Are you sure?"

"Of course I'm not sure. Why do you think they're called blackouts?" She wound up, ready to fling more abuse but saw his scorched costume and soot covered face. "What's with you? Did something terrible happen?"

Franklin didn't want to be the one to tell her, but there was no one else to do the job.

"Well, you know how Buster hates my car, how he always finds ways to make me look bad?"

"Ye-es."

"I guess my car finally had enough. Tried to kill him. With me behind the wheel." Franklin tried to assess her reaction. She rolled her eyeballs, drooled, and then collapsed face-down on the bed. Nothing he could pin down as a confession-like look of guilt.

"Funny, when you think about it. How it just took off, all by itself. Ran over a fire hydrant, nearly flattened old lady Cavallo and her cat, Sasha. Then, zoom, up into a garage where it—" Franklin tried to chuckle but didn't have much luck. "Where it—this is kind of the funniest part—where it blew up. Booooom!" Franklin flung his hands in the air and did a finger waggle of raining debris. "Buster and I dived out of the car just before it rammed the back wall and exploded. Otherwise, Red would be serving clown burgers at the Big Top today."

Franklin stayed fixed on Lucy.

"That would've been pretty funny to someone who hates clowns. Wouldn't it?" Franklin kept watching her for a reaction. "When you think about it?"

Lucy was still face down, but she reached out her hand for help getting up. Franklin gripped it to get her upright, taking another quick look as he pulled her toward him.

"What are you checking for?"

"Nothing."

She took a long, languid swing at him with her other hand.

"Then check somebody else!"

Her muscles were still rubbery and unreliable as she flung herself around the room. She pulled her clothes out of drawers, stuffing them into her bag. She caught sight of herself in the mirror, wearing only the tee-shirt and panties. She yanked the sheet off the bed and wrapped herself in it.

"Keep your eyes to yourself!" She went back to packing, one hand holding the sheet up, the other flinging clothes at the bags on the bed. She stopped and straightened up, her arms locked across her chest. It seemed to Franklin she meant to keep herself from flying apart rather than anchoring her modesty.

"You don't think it was me, do you?" She pushed her hair out of her face and plunked herself down onto the bed. She looked small and overwhelmed at last. "It's not my fault! What've I ever done to you?"

"Me?"

"You clowns! All of you clowns!" Her shoulders slumped and she threw her head back, her eyes closed. A chuff of helplessness burst out of her. She gripped the pillow to her chest.

Behind her closed eyes Lucy saw herself dolled up for her sixth birthday. She presides over a party at the kitchen table surrounded by her young friends.

At one end of the table, a big party clown does cheesy magic gags for the kids. He plays his tricks on his long-suffering partner, his wife, doubling as a short, butterball of a clown.

"I loved clowns. What'd I know," Lucy said to Franklin.

Lucy remembers her dad being at one end of the room, his pointed birthday hat set at a jaunty angle. Her mom watches from the shadows of the archway to the dining room.

The big party clown pulls a scraggly bunny from his top hat as he catches a glance from Lucy's mom. He hands the bunny to his clown wife and scampers around the table. He pulls goodies from his pockets, dropping handfuls in front of each of the kids. When he reaches the archway, he turns his pockets inside out. No more goodies. With a swoop of his hands, he signals that he's zooming off to fetch more.

He backs out of the room, waving bye-bye, pointing for them to watch the bunny. The kids lean in and laugh as the clown wife dances the scraggly bunny on the table top. But she's more interested in watching the big party clown leave.

"Every year. Same clown, same schtick. Until one birthday, it came time to blow out the candles like always," Lucy said to Franklin.

The kids are older, the big party clown and his wife are doing the same gags. The big party clown drops goodies in front of the kids as he dances around the table. He fades away into the hallway. The bunny dances. The clown wife watches the big party clown leave.

The cake is already in front of Lucy, the candles blazing. She looks around.

"I went to find Mom. I didn't want her to miss it," Lucy said to Franklin.

Young Lucy goes from room to room, searching for her Mom, until she reaches the bedroom door.

She pushes through and stops.

The big party clown straddles Lucy's mom, her bare legs waving.

Neither of them notice the door wide open, the light pouring in on the two of them.

Behind young Lucy, the clown wife appears. She rips off her wig and flies at the big party clown. The room explodes. Sheets, pillows, lamps, and clothes go flying as the clown wife chases the big party clown around the bedroom and into the hall. They skitter along, bouncing off walls, back into the kitchen and a wall of children.

The big party clown dives for the kitchen table, sliding across, blasting through the cake. He tumbles onto the floor, bounding back up on his feet and out the back door.

Across the backyard they run. The big party clown weaves through the swing set, leaving the clown wife tangled up in the chains. He jumps the hedge and makes for his car, the clown wife still on his heels. The kids are right behind, whooping with glee.

The party clown manages to get his car started and pulls into the street, the clown wife chasing him all the way. The kids pour out onto the front lawn, cheering.

"People still talk about that day," Lucy said to Franklin. "Last birthday party Lucy ever had." She buried her face in the pillow.

Franklin mouthed the freshly discovered and wonderous word. *Lucy.*

"Dad had enough. He divorced Mom and left us. I hate clowns."

"All of us?"

"Right. A greasepaint smile and a fake nose just screams 'trust me.'" She flung the pillow. "You clowns started it! I've been trying to get away from you ever since."

"So what's with keeping a scrapbook?"

She looked like she would deny it but gave up. "Trying to figure out where the tornado will strike next. Maybe find a way to outrun it." She slumped. "Unless I'm the tornado." She gored Franklin with her eyes. "Did you take it? Use it against me?" She flopped backward onto the bed.

"Buster has it."

Lucy chuffed and rolled her eyes. "Of course he does. What's he plan to do with it?"

"Use it to blackmail you into living happily ever after with him."

"And you wonder why I hate clowns."

◆ ◆ ◆

Franklin polished the rim of his glass with his finger.

"The most wonderful girl in the world, and we're both screwed by one clown years before I ever meet her."

"You don't think her mother's got something to do with it?" asked Red.

"The clown's the one with the penis," said Franklin.

"Every damn one of them it seems." Gladys raised her glass. "Present company excepted." She thought a moment. "Sorry. You know what I mean." She took a sip. "You didn't say why you ended up in jail."

"Because testosterone is thicker than blood. Lisker wasn't finished with Buster."

◆ ◆ ◆

The police were packing up their gear. The flat bed with Franklin's car had already gone. Lisker lifted his clown-haired topper and mopped his bald spot with a big red handkerchief.

"Living a lie, preying on fellow clowns," said Lisker. "'Cannibalism in Clown White.' How do you like that for a title?" He pulled out a notebook and jotted it down. "Don't want to forget."

"How could he be the Baggy Pants Slasher?" asked Buster. "He was driving the car."

"Never underestimate a criminal mastermind. What better way to throw off suspicion than by killing himself and making it look like he did it. I mean the Slasher did it."

"Defeats the whole purpose of being a *serial* killer, doesn't it?"

"Leave this to the professionals, kid. I've been at it a lot longer than you. I know the criminal mind." Lisker's eyes narrowed. "Unless you're working some kind of reverse psychology on me. That's it, isn't it? You're try to make me think it's *not* your brother so I *will* think it's your brother and forget all about the girl, what's-her-name, back at the bar."

Buster shook his head, trying to straighten out the logic. "Protect what's-her-name? You think I'd sacrifice my own brother to protect someone I hardly know? A stranger? Who haunts my every waking moment? Who just might be the one to make every one of my sexual fantasies come true? You mean *that* girl?"

Lisker fixed Buster with a hard, skeptical eye, nodding.

Buster could only stare back with his own ever-widening eyes of innocence. Buster's eyebrows finally ran out of room.

• • •

"It's not you," Franklin said to Lucy. You're not the tornado. Never were. Those blackouts? Somebody's causing them."

"Why?"

"Make it look like you're the Slasher. Make sure you never have a solid alibi. Keeping you on the run. If you're always a stranger wherever you go, who's going to vouch for you?"

"Who'd do that?"

"That private eye has plenty of motive."

Lucy frowned, her face dark and angry.

"Every time I turn around, he's right there watching. Halfway across the country. Every time one of you clowns turn up dead, he's right there. After one of my blackouts. You think somehow he's doing it?"

"I can't prove any of it. Yet. But he keeps saying how he can sell the story for a fortune. Sensational crimes. Sexy killer. He needs to pin the crimes on you so he can finish his book and sell it for millions."

"You realize what it means? I don't have to keep running." She hopped up off the bed, the sheet dropping to the floor. "I'm going to kill him."

"Whoa! You'll find yourself one step ahead of the tornado again."

"What am I supposed to do?" She stalked back and forth. Franklin tried hard not to stare at those pantherine muscles of her thighs.

"What?" Lucy stopped and looked down at herself. "Crap." She took the sheet up off the floor and wrapped it around herself again.

"I never thought I'd actually say 'thank you' to a clown. You may have saved my ass."

"It's an ass worth saving. And I'm sorry, it just popped out." Franklin's faced twisted up in a grimace he managed to unwind into a bit of a goofy smile at her.

"You don't know when to shut up, do you?"

"Occupational hazard and psychological defense mechanism. Commercial grade. Like wearing a titanium jock strap."

"I'm trying to figure out how to say 'thank you.'"

"A plate of cookies? Knitted socks? Jug of homemade whiskey?" Franklin's breath became more and more shallow.

"Great ideas. For a housewarming."

"Right. Nix that idea. It's pretty warm in here already."

She moved toward Franklin. He backed up, not sure how much of his thoughts she could read on his face.

"All this time you've been trying to get rid of me," she said. "Is it because you can't stand me? Or because you like me?"

"Oh, I never gave it any thought."

"You're lying."

"I seem to remember one of us calling me out for having a fake face."

"Ooooh, still mad about that, aren't you?"

"It's a very authentic face. It just happens to be painted on."

"Isn't it about time I get to see what's behind it?"

She took another step closer but caught her foot in the sheet and tripped into his arms, knocking them both to the ground. A gasp burst from Franklin as he hit the ground with Lucy landing on him. He didn't have to lose his balance. But he wouldn't have missed this for the world.

"It's true." Lucy prodded at him. "You *are* high grade rubber under all that stuff." She lifted herself slightly, braced on her arms, looking down on Franklin. "Here is where you show the rescued maiden your true identity."

"It is?" His heart filled up with hope, sloshing over, and washing away all good sense.

"Unh-hunh."

Staring up at her, he could see her eyes were even deeper, if such a thing was possible, feeling the definition of her body all along every inch of his own.

Lucy licked her thumb. "Let me help get you started." She reached to rub off his make-up.

He grabbed her wrist, smiling. Even her saliva was beautiful. "Am I supposed to make this easy for you or am I supposed to put up a fight?"

"Wasn't in the super hero manual, was it," she said, pushing harder to thumb off his make-up as he reached up with both hands to resist her. "If this is all you got, it won't be any contest. I want to see what my hero looks like under all the secret identity goop."

Surrender never seemed so delicious. He was ready. This time he was ready to let his arms go slack, let her wipe her beautiful saliva all over his face and give himself up in a way he'd never given himself up before.

Gun barrels sprouted all around her head, pointed at his face.

"Police! Don't move!" shouted a crackling male voice.

"We've got him, ma'am. You're safe now!" said a female voice, crackling on the same frequency.

Blue arms snaking out of armored vests took Lucy at the elbows and pulled her to her feet.

"You were very brave," said a third officer, escorting her out of the circle of blue uniforms surrounding Franklin.

Seeing past the weaponry, Franklin found himself at the center of a heavily armed squad of officers in tactical gear. Painted up as clowns.

"Suspect is in custody," said another of the officers, talking into the mic clipped to his shoulder, a frizz of green hair spewing from under his helmet.

Two of the officers rolled Franklin over, cuffing his hands behind his back and pulling him to his feet.

"You're under arrest," said the taller of the two officers as they held Franklin erect.

"You clowns have your own cops?" shouted Lucy, her eyes wide.

"Founders Day, ma'am," said the female officer. She wore red bow lips and long, fake eyelashes.

"Community outreach," said the tall cop, a tiny propeller beanie perched on his helmet.

"I'm under arrest?" Franklin tried to shake off the hands holding onto him.

"We have evidence you could be the Baggy Pants Slasher."

"You're kidding me!" Franklin looked from Lucy to the officers.

"Do we look like we're kidding?" asked the shorter one.

Oh, now is not the time for pointing out to cops carrying high-caliber weapons they look like a militarized circus poster standing there.

"You have the right to remain silent—" another officer recited at him.

"So that's what I did," Franklin said to Gladys. "You know, I was kind of hoping she'd speak up. Say something. Like, 'he was with me all this time.' Or, 'he's the one who figured out who the real Slasher is.' But she didn't."

Franklin saw Lucy's face working, like she was dredging up the nerve to say something in his defense. But she didn't.

Like Jeannie Krebs.

Jeannie and her posse are all standing in his room, Lucy in the middle. The whole lot of them watch, none of them saying a thing.

Lucy's mouth moved. Franklin wanted to make out the words 'I'm sorry,' from her. But the heated glare of the angry little-girl eyes fixed on her cook away any remorse Lucy might have felt. Instead, Lucy faded back among the ranks of the cool girls surrounding her.

The officers turned and marched Franklin toward the door. Franklin looked away from her.

"What am I supposed to do," Lucy finally said out loud as they passed by her.

"Get lost," said Franklin. Lucy recoiled as if popped in the face with a pie.

Franklin looked back at her. "Now. While you have the chance. Get lost," he said again before they got him all the way out of the apartment.

Outside, Officer Joe stood by the door, looking hangdog. But he didn't say anything either. The other officers half-carried, half-pulled Franklin down the stairs. Officer Joe followed them down to the street.

Franklin stared in amazement. They seemed to have every police car, van, and scooter from the tri-state area parked on the street.

He must be big news.

chapter thirteen

DOWN AT CENTRAL BOOKING in the old municipal building midtown, Franklin stood against a peeling yellow wall. He held a police placard at chest level, getting his mug shot.

"Face front. Chin up," said the officer behind the camera. The officer wore a carrot-sized nose, orange yarn-haired wig, and derby.

Flash.

Franklin flinched.

"Turn to the right. Chin up."

Flash.

"Turn to the left. All the way. Head back. Your nose is out of the picture. There. Stop."

Flash.

"Your own brother had you arrested?" Gladys asked Franklin. "Ain't that a kick in the cashews."

"Like I said, even when he's not there, he's there," Franklin said to Gladys.

The detectives stuck Franklin in a police line-up. To make it fair, they rounded out the line of suspects with desperadoes from the Arcadia High School Marching Band. Franklin, still in his clown get-up, squinted into the brilliant white light shining in his face.

Franklin slid a glance to his left, checking out the short, squatty tuba player, and a glance to his right checking out the bean-pole piccolo player. He leaned forward to see the drum majorette in a spangled leotard and nude tights.

"Number Two, get back in line!" came the metallic voice of the detective over the speaker.

Franklin stepped back with a sigh. Yeah. I'm going to prison. Inside his head, Franklin gave them his meanest, hardest jail face. Nothing to see here but a veteran jailbird, ready for another stretch in the slammer. Outside, his smiling clown face came across more like a sad, old bassett hound ready for a ride to the vet.

Behind the glass, a busted-up Big Rig eyeballed Franklin through the one-way window.

"Looks like the guy I landed on at the gas station. I was moving pretty fast, but I'm sure it's him."

Buster and Lisker leaned out from behind Big Rig, staring at Franklin on the other side of the glass.

"Is the suspect your brother?" asked one of the detectives.

Buster squinted, leaning close to the one-way glass.

"I heard he was adopted," said Buster.

◆ ◆ ◆

Across town, golfers overran the links with some serious clowning. Goofing on each other, cavorting for the gallery, clowns worked hard to best each other in driving, putting, and full-scale jokery.

Golfers used short-handled drivers and pool cues for putters. They brought out the exploding balls and canary-filled golf bags. They harassed and pestered each other with blow-outs, penny whistles, and swazzles.

Mayhem overtook the greens, the bunkers, and the water hazards. But nothing that could be called nefarious.

On the ninth hole, Buzzer, a hobo clown with a lime green tam and matching argyle socks lined up for a putt. He couldn't resist using his putter to goose a woman in the gallery.

From out of the trees and over the rough, a souped-up golf cart flew at the crowd. Its unmufflered engine tearing the air. At the tiller, a demonic clown all in black aimed the cart straight at Buzzer. A stocking mask painted over with slashes of white for eyes and mouth covered the demon clown's head. A wig of dull white yarn under a black knit watch cap topped the horrific face.

Buzzer had only enough time to drop his putter and run for the nearest water hazard. He dived in head first, plowing up the soft shallow bottom, his feet still kicking.

The cart carved an arcing turn, throwing up dirt and grass as it skirted the hazard's edge. The demonic clown gunned the motor and aimed at the knot of clowns still gathered around the ninth hole pin.

The cart scattered the clowns, geese-like, sending them to follow Buzzer into the water, leaping for bunkers, or dashing for the trees to escape the marauding cart.

◆ ◆ ◆

Franklin stepped out of the police station, squinting at the brightness of the late afternoon sunshine. He carried a manila envelope with his personal effects tucked under his arm. He stopped at the far end of the long walkway leading from the entrance of the police station to the street. Buster stood by his clownmobile, its engine idling.

Cop cars, sirens screaming and emergency lights spinning, streamed out of the garage. Bouncing, they made the turn onto the street, whipping past the spot where Buster stood by his vehicle.

"Hey? Need a ride?" Buster called out, waving at Franklin.

Franklin cut across the grass to avoid him. Buster hopped back in his van and sped to catch up with him. Franklin ignored him and kept walking as Buster creeped alongside.

"You let her get away!" Buster shouted out the window at Franklin.

"You had me arrested," Franklin shouted back and kept walking, not looking Buster's way.

"I told you! He tricked me! He's slick. The private eye may act dumb, but he's a pro at getting information out of a guy. I kept trying to tell the cops, it was artificial incrimination!"

"Oh, please!" Franklin stopped and threw his head back. He wished the sky would open up and crack Buster in the ass with a lick of lightning.

Buster shoved the gear into park and killed the engine. He hopped out, coming around to face Franklin.

"It's not all me, Frankie-boy. Did you say a single word? No. Just let them arrest you, fingerprint you, take your mug shot, and stick you behind bars."

With great deliberation, Franklin deigned to look at Buster. Oh, the density that is Buster.

"I bought her a little time. So she could get away from here!"

"No. You got yourself arrested so she'll see what a big hero you are and forget all about me."

"That is *really* stupid."

"Of course it is, Captain Wondershorts!" Buster flung his arms out and slapped his sides. "You are always doing sneaky things to get women to notice you. The sneakiest has to be pretending you don't want them to notice you at all."

Franklin chewed on that thought for a moment as he took his things out of the envelope and refilled his pockets.

"Okay. Thanks for bailing me out. We even now?" Franklin handed Buster the empty envelope and kept walking.

"I didn't bail you out. Somebody called 9-1-1 saying the Slasher was on the loose at the golf course. Cops didn't say anything to you about it?"

They might have. Franklin had been keen to get away. He hadn't paid much attention to anything but Officer Joe opening the door to his holding cell. Officer Joe might have said something like, "The Chief's cutting you loose for now. Don't leave town." Franklin took his stuff and got the hell out of there.

Footsteps came pounding down the walkway behind them. The private eye lumbered up to them, holding down his clown topper to keep it from blowing off.

"Hey! Sorry!" he shouted as he got close to them. He did a little cross-step to turn his whole bulk toward Franklin, never stopping as he came even with him. "No hard feelings, right buddy?" he huffed as he thudded by, aiming his body back down the road.

Franklin jack-rabbited after Lisker, tackling him. They collapsed face-first, rolling on the grass.

Lisker had his hands up, protecting his nose. "Hey! Gives! Gives! I already said 'no hard feelings!'"

"I'd like to see some bruising, so I know it's real!" Franklin shook Lisker by the lapels, bouncing his head on the grass.

"I—never—believed—for—a second—" he gasped out in time with his bouncing head, "—you—could be—the Slasher." He grabbed Franklin by the collar, making him stop. Uncrossing his eyes, Lisker said, "I let the other clown think he'd conned me so they'd lock you up. I knew I could flush out the real Slasher. It worked. Come on, let me up. I got a Slasher to catch. Before those cops hog all the glory!"

Lisker took a deep, deep breath, until his face became an overfilled, misshapen balloon. He let go with a gut-pop, bouncing Franklin off backward and butt-upward. The private eye rolled over, struggled back onto his feet and headed off, running. The taillights of the last cop cars were already disappearing down the road ahead of him.

"You still think there's any way he could be the Slasher?" Buster stood over Franklin.

"Yeah, I do." Franklin got to his feet.

"If it's not him out there at the golf course, who is it?"

Franklin froze for a whole, long moment. He smiled.

"Someone who doesn't like the idea of me sitting in jail."

"Who?" asked Buster. "Who? Come on. Who? I can't think of anyone."

Franklin stared at the cloudy void he imagined between Buster's ears. His gaze was so keen it made Buster explore his forehead with his fingers.

"What? Have I got something on my face?"

What Franklin saw was Lucy planting that kiss on him. That soul-shattering, politics-changing, rocketing-to-the-core kiss. All he wanted in the world was to be there when she cranked up the voltage. To be the bullseye when she fired off those lips of hers in earnest and at full strength.

"You thought it was the girl? Lucy?" Gladys asked Franklin.

"Too much to hope, I know. But I knew Lisker had to be thinking the same thing," Franklin said to Gladys.

"Gimme your keys." Franklin held his hand out to Buster.

"What for?"

"I have to get there before that private eye does."

"He's in his car by now. You'll be too late."

Franklin held up Lisker's keys.

"Ooooh, you stuck your hands in his pants pocket? Yuck!" Buster shook his hands to fling off any second-hand cooties.

"So gimme your keys."

"No." Buster clamped his hands on his pockets.

"Why not?"

"Give you the chance to be the hero again? Not happening, Frankie-boy."

Franklin put up his fists and danced around Buster.

"You want to fight me? Right here in front of all these cops?"

"All the cops are gone. Chasing the Slasher." Franklin advanced on Buster. He moved closer and closer to Buster in a slide-step hop, his fists up, punching at him with tiny, twisting jabs.

Buster snorted a laugh at Franklin's freakish stance. He took up a stance of his own.

Holding his left fist straight out, Franklin spun his right fist, a haymaker of a windup. He cocked—and stuffed his left hand into Buster's pocket, plucking out his keys. He shook them at Buster and smiled, spun and dashed down the steps, jumping into the clownmobile. He gave Buster a wave and roared off down the street.

◆ ◆ ◆

Back on the golf course, the demonic clown ripped over the greens, jousting at clowns with the golf pin, tripping the fleeing funsters with the flag. The four-wheeled maniac speared their convenient backsides as they crawled for safety.

◆ ◆ ◆

Franklin flew down the road, whipping through traffic and weaving between lanes, in and out among the other cars. Drivers gawped, cursed, and pointed, all staring at Franklin just as maniacal behind the wheel.

◆ ◆ ◆

The demonic clown flung buckets of golf balls under the feet of clowns in flight, sending them slipping and sliding on the pathways, landing butt-downward with a coccyx-cracking thud.

The demonic clown stopped the cart and turned to listen.

In the distance, closing fast were the sirens of the converging police cars.

The demonic clown steered the golf cart for a service road and came out by the maintenance shed, running the cart in behind a parked turf truck.

Outside the entrance of the country club, police cars converged, roaring through the gates.

The turf truck driver, headphones clipped over his ears and bopping to his tunes, climbed into the cab. He started the engine, put the truck in gear and drove out of the maintenance yard. Steering for the entrance, the turf truck parted the oncoming police cars still filing in and heading down the main drive.

Franklin had to slam on the brakes as he reached an intersection, the light turning red against him. He locked up the brakes, sliding to a stop inches short of the crosswalk.

The turf truck roared through, followed by the demon clown in the golf cart close behind. The caravan of police cars with sirens warbling came ripping along after.

Franklin whipped the wheel hard and followed the frantic train.

The turf truck driver, deep into his music, steered the truck into highway traffic, oblivious to the police vehicles closing in behind him. He remained lost in a great, air-drum solo, wrists on the steering wheel, head banging and hair shaking.

The first police car to reach the truck spotted the rope tying the cart to the rear of the turf truck. The officer raced forward to wave the turf truck over to the shoulder.

"Pull over! Pull over!" the officer shouted through his loudhailer.

The turf truck driver saw the posse of police cars bracketing him front, back, and sides. The police car on his left swung in close, still waving at him to pull over.

The driver slammed on the brakes and steered for the shoulder. The golf cart rammed the rear of the truck, shattering and rolling off the pavement.

Police cars swerved and slid as they braked hard, tires screeching. Cops piled out, guns drawn, running for the destroyed cart.

Franklin pulled up behind the police cars, jumped out, and chased after them. He pushed through the officers gathered around the pile of debris.

They turned the body over.

It turned out to be a spray-painted mannequin, its face pushed in and dressed in a black jumpsuit. From the name tag stitched over the pocket, it must have belonged to some janitor named Phil. One of the cops held up an old mop head of a wig and black knit cap knocked off the mannequin.

"Friend of yours?" asked one of the cops, holstering his weapon.

"Just one of the clowns," said Franklin. "Lousy bridge player. Always the dummy."

"You got any idea who's behind this?" another of the cops asked Franklin, but not like he believed Franklin did.

"Clearly someone who has no respect for the game of golf." Franklin eased backward. He turned and ran for the clownmobile. He jumped in and roared off.

♦ ♦ ♦

"You didn't tell them about the girl?" Gladys asked Franklin.

"Seeing the dummy, I couldn't be sure who'd done it. Did she? Or did Lisker rig it so he could be at the police station while the Slasher appeared to be on the loose. Standing there, having all those cops looking at me, made me think it could be his plan for me to rat her out."

"You know, I had a thought. What if the private eye and the girl are in cahoots? You know. Working together?"

"How do you mean?"

"You're saying there's supposed to be this big payoff if he gets his book deal, right?"

"Right."

"What if they're both in on it? He's the brains. She's the beauty."

Franklin lit another cigarette. He studied his reflection in the mirror behind the bar. "Hunh." Franklin considered that angle. He waggled his finger at Gladys, the smoke of the cigarette dancing in the lights from behind the bottles. "Now that is interesting."

"Just a thought." Gladys drew on her own cigarette. "What did you end up doing?"

"Went back to my place to find that thing." Franklin pointed at the scrapbook lying on the bar between them. "Most likely Buster still had it hidden somewhere. Seemed like a good idea we should get rid of it before Lisker got to Buster. If he could talk Buster into thinking I was the Slasher, it'd be a snap for him to fleece Buster for the scrapbook. Put another nail in Lucy's lucky horseshoe."

• • •

Franklin found the front door of his apartment still open and the lights off. The afternoon daylight outside made the darkness inside the apartment more sinister.

He grabbed the giant soup ladle from the umbrella stand. Franklin steadied the wobbling utensil with both hands, in case it wasn't Lucy or Lisker hiding in the dark.

"Buster?"

Franklin heard a lot of scrambling around and hissing. Like the sound of air squeezed out of Buster's rubber girl-friend. Or a large snake busy with consuming Buster whole. He could live with that.

"You're in big trouble if you're allergic to giblets!" Franklin flipped on the lights.

Lucy slipped out of Franklin's bedroom, pulling the door closed behind her. Bare-legged, Lucy wore a garish, multi-color, over-sized jacket.

"What are you doing here?" she hissed, holding the jacket closed.

"Me? What are you doing here?" Franklin was angry she'd put herself in danger to get him out of jail. But he was relieved to see her. Okay, he was delighted to see her. De-lighted she wasn't mashed under a turf truck, torn apart by wild clowns, or carted off to jail in handcuffs and leg irons.

"I had some unfinished business," she said.

Franklin's mouth went dry and his breath left him. He bit his lip to moisten his tongue that had gone into hiding, clinging to the roof of his mouth.

Franklin believed he'd found the woman for whom he would, without hesitation, risk life, limb, and dignity. How hard could it be to put all of that into a few measly words?

"Seeing—uh—seeing the golf cart in pieces all over the highway, thinking of you in it—" Franklin stopped. Those few measly words were harder than he thought. The poetry in his head turned into prattle as it left his mouth.

"What makes you think it was me?" Her eyes drilled holes through him, leaving smoking scorch marks on the wall behind him. Somewhere a smoke detector goes off.

"Right. Right. No way it could've been you. Silly me. I just meant to say—" Franklin stopped. He closed his eyes to concentrate as he charged through the concertina wire of his emotional defenses.

He shook himself. Look at her, you jerk. Look at her. He opened his eyes, looked at her for all he was worth, and began again. "I just have to say—" he said, stumbling into another pocket of dead air.

"Say what?"

"I just have to say—" Like an image swimming into clarity, Franklin realized how she was dressed.

"—you're not wearing any pants."

"Hey! Surprise, Frankie-boy. Guess who I found?"

And—neither was Buster.

Buster danced on tippy-toes out of the bedroom. He stayed hunched over as if the slight crouch would make up for the fact he wore nothing but his boxers and socks.

Of course.

The air went out of Franklin. All the air. Everything. In his lungs, the accidental gulp of air in his belly, even the methane built up in his intestinal tract. He turned into a fart-fart-farting balloon. The leaden load of his heart in his shoes pinned him to the floor. It was the only thing that kept him from flying around the room.

"You're going to do it again, aren't you," said Franklin.

Buster, still in that ridiculous crouch, took Franklin by the arm, moving him back, away from Lucy. "You know how it's always been with you and me? Share and share alike?"

"What? Rent? Pistachio ice cream? Amoebic dysentery from the looks of you?" said Franklin. "I hope."

Buster straightened up. "It's not my fault I don't like any of the girls I like."

Franklin rattled his brains, hoping it would re-arrange Buster's words into a coherent thought.

Nope. Didn't help. The idea kept buzzing around with no intelligent place to land.

"Someone like her comes along, it changes everything. The way you kept harping on how she could be the Slasher—"

"I didn't harp."

"—I was sure she'd gone out of my life forever. The only thing left was you, me, and that long, lonesome highway into the sunset. I came home, and what do I find? Her. In her underwear. When a girl gives off signals like that, it's got to mean something, right?"

Franklin didn't say anything.

"Right?" Buster asked again.

"I used to think you did it on purpose. Ever since fifth grade. Just to screw with me."

"You still mad about that? I punched you once. Once. And not very hard."

"Every time you do this, you might as well slug me."

"Okay. All right." He turned his shoulder to Franklin. "You want to slug me back? Go ahead. Get it out of your system once and for all and stop whining about it."

"You can't help yourself, can you? It's a condition with you."

"You're saying I'm a mental case?"

"I'm saying you're delusional if you think a woman like her would give you a thought for more than two seconds."

"We were kind of in the middle of something." Lucy came up to stand beside Buster, running her hand up and down his bare bicep. "So—if you're not going to slug him, we've got a little business to take care of."

Franklin stood in perfect synaptical disorientation, staring at her. "Him?" The word finally came out more of a squeak than the bark of laughter he'd intended. "*He's* your unfinished business?"

Still, she flinched.

"You're the one said I should settle down."

"Occupying the same spot in the time-space continuum with Buster isn't what I'd call settling down."

"Like Bustery-boo here says—" said Lucy, her voice softer, smokier.

"Bustery-boo?"

"As long as the Slasher's on the loose, I need an air-tight alibi." Lucy poked Buster's bicep. She added a smoldering undulation that didn't seem possible in a creature possessing an endo-skeleton.

"That's me," said Buster. "Air-tight, water-tight, rock-solid, iron-clad, and gold-plated. Face it, Frankie-boy. When a girl's in trouble, who's she need more? The straight arrow good guy super hero? Or the guy who can lie for her with a straight face?"

The impulse to flee washed up Franklin's legs, tingling his every nerve.

Buster put his arm around Franklin. "I get the way you must feel. But you know, circumstances, no matter how bad they seem, can turn out to be the very thing you needed? How they change your life? And you see the world in a brand new way? This is one of those times."

"I should've stayed in jail. I missed baloney sandwich night for this? The other inmates tried to tell me it'd be the highlight of my incarceration." The urge to flee was now an emotional imperative. The fluttering in his guts demanded obedience.

Franklin aimed himself toward the door.

He stopped, surprised at himself. It may be that he'd reached the point at last when he needed to speak up and quit blaming Buster for his own failures.

Franklin straightened up. I'm going to turn around and tell her exactly how I feel, he told his craven self. You can't make me, his craven self said back to him.

Franklin managed to turn himself around to face them. "Not this time, Buster." Franklin focused on Lucy. "I just have to say—"

Buster jumped between Lucy and Franklin. "You said it yourself. I can't help myself. Don't make me do something I'll regret."

Franklin stuck out his chin. "You go right ahead."

"Oh, Frankie-boy, you're asking for it."

Franklin closed his eyes, ready to take whatever Buster had to dish out, ready to take Buster's best shot for Lucy.

"Don't close your eyes. I want you to see this."

Franklin opened one eye, ready to shut it when the fist flew at his face.

It wasn't Buster's fist. It was the hand-drawn real estate flyer with the smiling house, the legs sprouting from the windows and the promise of the free massage. Buster dangled it in front of Franklin's face.

"I did it. I called the number. I know I said you'd never catch me doing something so creepy. But I did. You see how desperate I was?"

Franklin took the flyer, studying it. "You called for the free massage?"

"How can you not feel sorry for me?"

"Sure, sure," said Franklin, no longer listening, now engrossed in the flyer.

"Hey, I got an idea. You go. I'm betting you could use a free massage after the day you've had."

Franklin looked up from the flyer, staring into space.

"Sound like fun?" asked Buster, giving Franklin a light tap on the arm.

Franklin didn't answer, only stared. Buster leaned his head next to Franklin's trying to see whatever it was Franklin had fixed on.

"She'll be expecting you," said Franklin, still staring.

"I didn't give her my name." Buster snorted a laugh. "I said I was desperate, not crazy." He slipped his arm around Lucy's shoulders.

Franklin had begun to nod, flicking a glance at Lucy, then the flyer, then Buster.

"Wha'd'ya say? Buddy?"

"I say—" said Franklin. "—I say, it looks like you two have figured out how to make it work. Make a relationship built on extortion and mutual suspicion work. Not many people can pull that off."

Buster frowned. "So—you're happy for me?"

"Strangely happy. Unnaturally happy. Abnormally happy. I think I'll go drown my happiness at the Big Top. Who in their right mind would want to miss a Happy Hour with this waiting for them?" Franklin shook the flyer at them.

Buster said to Lucy, "Didn't I tell you he was a good sport?"

"Franklin." Lucy slipped from under Buster's arm and followed him to the door.

"If you'll excuse me. You're working on your alibi and I'm in desperate need of a massage." Franklin held up the flyer again.

"You should hang onto this." Lucy held out the scrapbook. "Buster planned to hide it in your room."

He lowered the flyer. "As you probably noticed, Buster's always one step ahead of me."

"Take it. You don't want the cops finding it there. They'd get the wrong idea. All over again."

"Thanks." Franklin didn't know what else to say.

"One more thing," said Lucy.

Franklin waited, with only the faintest of hope in what she might say next.

"Do you have any more duct tape? This will not be enough." She held out the nearly used-up roll.

Franklin left before any of a dozen unwholesome and unwelcome images took root in his overactive imagination.

♦ ♦ ♦

"What's the big deal about the flyer?" asked Gladys.

"You left it, didn't you," said Franklin, "hoping to snag a clown."

Gladys twisted her lip, knocked off a bit of ash. She said, "Okay, okay, Sherlock. I did. But if you knew it was me all this time, why'n'tcha say something when I first got here?"

"Because I kept hoping Lucy would change her mind about Buster, and Buster would show up. Or call. Or something."

"All this time I'm waiting for the big guy to show and it's only you. Pardon my saying."

"How'd you know he was a big guy?"

"I don't know. Sounded like a big guy over the phone. You clowns all sound alike in the dark."

"You disappointed?"

"Oh, I'll get over it," Gladys shrugged. A new thought seemed to hit her and she said, "You left Lucy alone with him thinking she could—*skkkkkkk*?" Gladys drew her thumb across her throat. "That's cold."

"That's not what I was afraid of her doing to Buster."

"If it wasn't that, what did you think she'd do?" It took a moment before Gladys's eyes popped open wide. "Ohhhh."

"Riiiiight."

"My money still says she's in cahoots with the private eye. She was waiting for you to leave so she could finish off the big guy."

"If she does, it's because Buster is Buster, not because Lucy's the Slasher."

"If Lucy was my girl," Red said more to Gladys than Franklin, "I'd punch Buster in the nose. Settle it right then and there." Red lined up the bar fruit like he needed to give his hands something to do.

"She wasn't my girl," said Franklin.

"You said she was," said Gladys.

"I didn't."

"Somebody did." Gladys pointed at Red. "You did."

"Way he was drinking? Honest mistake." Red shrugged.

The telephone rang.

Franklin straightened up.

Red picked up the phone. "Hello. Big Top. Hello?" He listened for a long moment before putting the handset back in the cradle. "Hung up."

Franklin slumped again.

The clown clock over the bar chuckled the hour.

"That's it for happy hour." Red snapped the bar towel off his shoulder.

"Looks like neither of us got what we came for." Franklin drained his glass and set it down.

"No Buster," said Gladys.

"No Lucy," said Franklin.

"I had my heart set on it being the big guy," said Gladys. "No offense."

"None taken."

"So, what now?"

"I am going to give up clowning. Go straight-faced."

"Aw, come on. I was just getting used to you as a clown."

"No, no. Like I told Red here, it's time to kill off Franklin."

"Oh, let me take care of that for you," said Gladys. "There aren't enough clowns in the world to go around."

"Too many if you ask me."

"It's like I always say."

"What?"

"A clown in the hand is worth two in the tent." Gladys crushed out the remains of her cigarette. "Hey, why not let's go to your hideout at the amusement park? You can show me how good a clown you are. I been around more'n a few in my time. Maybe I can help before you do anything rash."

Franklin raised an eyebrow at her.

"No funny stuff, I promise. I mean no *funny* funny stuff. You gotta admit, I've had tons of experience with clowns. I hate to see it when clowns up and quit."

"Why the hell not." Franklin slapped the bar. "But if it doesn't work out, the makeup's coming off."

"Fair enough." Gladys slapped the bar right back at him.

"Ever see a clown without his makeup?" asked Franklin.

Gladys drained her glass, bit off the cherry, and dropped the stem back in the bottom. "Always a first time," she said, chewing.

"That makes two of us." Franklin slipped off the stool, steadying himself with a hand on the edge of the bar.

Gladys slipped off her own stool, knocking against him.

"Sorry, no funny stuff." She put up her hands, wiggling her fingers.

"Of course not." Franklin straightened his collar and wig.

"Hey!" called Red. "What'll I say if anyone does show up looking for either of you?"

"Drinks are on them," said Franklin and turned to Gladys. "Beats a pie in the face any day."

Gladys laughed, which caused Franklin to laugh. They tottered out the door, still laughing.

In the parking lot, Franklin unlocked the passenger side of the clownmobile. He did a sweeping bow, inviting Gladys to step aboard. She got one foot onto the running board and stopped.

"Should we be driving?"

"We could both sit in the back, but we'd never get there."

Gladys winked at him and gave him an elbow to the ribs.

"I mean, who'd drive?"

Gladys gave him another elbow and another wink.

"We agreed. No funny business."

Gladys blew out her lips in disappointment. "I kinda hoped you forgot."

"Clowns have long memories." Franklin gave a little twist of his nose, thinking. He held up a finger and reached into his baggy pockets, pulling out three balls. He did a quick pattern, juggling the three balls. He flipped them into the air, did a quick spin, catching the first, then the second, then—no third.

"Hmmm." Franklin gazed up into the night sky, waiting for the third ball to drop.

He frowned, still waiting.

"Where'd it go?" Gladys watched the sky overhead.

Franklin grinned and held out the third ball.

"I guess my reflexes are still good."

"I feel safer already." Gladys climbed into the passenger seat.

Franklin slammed her door and scampered around to the driver's side. He did a quick look around the parking lot before climbing in behind the wheel.

"Buckle up and let's see what this thing can do." Franklin floored it, throwing Gladys back against the seat. The clownmobile swayed as it whipped out onto the street.

"Be careful," she shouted at Franklin.

"Why? It's not mine!"

chapter fourteen

THE HEADLIGHTS OF THE CLOWNMOBILE swept back and forth as Franklin steered for the front gate of the amusement park. The vehicle weaved, bouncing hard over the potholes. A hub cap banged loose and rolled off into the dark.

Franklin and Gladys climbed out.

"I'll get that later," said Franklin, listening as the hubcap rattled to a stop somewhere in the night.

"At least we got here in one piece. That's something." Gladys twisted her hair back into place and yanked her skirt straight.

"Does it seem dark to you?" asked Franklin.

Night was full on now, but the security lights weren't lit. It made for a deeper darkness so far from town, out away from everything.

"Works for me."

Franklin reached the front gate, Gladys just behind him. The lock hung opened, the gate rolled part way back.

Franklin glanced around, trying to see into the gloom beyond the gate.

"We going inside? It's too spooky out here."

Franklin hesitated before leading her across to the circus pavilion, through the arcade of closed shops, rides, and games.

He stopped short and Gladys ran into him.

"What?"

What he saw was the rear end of the dark sedan, parked behind the shrouded Tilt-a-Whirl. What he said was, "Black cat. Bad luck."

"Where?"

"Already gone. Guess he had a prior engagement. With a rat."

He pointed toward the big metal tent of the circus pavilion. "Over there."

Once they were inside the pavilion, Franklin connected the work light.

"Ta-da!" Franklin threw out his hands and gave Gladys a great big smile. "Here we are."

"Here we are. I can't believe I'm getting a clown show all to myself." Gladys turned away, opened her bag and took out a mirror. "Lemme freshen up before we get started," she said as she daubed at her face.

"Take your time." Franklin crossed his arms.

"I guess after Lucy," she said, still daubing, "this makes me the second woman you ever brought here alone."

"Oh, I don't think so."

"There've been others? You clowns. You're all such lady killers."

"Like I said, I've always had the worst luck with real women."

Gladys stopped, her back still turned to Franklin. "Makes two of us," said Gladys. "I've always had the worst luck with clowns. And most of them? Can't make me laugh to save their lives."

Gladys turned on Franklin. She wore white gloves and a grotesque clown face, painted with a slashing red mouth, smeared white eyebrows, and daubs of rouge for cheeks.

She raised an enormous knife overhead. The blade gleamed crimson, reflecting the red light of the exit signs.

"Hah!" Franklin hopped, his fingers machine-gunning at Gladys. "I knew it, I knew it!" Franklin pranced around in a victory dance. "I knew you were the Slasher. I knew, I knew, I knewIknewIknew," he sang. He stopped and crossed his arms. "I knew all along it was you."

"Funny." Gladys took a step toward Franklin. "I knew all along you knew it was me, too."

"But the kicker? When you said, 'I had my heart set on it being the big guy.' How would you know that? He never said it was him. So how could you know?" Franklin cupped his elbow in his hand as he tapped a finger to his cheek, a clown in deep thought. "Unless you made only one flyer, meant for Buster. Like you did for Big Rig." Franklin put his hands on his hips, through being silly. "I knew you'd have to do something to keep me quiet."

"Funny." Gladys took another step toward Franklin. "I knew I'd have to do something to keep you quiet, too."

"But I had a plan."

"Funny." Gladys took another step toward Franklin. "I had a plan, too."

"All I had to do was keep you busy. You think I tell every Tom, Dick, and Harry Houdini my whole life's story?"

"Funny." Gladys shifted the knife in her hand. "I had to keep you busy, too. You think I care anything about some clown's miserable life story?"

"Well," said Franklin, ready to land the clincher, "I called the cops and told them we'd be here, and they could catch the Slasher in the act. All I have to do is give them the signal." He held up a silver police whistle.

"Funny, I called the cops, too."

Franklin stopped, lowering the whistle. "You did?"

"Un-huh. I told them a loudmouth clown was planning a great big Founders Day joke at the amusement park. Pretend he was in danger. Then, when all the cops show up, he and all his clown buddies would have a great big laugh on them. A little pay-back for arresting him in the first place."

"Uh, what did they say?"

"The chief of police, himself, thanked me for being a conscientious citizen."

"He did?"

"He also said how much better off this city would be if he could get rid of all the clowns."

"He said that?"

"Mmm-hmmm. And I told him how good it made me feel to do my part. So, no cops. Just you and me and this big old circus tent. You know what I like about this place?"

"The cotton candy's fresh? I could run get us some before we get too wrapped up in all the running and screaming."

"I like how far away it is from everything."

Franklin fumbled the whistle to his mouth and blew. Nothing but a wheezy whisper. He blew again. Same wheezy whisper.

Franklin danced backward as Gladys advanced.

"It's no good finishing me off. I told everyone it was you, Lisker. The minute you showed up for happy hour at the Big Top, I knew I'd been right all along. Your disguise couldn't fool anyone."

Gladys stopped. "Disguise?"

"Going around pretending to be a clown junkie. I give you that. It would be the perfect disguise for scoping out the town, picking your victims—if you knew the first thing about dressing like a woman."

"Disguise?"

"You should go back to department store security. Maybe they'll put you in women's wear. No, wait. That's right. They'll put you in jail."

"Oh, you did *not* just tell me I looked like some saggy-assed private eye in drag." Gladys peeled off her jacket, tore open her blouse, and sent buttons flying. She revealed a genuine female-type bosom bound up in a brassiere requiring industrial underwire. She shucked her blouse to the sawdust.

"Oops," said Franklin. That's a lot of cleavage for a saggy-assed private eye in drag.

Again! Again, Franklin's imagination had gotten the better of him. Because, even in this light, he could see she looked far more attractive than he'd realized. Why hadn't he seen that? He should have seen it. And why? He gave himself a mental smack in the forehead. Because—because because because—he'd so convinced himself he was right about the Slasher. He might as well be looking at the world through welder's goggles. Note to self—scratch ace detective off the list of career choices when he gives up clowning. If he lives long enough.

"I know this place like the back of my hand!" Franklin backed toward the front door. "There's no way you'll be able to find me out there. I can hide for days if I have to." He spun and grabbed for the slam bar on the doors.

Chained and padlocked!

Gladys chortled, dangling the key before dropping it into her brassiere. "Come and get it," she said moving closer. "How does it feel to be the butt of this joke, clown?" She raised the knife, picking up speed. "You break up my marriage! You give me diseases! Dancing, smiling. I'll carve that stupid grin right off your face!"

Gladys let out a hideous howl and flew at Franklin, swinging the knife in scything sweeps. Franklin hopped backward, his elbows flapping to keep his hands away.

Franklin churned up sawdust, dashing for the other door, slamming hard against it.

Chained and padlocked, too!

She was almost on top of him.

"Waitwaitwait!" He held out his hand. "I've got one question."

She slowed. "Only one?"

"Why a knife? That's not the special Baggy Pants Slasher ingenuity we've all come to know and admire. Would you like a little time to work up something more creative, more your style? I'm happy to wait. I'll go have a smoke, give you all the time you need."

"Because I want to feel this one." Gladys licked the blade and savored the taste.

Oooh boy.

"Hey, if this is because I said you didn't know how to dress like a woman, it's only because I thought you were a guy, right? So, naturally, a woman looking as terrific as you do and me thinking this whole time was really a guy, couldn't be that gorgeous, so you had to be a guy. I mean *he. He* had to be a guy. Had me fooled completely." Franklin gestured toward her bosom. Maybe it made as much sense to her as it did inside his head. Worth a try.

"Enjoy the view, clown. It's the last real woman you'll ever see."

Franklin did a diving tumble forward under the swish of her blade. He sprang to his feet, bounding out of her reach, and raced toward the piles of props stacked around the center of the ring.

"It's not too late to surrender!" Franklin would have preferred Gladys as a man in drag. As a woman dressed as a woman, she moved like a cat in those killer heels of hers.

His clown brain hijacked his critical survival instincts. His distracted neurons considered fight, flight, or funny in response to his present danger. Anything a killer wore would be killer. He hoped he lived to work it into a gag.

Panic won the day and Franklin shot up over the blocks, stag-leaping between the bull tubs, Gladys right behind him. Up a ladder, down onto the mini-tramps, bounding first to one then the other, then back again as she slashed at his kicking legs. He bounded over a stack of pads, slamming down onto a pile of giant beanbags, Gladys flying at him.

Lying there on his back, he spotted the ventilator openings in the roof overhead just as Gladys filled his field of vision. He rolled out from under her a bare moment before she landed flat, driving the knife where he'd been, slicing into the mat.

He ran for the mini-tramps again. He'd never get up the ladder in time. But if he could bounce high enough, he might reach a rafter. Then he could pull himself up and climb out the opening in the roof.

He bounced and grabbed for the rafter but missed and came back down on the mini-tramp. The rebound sent him skyward again, his hands waving to grab a rafter. He missed again, landing on the mini-tramp again and bounding upward once more. He had to keep his knees tucked to avoid Gladys's hacking and slashing. She kept swinging at him with that impossibly bright and terribly sharp blade. Slashing and bouncing, slashing and bouncing.

Until she kicked the mini-tramp out of the way and he landed hard, splayed out. He scuttled to his feet, backing away, into a stack of chairs, the pile falling over on him. He grabbed one and held it out between them. They circled each other.

She stopped, reached down, and grabbed the end of the mat Franklin stood on. She gave it a yank, pulling his feet out from under him, knocking him backward. He landed on another of the mini-tramps and bounced back at Gladys. She had no time to raise the knife to impale him as he flew toward her. Franklin slammed into her and knocked her to the floor, sawdust billowing everywhere.

It took him a bare second to realize he was straddling her. He clamped her wrists as they battled for the knife. He bore down on her arms with all his weight, which wasn't much against a homicidal maniac. He managed to pin her wrists to the floor. They were nose to nose, hot breath to hot breath.

"Is that a banana in your pants or are you just scared stiff to see me?" said Gladys, raspy and warm.

Franklin banged her wrist against a wooden box until the knife knocked free and tumbled to the sawdust.

Gladys howled and flailed with her legs, trying to hook him with her heel, only managing to kick him in the back of his head.

The front doors blasted open, sheared from the frame, snapping the chain, wood splintering. The front end of a tour bus crashed through, crumpling aluminum, coming to a stop halfway inside the arena.

There was a pneumatic hiss and Lucy, dressed in Buster's clown costume, stepped down from the bus.

"Lucy?" asked Franklin. He looked down at Gladys, who smiled, her bosom heaving, her bra glittering in the half-light.

Franklin, relieved, had to chuckle. "It's not what it looks like."

"Mother!" shouted Lucy.

Franklin's eyes and mouth sprung wide open, looking first at Lucy then at Gladys.

"Boyoboyoboy, there is no way in the world this is what it looks like!"

Even from there, Franklin could read the flashback in Lucy's face. As she saw herself all grown up, still wearing her little-girl party dress. As she stood in the doorway of her mother's bedroom. As she watched her mother's feet flail in the air. As she watched the big party clown rocking and rocking against her mother, his head thrown back. As she watched herself tumble into the dark cavern of his big red mouth open in a yodeling O of ecstasy.

"Honey?" Gladys said to Lucy. "Find me something heavy."

"What for?"

"To kill him with! Look around. There's gotta be some-thing handy in all this junk."

Franklin could see in Lucy's eyes that she was con-sidering it.

"All these years? You let me go on, thinking I was the one? And those blackouts when I was a child? That was you, wasn't it."

"I had to give you something to make you sleep. It's not like I could run out and get a babysitter. Now, do what momma says."

While Franklin watched Lucy consider braining him, Gladys crept her hand closer and closer to the knife on the floor.

Lucy dodged past the two of them and snatched up the knife.

"That's my girl! Stick it between his ribs right above the waist. Up to the handle. That way you get his liver."

Lucy stood over them, her breath coming hard and shallow.

"Baby? You think you could do that for momma?"

What Franklin sees is Lucy rearing back and flinging herself at him, his brain filling in all the gory details. The icy shock of cold metal piercing his flesh, the wetness as he bleeds out. His brain rockets through the cascading images of his end. Officer Joe covers him with a sheet much too short, leaving his clown shoes sticking out. Lucy and Officer Joe stand over him as Lucy, cuffed and bracketed by two officers, gives her statement. She tells them how she went a little bit crazy, stabbing and stabbing the clown sitting on her mother. What surprises her most, she says, is all the blood. Her momma always told her clowns were filled with sawdust. And all Franklin can think is, if he's dead why can he still hear them?

Franklin snapped back to reality.

Lucy was still studying the point of the knife, and he was still sitting on Gladys.

"You can get off her. I'm not going to use this on you."

Gladys gave up, her head falling back as she closed her eyes and blew out a long hard breath of disappointment.

"You are exactly like your daddy," said Gladys. "Soft-headed over clowns. Blaming me and letting the clown off the hook."

Franklin stood up, handed Gladys a red ringmaster's coat from the pile of costumes. She refused to take it, so he laid it over her bosom. "I'll, uh, let you button it yourself." He turned to Lucy. "How'd you know where to find us?" His eyes kept shifting between Gladys and Lucy as Gladys rolled onto her side and got to her feet.

Before she could answer, Lisker called out, "Mine! Mine!" He raced across the ring, pushing past the debris.

He grabbed Lucy around the waist, yanking the knife out of her hand.

"Ah-ha! Gotcha!" he shouted, holding onto the thrashing Lucy. "Never mind us," he said to Franklin. "We'll slip out as soon as I get the cuffs on her."

"Relax. It's not her," said Franklin.

"I was hoping for a really big capture," he said to Lucy, working her wrists into a zip tie as she struggled. "Lots of law enforcement, all the major networks."

"It's not her, you idiot!" Franklin punched at Lisker's shoulder, trying to get his attention.

"Here, hold this for me, doll." Lisker handed the knife to Gladys and turned back to Lucy. "Can you be happy with a citizen's arrest? We'll make it official with a justice of the peace."

"That's not the Slasher, you imbecile!"

The words finally seemed to land. "All right, Miss Marple, tell me who *you* think it is?" Lisker put his hands on his hips.

Franklin dropped his chin to his chest and pointed at Gladys. "Her."

Gladys dumped a blue plastic barrel over Lisker. She kicked it, flipping it, trapping him upside down, and knocking Lucy to the ground.

"Okay. Where were we?" Gladys came toward him, resting the knife point on her fingertip.

"You were about to give up your life of crime and turn yourself in? I hear there could be a movie deal."

"I told you. I want to feel it."

"Mother, not this one!" Lucy kicked, trying to get her feet under herself.

That was ill-timed. For Franklin. Because he stopped, his very hungry heart chewing on what she could possibly mean. It was perfectly timed for Gladys. All she needed was that single, heart-stopped second to reach Franklin. She grabbed him by the collar, yanked him close, and put the blade to his throat.

"It's funny, isn't it? If you'd said something back at the Big Top about Buster not showing up, you wouldn't be in this pickle now, would you?" She moved the blade to his jugular. "You know, it's like you said. Even when Buster's not there, he's there." She hissed into his ear, "Lights out, clown!"

Lights went on all over the place.

A horde of clowns, the whole gang from the Big Top, ringed the four of them.

"How'n hell'd you all get in here?" Gladys growled, but her eyes sparkled, a cannibal at the banquet.

"They know this place like the back of their hand, too," said Franklin, smiling. "Hey, guys! Look what I found." He waved at them, not moving his head, the knife still at his throat.

"Frankie!" shouted Stubby. "You gonna hog that clown junkie all to yourself?"

Fricka-Frack called out, "Where're your manners? We ain't been properly introduced."

"Let's have a little etiquette if you please," said Skinny. "And you know what that means?" Skinny put a hand to his ear, waiting.

"Blanket toss!" the clowns shouted back. They swarmed over Gladys, covering her up in the blanket. They trundled her to the middle of the ring and heaved her into the air. She squealed as they lofted her, then gave out with a *whoof* when she landed. With a whooping woo, they heaved up again. The clowns managed, with a little practice, to snap the blanket and tumble Gladys head over heels.

"It's all in the wrist," said Skinny as Gladys did another layout into the blanket.

"Police!" came voices as cops breached the door and poured into the ring.

The clowns caught Gladys and wrapped her up in the blanket. They dropped her to the floor, everyone planting a foot on the bundle.

"Franklin!" Officer Joe stepped forward, his weapon drawn, two more officers behind him. "What's going on here? Old man Kanega's going to pee his overalls, you guys throwing a party here without his permission."

Officer Joe came over to the squirming bundle.

"What's under the blanket?" he asked.

"What blanket?" asked Noodlenick, a character clown in a trout-tailed fishing hat. Everyone gave Officer Joe the same deep shrug. Like they'd practiced it.

He waved them back and unrolled the blanket. Gladys staggered to her feet, reeling, enfeebled and dizzy, trying to swipe at him with the knife. Officer Joe holstered his weapon, caught her arm, and lifted the knife from her grasp. He summoned another of the officers to take the knife. Then he snapped his handcuffs on her.

"I didn't think you were going to show up," said Franklin.

"All the pranks this week? Chief wasn't going to let you clowns sucker him in again. Until we got a call about some clown stealing a tour bus and how Funtime was lit up like Christmas. He had to let us check it out."

"Where'd you guys come from?" Franklin asked the clowns.

All the clowns pointed at Lucy who was getting the zip-ties cut off her by the other officer.

"I tried calling the cops. They thought it was part of the joke."

"You okay?" Officer Joe asked Franklin.

"I'm fine," said Franklin.

Officer Joe lifted Franklin's arm into the light. "That fake? Or should we take a few minutes to worry about it?"

Franklin's sleeve glistened in the light, soaked in blood.

Franklin looked at Lucy then at Officer Joe. "Just a scratch," he said. Then he fainted.

chapter fifteen

THE SPARKLIES FILLING FRANKLIN'S HEAD dissipated. He could feel cold metal on his backside as he sat on the rear step-up of an ambulance. It was still night and the cop cars filled the main thoroughfare of the arcade. Spinning emergency lights flashed off the clapboard and sheet metal of the buildings. It had gotten colder. Or at least Franklin felt colder.

He realized Lisker stood next to him.

"Sorry about the little mix up with the Slasher," said Lisker.

Franklin looked up at the private eye touching the bandaged spot on the top of his head, his remaining hair all askew.

"And I'm sorry I ever thought there was any possible way you could be a criminal genius," said Franklin.

"Hey, it's okay, kid, I get that all the time. Comes with the territory. You get used to it." Lisker winked, pulled the trigger on his finger-pistol at Franklin and clicked his tongue. He turned and left Franklin sitting there.

Lucy stood by the police cruiser. Gladys sat in the back seat. An officer searched through the contents of her purse spread out on the cruiser's trunk lid.

Lucy had been glancing over as Karla, the EMT, cut Franklin's sleeve open and worked on his arm.

Franklin kept his head turned toward the spot where Karla dabbed up blood with a gauze pad, but his eyes stayed fixed on Lucy. She appeared to hesitate before walking toward him.

It gave him an icy feeling all down his spine. He wasn't sure what to say to the girl of his dreams, whose mother was his worst nightmare.

She stood over him a long moment.

"Hey," said Lucy, shifting from foot to foot like her shoes were too tight. "They got you patched up?" Lucy nodded at Karla.

"No more extra orifices." Franklin raised his arm.

"Ennnh!" Karla frowned and took his arm in her hand again.

"Missed you at happy hour," said Franklin. "Heck of a floor show. Some cut-up tried to skin a clown. You'd have loved it."

"Look. I had no idea my own mother—" Lucy burst out, hesitated, and tried again. "My being—" she stopped.

So much for seeing the humor. Franklin left her dangling a tad too long before he gave her what he hoped passed for a sympathetic shrug. "You don't owe me an explanation."

"No, I don't," said Lucy. "I don't owe you anything. If you hadn't stuck your big red nose in my business at the bus stop, lost my wallet, run off and made me chase after you, I'd be gone. You'd never have laid eyes on me. Or my mother. So, no, I don't owe you an 'explanation,'" she said, making air quotes.

Watching her, angry like that, Franklin realized people don't know what they're talking about. Angry women are not beautiful. They're scary. She's scary. It hit him that it could mean he was getting over Lucy. It could mean he'd taken that all-important first step toward recovery. It could mean he was on his way to getting out from under the hopeless romantic monkey on his back. Boy, glad that's over.

"What the hell were you thinking? Going off with some strange woman that way?" she asked without as much heat this time. "That's the kind of thing Buster would do. I expected something better from you."

Great. If she expects something better, is it possible she *wants* something better? From him? So much for the long lonesome road toward recovery. Most agonizing five seconds ever. He turns around and picks up the hopeless romantic monkey. It gibbers and capers, glad to see him after being gone so long.

"I'd already figured out she was the Slasher," said Franklin. He didn't mention how he thought her mother looked like Lisker in drag. "She used the same trick on Big Rig."

Lucy winced.

"Why didn't you call the cops. Leave it to them."

"I did. But someone needed to keep her busy till they got there."

"They had no intention of being there."

"Uh, yeah. It didn't go like I planned."

"Why would you do that?"

"Only way I could prove to Buster and Lisker you couldn't be the Slasher."

"Why put yourself in danger? For someone you hardly know? Someone who can't stand the sight of you in that face of yours?"

Not ready to give an answer to such a question, he asked her instead, "How did you figure out where we were?"

"Same way. Buster said something about Big Rig and a flyer."

"Ah. Buster."

"I went looking to warn you. When I got to the Big Top you two were already gone. Red told me she'd asked you to bring her here."

"Why did you come after me? Even if you didn't know—what she planned."

"What do you mean, even if I didn't know? Don't you believe me?"

"There was nothing to stop you from leaving town after you finished with Buster. How is he by the way?"

"Don't worry. He's still breathing. I didn't—"

"—have sex with him," said Franklin at the same moment Lucy said, "—kill him."

"Sex?" Lucy shouted, flinching backward.

"Kill?" Franklin shouted back at her.

"Stay still," said Karla, straightening up and putting her hands on her hips.

"Is that all you clowns ever think about?" Lucy turned to Karla as if to connect with her, woman-to-woman, at the stupidity of men in general and clowns in particular.

"What else is there to do for two people in their underwear looking to pass the time?" asked Franklin. "I knew you weren't going to kill him. Who the hell knows about the other." Franklin stopped. He flicked a glance at Karla, apologizing on behalf of all men everywhere. Franklin looked up at Lucy. "I mean, it's okay. It's what Buster's famous for. What am I supposed to say?" Franklin looked to Karla once more, this time for confirmation. But Karla put her hands up and gave Franklin a jut-jawed refusal to let them draw her in. She went back to work on Franklin's arm.

"You could say thank you. I did save your sorry clown ass twice. In case you're keeping score."

"Why would someone who hates the sight of me made up like this do something like that?"

"Does it matter why?"

"Is it to make sure I'm still good for the seventeen hundred dollars and sixty-two cents?"

"You," said Lucy, all the anger sparking out of the finger she jabbed at Franklin, "are a hopeless dick."

Lucy spun on her heel and walked away, back toward the police cruiser.

He realized he hadn't asked her what exactly she did to Buster. He also realized he didn't care.

Franklin, still sitting on the ambulance step, sees the circle of addicts in the darkened room. The hard, narrow light shines on him.

"Hi!" says Franklin. "I'm Franklin, and I'm a hopeless dick."

"Hi, Dick," the rest of the group calls back to him. And so it goes.

"Okay," said Karla, "Climb in. We need to run you over to the hospital, get you checked out." Karla kept her hand on him as he got to his feet. She steadied him as he stepped into the back of the ambulance and directed him to the bench seat. She looked back at Lucy as she stalked past the police cruiser without stopping to look in on Gladys. "Your girlfriend can ride along if you want."

"You'd have one more bloody orifice to stitch up on me if she did."

Karla nodded and closed the doors on him.

The EMTs mounted up, flipped on the siren, and pulled out of the parking lot.

◆ ◆ ◆

Franklin made it back to his apartment a little past two in the morning. He'd been in the hospital emergency room the whole time, where he'd learned a very important thing.

He learned that he hadn't learned a single solitary thing from the last three days. Unless he counted that brainstorm as having learned something.

He let Heidi the charge nurse and Joyce the treatment nurse have their way with him. All it took was a little batting of the eyes, a little puckering of the lips. They sweet-talked him into entertaining the kids still stuck in the waiting room. They enticed another two hours out of him for mere promises of off-duty delights.

Until the cops brought in a severely inebriated fifty-five-year-old man they picked up for threatening a parking meter with a squirt gun. Spotting Franklin, the guy barricaded himself in the toilet. Convinced the Grim Reaper disguised as a circus clown had snuck in to look for him, he refused to leave. The attending physician chased Franklin home.

Franklin was one used-up clown.

When he reached his apartment, the front door stood open. He stepped through and paused before calling, "Buster? Are you here?"

He sidled in further, standing in the little alcove by the front door, listening. He called out again, "Buster?"

From his bedroom, Franklin heard muffled cries.

"Okay, okay," said Franklin. "I hear you. At least you're breathing."

Franklin came and stood in the doorway to his bedroom.

"Yep," said Franklin. "That's probably illegal. Did you sign an abdication of personal dignity consent form?"

Buster lay stretched out, jay-bird naked, duct taped to the bed posts, looking ready for a little unregulated domination.

Franklin pulled out his mobile phone, squinting to see the screen as he thumbed the numbers. He put the phone up to his ear. "Hold on a sec." Franklin held a finger out to Buster. "This is too good not to share."

There came another, more violent *agh-agh-agh-agh-agh* from the bed.

"No, no, don't worry, no pictures," said Franklin waving the phone around. A flash went off. "Except that one." He studied the screen. "You moved." Another flash went off. "And that one." A third flash. "That's the last one, honest. I promise I won't post them on our clown page. He studied the pictures and said, "Oh, we have to do these up in frames for Mom's mantel this Mother's Day."

A voice from his phone caught Franklin's attention and he put it back to his ear, again holding his finger up at Buster.

"Yes," said Franklin, taking on a hissing, whiskey-whisper of a voice with a shady foreign accent. "I'm a snitch for one of your officers, y'know, and I, uh, got something for 'em." Franklin listened a minute and said, "No, no. I tell you who I gotta talk to." He moved out of the room, leaving Buster stretched out on the bed.

In no time, flashing red and blue emergency lights were outside the apartment complex. Franklin peeked through the curtains.

"We got company," Franklin shouted back at Buster. "No, no, don't get up! I'll let them in." He opened the door.

Officer Sunshine stood at the door, breathing hard. Down on the street an ambulance rolled up behind the police cruiser.

"That's a lot of stairs," said Officer Sunshine. She steadied herself, cocking a wary eye at Franklin. "This isn't one of Buster's clown jokes, is it?"

"No, nothing the least bit funny about it. I remember how close you two were, I thought you should know."

"Were?"

"Are," said Franklin, touching his face, embarrassed by his slip. He pointed. "That way."

Officer Sunshine turned and waved for the EMTs who'd been waiting at the bottom of the steps.

"Come on up. The more the merrier." Franklin called down to them.

The two EMTs jogged up the stairs and followed Officer Sunshine inside. Franklin fell in step with the shorter EMT and asked her, "Did you know the deceased?"

"Deceased?" she asked, "We didn't get a DB call. Is the vic deceased?"

"Eventually." Franklin followed her across the living room. "Like the rest of us."

They all crowded around the doorway of Franklin's bedroom, looking in on Buster.

"Dang!" said the tall EMT.

Officer Sunshine gave out with a deep sigh and said to the EMTs, "No need for you to hang around."

"False alarm?" asked the short EMT, eyeballing Franklin hard.

"Log it as a 'good intent' call. He won't be needing you. But," said Officer Sunshine, "I have to go get my taser." She fairly skipped back out the door and down the steps. The EMTs followed her outside, the tall one still shaking his head.

"Should've got pictures," he said to the short EMT.

"Hey," said Franklin, leaning on the door frame, smiling at Buster. "You know how circumstances, no matter how bad they seem, can turn out to be the very thing you needed? How they change your life? And you see the world in a brand new way?"

Buster groaned against the duct tape, his head dropping back on the pillow.

Officer Sunshine returned, taser in hand.

"This," Franklin pointed at the taser, "is one of those times."

"This? Just a precaution," she said. She studied her watch and did a silent count down, then said to Franklin, "Good thing I'm off-duty. This could take a while."

"If you'll excuse me, I'm off to watch the submarine races in the park," said Franklin. He checked his fingernails. "I could use a manicure while I'm at it."

Officer Sunshine removed her cover and unbuckled her Sam Brown, flinging both onto the chair. "This is going to be instructive."

Officer Sunshine pulled open her shirt and nudged the door closed with her boot heel. Buster's muffled yowls were the last thing Franklin heard as he left the apartment.

chapter sixteen

A LITTLE PAST NINE-THIRTY in the morning Franklin steered the clownmobile into the bus station parking lot. He swung around and stopped in front of the whitewashed station building. Lucy sat on the bench against the wall in the shade of the station. She'd piled up her luggage on the bench beside her.

"Hey," said Franklin, leaning out the driver's side window.

"Hey," said Lucy, turning to look up at him, shading her eyes. The morning sunlight glinted off the chrome of the clownmobile. She winced and turned her head. "You ever wash that stuff off?"

"Got a birthday party. Couple of German Shepherds. Owner swears they're better than family," said Franklin. "Traded with Noodlenick. Took the dogs and gave him my bachelorette party. They say pets might be a coming thing. Cats. Birds. Fish."

"Just as well, I guess. Never would have recognized you naked. Your face. Your face naked."

He got out of the van and closed the door. He stood with his hands tucked into the hip pockets of his costume.

"Are you here to see I leave town for sure this time?" She held up her bus ticket. "In case you need proof."

Franklin smiled. "I've got a few minutes before I have to be there to throw out the first mailman." He cleared his throat. "All right for me to sit down?"

Lucy didn't say anything, but scooted ever so slightly aside to give him room. She put her ticket back into her shoulder bag, ignoring whether he chose to sit or not.

Franklin took his clown purse out of his pocket and sat down next to her. He snapped open the purse, blew into it, made a show of wiping the dust from his eye.

"Isn't there a snake that's supposed to jump out?" asked Lucy.

Franklin took out a roll of bills, peeled off the rubber band, and handed the roll to Lucy.

She hesitated, then lifted her hand to take them, but still hesitated. Franklin nodded for her to go ahead. She took the bills and counted them.

"And the sixty-two cents?"

Franklin reached deeper down into the purse and took out the coins, dropping them one by one into her hand.

She studied the coins in her hand. She picked out one and handed it back to him.

"Canadian."

"I'll have to owe it to you. Got a forwarding address?"

"Not yet."

She held up the wad of bills. "Where'd you get this? Hock a pair of your shoes?"

"Buster. He bought some pictures I took."

"You found him."

"Hard to miss."

Lucy rubbed her fingertips at a spot on her forehead. "Yeah, a girl's gotta do what a girl's gotta do."

"Sorry for thinking—what I was thinking."

"Forget it."

"Kind of a habit. Thinking the worst where Buster's involved."

Lucy kept watching down the road as she nodded, not adding anything.

"Anyway, thanks for showing up when you did. You'll appreciate knowing I've added superhero to the list of things I will leave to the professionals."

"Glad I got there in time," said Lucy.

"Quite an entrance. You'd be a natural."

"Natural what?"

"Clown."

"No way."

"Anyway, I'm glad it worked out."

"Me, too."

"Very glad, if I'm honest."

"Me, too."

"Beyond glad is more like it."

"Me, too."

Lucy and Franklin stared off in opposite directions.

"I had no idea she'd been following me ever since I left Bakersfield."

"It's okay," said Franklin. "You don't have to tell me anything. It's not like you and I share the same special adhesive bond you found with Buster."

"I can't tell if you're trying to be funny or if you're feeling sorry for yourself."

"Good. Comedy's useless if you can't hide behind it."

"You don't make it easy."

She closed her eyes and clenched her lips hard together.

"I hadn't planned to say anything. I planned to leave and let you think whatever you wanted. But here you are. So, I might as well tell you."

◆ ◆ ◆

The day of the mayhem at the golf course, with cops bearing down, Lucy hid in the bushes. She threw away her clown wig. She pulled off the stocking mask cut from her tights and painted with slashes of white and red for eyes and a mouth.

She watched as the turf truck rolled away, the golf cart roped to its frame.

"I didn't have much time. I was hoping the knot on the cart would hold long enough. At least until I could get back to your apartment and ditch the costume," Lucy said to Franklin.

"Pretty clever. The police had to chase it all the way onto the interstate before they could get the truck stopped. Made for a spectacular crack-up," Franklin said to Lucy. He didn't mention how it made his guts turn to water, watching the cart slam into the truck and roll off the roadway, scattering pieces all over.

Lucy stayed hunched over in the bushes as she peeled off the black clown jumper she'd been wearing. She had another, more colorful jumper underneath. She popped a clown topper onto her head and adjusted the yarn fringe of red hair.

"I used one of the clown suits I found in your room."

Great. Something else with her smell on it that he'd never be able to wash out. He might as well go ahead and burn it to save himself the heartache.

Lucy dashed for the stairs to Franklin's apartment and scampered up the steps. She took the key from the mailbox and opened the door, letting herself in.

"My plan was to slip in, get my clothes, find the scrapbook wherever Buster hid it, and get out of there."

Lucy was in Franklin's bedroom, stripped down to her bra and panties, when she heard the front door open. She dropped down onto the floor beside the bed, out of sight of the door.

Buster, carrying the scrapbook, pushed in to the room. He sidled around the bed to the nightstand, and opened the drawer, wedging it in under Franklin's socks.

He straightened up, very still, then whipped around, catching Lucy ducked over and waddling for the door.

"Hey!"

Lucy screamed and grabbed the black jumper off the bed to cover up her near nudeness.

"What're you doing here?" they both shouted at the same time, at roughly the same decibel level of panic.

Lucy spotted the scrapbook just as Buster recognized the demon clown suit.

"Aha!" they both shouted at the same time, at roughly the same decibel level of gleeful smugness.

At the same nanosecond they both broke out of their panic. They realized they were both holding their own incriminating objects in plain view. They whipped them behind themselves.

Lucy covered up her nakedness with her bare arms.

"You're going to hide that in Franklin's room?"

"I'm doing you a favor. The kind of favor that make girls throw themselves on their rescuer and smother him with kisses. If Lisker finds this and shows it to the cops, they can't help but think you're the Slasher."

"It wasn't me! Okay, in the golf cart, that was me." She flailed and slapped her thigh. "Franklin's in jail!"

"Well, I hope you're happy. They let him go!"

"That's no surprise. Nobody'd believe he could be the Slasher."

Buster waved the scrapbook at her. "They will if we give them a smoking gun—smoking scrapbook."

"You'd do that to your own brother?"

"You need a fall guy. I need someone to spend the rest of my life with. He needs to be a hero. Looks to me like it works out all around for everybody."

Lucy edged for the door. Buster leaped to cut her off, pinning her in the corner between the wall and the bed.

"If you aren't the Slasher, who's to say it couldn't be Franklin? What makes jail better than spending the rest of your life with me?"

"Time off for good behavior?"

She broke for the other side, over the bed, bounding for the door. Buster dived across the bed, grabbing for her hand.

"I'm willing to overlook your homicidal tendencies if you are!" shouted Buster.

"He's your brother!"

"He'd do the same for me."

"That's crazy!"

"Love is all about sacrifice. Sacrificing your brother. Your best friend. Your principles!"

Buster pulled Lucy down onto the bed beside him, gripping her hands. Lucy rolled backward off the bed, onto her feet. Buster whipped over and body-blocked her, pinioning her arms. He tried to kiss her as she played keep-away with her mouth. She snaked her body causing him to smile. She slithered down out of his embrace, but he pivoted and caught her up in his arms again. She gripped the fabric at the shoulders of his jacket, keeping her mouth out of range of his lips.

Somewhere a police siren wailed.

"Listen," said Buster, "they're playing your song."

Lucy, breathing hard, nostrils flared, kept her lips tight together in case Buster decided a french kiss was next on the menu. Her eyes rocketed side to side, her mind click-ety-clacking as she calculated an escape. She saw a roll of duct tape among a pile of small tools.

"I keep it handy for putting quick gags together," Franklin said to Lucy. "Honest."

Lucy fixed her eyes on Buster's face, trying to read him. She saw her chance. It's possible she saw in Buster's eyes, swimming in all that clown make-up, an honest effort to be tender in victory. It might be an opening she could exploit.

"Okay, okay. You win," said Lucy, relaxing. "You're right. The way the private eye is working to pin this on me, I do need an alibi." Lucy stroked and smoothed the fabric of his jacket shoulders.

Buster pulled Lucy to himself. "Air tight."

Lucy gave out with a grunt. "Iron clad."

Buster gripped her closer. "Rock solid."

Lucy used her forearms to lever herself backward to look him in the face. "No questions asked."

Buster embraced her, hunching over, resting his chin on her shoulder. "Curiosity kills the cat."

She managed to push him back far enough to make eye contact with him again. "We should do something to celebrate."

From the living room, Franklin called out, "You're in big trouble if you're allergic to giblets!"

"Damn," said Buster.

"Quick, give me your jacket." She yanked at Buster's jacket, pulling it off him and slipping into it. She stepped out of the bedroom, pulling the door closed behind her. Buster shucked his shirt and pants, pulling his undershirt over his head. He bounced around the bedroom working to remove his shoes.

"Buster was already down to his boxers," Franklin said to Lucy.

"He didn't get any help from me," Lucy said to Franklin.

Once Franklin left, headed for the Big Top, Lucy turned back to Buster.

"Lucky I had that flyer," said Buster. "Franklin would've ruined everything."

"Lucky for you."

"Lucky for you and me both, Franklin's desperate enough to fall for that free massage hoax."

"Hoax?" asked Lucy.

"After what happened to Big Rig? Of course it's a hoax."

"You told him you were desperate. You didn't tell him it was a hoax."

"He'd still be here if I had."

"So right now, Franklin is on his way to meet someone who could be the Slasher?"

"Maybe not," said Buster, but he didn't look convinced now. He brightened. "It gives us more time alone," he said by way of excuse.

"The least I could do was warn you," Lucy said to Franklin, "then slip away with the rest of the clowns."

"That's why you needed him out of his costume," Franklin said to Lucy, with a faint tinge of relief in his voice.

"Time's a-wasting," she said to Buster, advancing on him with a swing and sway that would melt a man of sterner stuff. She pushed him onto the bed and straddled his chest.

"Do we need that?" asked Buster, pointing at the tape.

"It'll help me relax. You know how I am about you clowns." She rubbed her hands up and down Buster's chest.

"You seem pretty relaxed already."

Lucy peeled a length of tape from the roll. She took the strip between her teeth and tore it with a sexy whip of her head.

"Hold it." Buster pulled a chain from around his neck. "My medic-alert badge. We don't need the EMTs showing up for a false alarm." He slipped it off over his head. "Okay. I'm ready."

"That'll be handy," said Lucy, her eyes a heady concoction of means, motive, and opportunity all in one juicy look.

"That's how Buster described it when the officer took his statement," Franklin said to Lucy.

"Oooh."

"Don't worry. She was off-duty. And out of uniform. All the way out of her uniform."

"That's a relief."

"It looked to me like you were about to make Buster's dreams come true."

"I had to make him think the same thing. You saw how I left him."

"Good enough reason to keep a roll of duct tape handy."

"I hoped if I wore Buster's clothes, I'd get past Lisker. In case he waited outside the apartment, trying to catch me."

Lucy stepped out of the apartment, dressed in Buster's costume. She swam in the pants, shirt, and jacket. The shoes were enormous on her. She'd piled up her hair to make the hat fit. The only way she could get down the steps without tumbling to the bottom was to walk like an inebriated duck.

"You'd have laughed," Lucy said to Franklin.

"Seeing you civilians made up as clowns always makes me laugh," Franklin said to Lucy. He wasn't laughing.

Finally reaching the bottom, Lucy straightened the costume, leveled the hat and did her best saunter down the street.

Lucy walked as fast as the shoes allowed, picking up speed as she got the hang of moving in the oversized flappers. She'd worked up a good head of steam, a wiggling waddle and arms flailing. She kept checking behind herself, watching for anyone chasing her.

"I felt I should at least call," Lucy said to Franklin, "and let you know what Buster said about the free massage being a hoax."

"You didn't make it."

"No."

Lucy walked past the filling station where the chartered tour buses were fueling for the trip out of town. Clowns stood around, or lined up to board, the drivers marking each passenger off their manifests. Cops checked faces in the crowd.

Lucy's eyes went wide. She kept her head down, moving faster and faster until she was skipping to get past the officers. She was almost past them. None of them had spotted her. Then Officer Joe whistled at her as she came even with him.

"Hey! All clowns on the bus!"

"Uh, gotta make a phone call," she said, giving him her best baritone. She veered and headed for the phone booth by the front door of the filling station's mini-mart.

Officer Joe kept watching, so she fished in the pockets for anything like usable change. Surprised, she found a quarter. She dropped it in and dialed for information.

"Big Top," she said into the phone, still using her fake baritone.

"Nobody tried to sneak on the buses," she heard Officer Joe say.

"How'd you know?" shouted Lisker. "They're all wearing grease paint!"

Lucy whipped around, keeping the mouthpiece of the phone in front of her face.

"We're checking every one of them." Officer Joe hefted the collection of manifests.

"Every single one?" Lisker didn't seem convinced. He looked around, taking his own inventory. He threw up his hands and stormed back to his car.

Through the earpiece, Lucy heard Red answer, but she'd dropped the phone. She moved to the end of the longest line of clowns boarding. As one clown climbed aboard, Lucy took a giant pace backward. Another clown up the steps and another backward pace. Until the last clown went up the steps and she'd moved behind one of the buses. Hunched over, she ran for the street.

"I went down the block and found a phone in front of the Barking Penguin," said Lucy. "It's a, it's a—" she snapped her fingers to prime her memory.

"Pub," said Franklin. "Lots of animal acts hang out there."

"Explains the rotten fish smell."

"I stay away from it."

"Anyway, I grab the phone and before I can dial, one of those buses pulled up next to me and stopped," Lucy said to Franklin.

Lucy stood at the little phone kiosk outside the Barking Penguin, keeping watch in both directions. She punched up Information on the phone's keypad. Before she could finish, a clown bus rolled up next to her and stopped, the door *wooshing* open.

The driver, as clowned up as his passengers, called out to Lucy, "I thought we got all you clowns!"

The Big Top Tavern's sheet metal clown was visible in the distance. Lucy started to tell the driver she was only going up the road.

Lisker pulled his car to a stop just ahead of the bus. He got out and squinted hard, watching Lucy.

Lucy hung up the phone, ducked her head, hefting her bags, and hurried for the bus.

"I don't know how the private eye figured out so fast it was me," Lucy said to Franklin.

"Lisker recognized Buster's jacket and hat on you. He made the connection."

"How?"

"Lisker found Buster first," Franklin said to Lucy. "Realized it must've been you who did it and took off after you."

"Did he at least check to see if Buster was breathing?"

"I think he saw Buster's predicament as the Slasher's big finish. He apologized for not cutting him loose, but he had a Slasher to catch, and Buster'd make a phenomenal last chapter. There's no satisfying some people."

It explained why Lisker stared so hard at her as she stood at the little phone kiosk. She dropped the phone and dashed up the steps, boarding the bus. "You talked me into it!" she said as the door hissed closed behind her.

"You're better off outta this burg," said the clown driver. "Ain't safe."

All the passengers on the bus blew kazoos and Bronx cheers for the town, giving it a hearty nose-thumbing. The driver steered the bus around Lisker's car and headed for the interstate.

Lucy kept an eye on Lisker's car as she squeezed through the rowdy crowd to the only empty seat at the back. She fit herself in, but couldn't relax, surrounded by clowns. She sat, tensed, up on butt-*pointe*.

Her seat mate, a big auguste clown elbowed her.

"Shucks's the name," he said, holding his hand out for a shake. "What's yours?"

Her face opened up wide because her brain had shrunk to pea-sized. "Frappe?" the only noun she could get out.

Shucks nodded a howdy-do and said, "So, did you kill 'em?"

"Kill?" asked Lucy, a slight edge of panic still in her voice.

"On the golf course?"

"Golf course?"

"What'd ya shoot? Pretty hard to keep score with the Slasher chasing us all over the green."

Outside, Lucy watched as the sheet metal sign for the Big Top went sliding by, the bus rolling toward the interstate.

"How far to the next rest stop?" asked Lucy.

"Don't need to." Shucks jerked his thumb toward the back. "Rolling Johnnie'll take care of us."

Lucy drooped into her seat. "Maybe it's just as well."

The town limits dropped behind them. The road began to cut through the sorghum fields on either side of the pavement.

She put her head back and closed her eyes against the carpet of hair and zany hats in ranks ahead of her. A honking car came barreling up beside the bus, drawing even with it.

"Lisker followed us," Lucy said to Franklin, "racing with the bus, honking and weaving."

Lisker drove like a madman, steering in close to the bus, then forced onto the opposite shoulder by oncoming cars. The road hadn't split into four lanes yet. Traffic came straight at Lisker, who kept honking and weaving, honking and weaving. It was an insane demolition derby in the making.

The bus driver picked up speed. Watching the traffic ahead and checking his side mirror, he kept the lunatic next to him in view.

Lisker managed to draw far enough in front and nudge in close to the bus, trying to force the behemoth to the shoulder.

Unable to outrun the maniac in the car, the bus pulled to the side of the road, jerking to a stop. The screwball in the sedan slid to a halt a dozen yards ahead. The driver picked up his mic to call the dispatcher. Lisker jumped out of his car, raced back to the bus and started pounding on the glass.

"Open up! Open up!" he shouted. "I know she's in there!"

Lucy, acting as confused as the rest of them, saw no way out. Then she did. A brainstorm.

"It's the Baggy Pants Slasher!"

The bus exploded with hyper-energized clown fright.

Clowns boiled out of the bus, out the windows, and through the door. Lisker scampered to herd them into a manageable line. The clowns trampled Lisker flat in the panic, mashing him into the gravel with a beating swarm of fleeing clown feet.

When the private eye managed to pull himself out of the Lisker-shaped crater, he climbed into the bus. He didn't find anyone in or under the seats. He slapped a headrest and ran back along the length of the bus and down the steps.

Lisker scanned the fields bracketing the road. A clown head popped into view before vanishing in the chest-high growth. He started for it, dodged an oncoming car and aimed for the spot where he'd seen the head disappear. But a dozen yards away a second head rose up and vanished. Lisker made for it, breasting through the waving stalks. A third clown head pop into view on the other side of the road.

Lucy peeked down from the overhead luggage rack. She watched Lisker in the field, chasing jack-in-the-box clowns.

Lucy slipped into the driver's seat, floored it, and steered the bus in a two-wheeled U-turn. Tires screeched as she headed the bus back toward town.

The clown heads all popped up as the bus disappeared back the way they'd come.

Lisker slapped at the leafy cane around him, watching the bus dwindle from view.

Moments later, the bus roared into the parking lot at the Big Top, taking out the metallic clown sign hanging over the street entrance.

The door hissed open. Lucy flew down the steps and ran for the tavern.

Inside, she slammed up to the bar.

"Franklin. Was he here?" she asked, breathing hard.

"Yes. He left with somebody," said Red, putting glasses away.

"Who?"

"Some blonde."

"Where did they go?"

"Kanega's Funtime Village. Out past the interstate," said Red. "He said he'd show her some of his clown tricks." He winked at Lucy.

"I'd have said to hell with it right then," Lucy said to Franklin, "but I saw the glass she'd been drinking out of."

"Is that—?" she started.

"White Russian with—" said Red.

"—a cherry," Lucy finished his sentence. "Red, let me use your phone."

"That's when I tried calling the cops. But they weren't interested," Lucy said to Franklin.

She hung up the phone. Lucy's eyes shrunk to slits. She slapped the bar, stewed a moment before asking, "You know where I can round up a bunch of clowns?"

"That's how you figured out your mother had been at the bar?" Franklin asked Lucy.

"White Russian with a cherry. Meant she was back to her old tricks, picking up clowns."

"Which of us did you think needed rescuing?"

"Isn't it enough for you I showed up?"

Franklin could say it was, but he wasn't satisfied. It kept gnawing at him. "You always make a habit of driving a bus through locked doors when your mother's out late on a school night?"

"Hey! My first time driving one of those things."

The bus jounced over the potholes, through the main gate, sending the two large gate panels of cyclone fence skittering. She heaved the wheel hard but took out the awning of the arcade games as she aimed at the main doors of the circus pavilion.

She gripped the wheel as the behemoth crunched the little marquee over the doors, rammed through, coming to a stop inside.

"I had trouble reaching the brakes."

She leaped down from the bus and saw Franklin sitting astride Gladys. Even through all the make-up, she could see the great big smile on his face.

"I wasn't *smiling* smiling. I was *relieved* smiling. Big difference," Franklin said to Lucy.

"The way you were smiling, I nearly left you both right there," Lucy said to Franklin. "But when she asked me to brain you, I knew it wasn't because you were a lousy lover."

"Thank you."

"I must've been in shock, thinking what it could mean. How she might be responsible for all the others."

That still didn't answer Franklin's question about why she went to such extremes to rescue her mother from a randy clown. Instead, Franklin asked, "So where're you off to now?"

"Back to Bakersfield. No reason to keep running."

"Gladys say why she did it?"

"She hates clowns."

"I meant, how she could let you go on thinking you might be the Slasher?"

"Oh. She hoped the blackouts would keep me thinking I could be the one, and I'd stay away from the likes of you. You guys. You clowns. Her way of keeping me safe."

Nothing for him to say about that. Franklin clasped his hands between his knees and looked off down the road. The bus pulled into the parking lot and up to the station.

"So, um," Franklin started, but the bus rolled up into the parking bay and its door opened.

Lucy shouldered her luggage and went to board.

"I still owe you that penny," said Franklin.

"Next time I'm through here. None of your clown bull-shit, either." She moved up the steps onto the bus.

"I'm good for it. Wouldn't think of stiffing a civilian. Too fond of my knee caps."

Now it was her turn to have nothing else to say. Lucy walked into the darkness of the bus, down the aisle to find a seat. Franklin watched her silhouette move along to the rear.

The door closed. Franklin stepped back as the bus pulled away.

This was not how it was supposed to end. One of them was supposed to fling off all the extra baggage, sweep the other up, declare undying love. She can climb a rope overhand, for Pete's sake. It should be a snap for her to toss him onto her shoulder and carry him into the sunset.

That was not her job. It was his. Either he could be safe, or he could be real.

The tail end of the bus was still in sight. Not yet through the traffic lights. There was still time. He sprinted for the clownmobile, hopped in, and twisted the key in the ignition. The starter clicked.

Nothing.

Buster appeared on the driver's side. Franklin rolled down the window.

"Thought you might like to have a souvenir." Buster handed Franklin the distributor cap.

Franklin watched the bus disappear into traffic.

"And I chained the hood down." Buster leaned in to Franklin. "You are going to pay, Frankie-boy."

Buster's head jerked backward. Franklin saw Trooper Sunshine holding a studded leather leash with Buster on the other end. Trooper Sunshine wore leather and denim civvies and sat astride a huge motorcycle, 600ccs if it was a cc. She twisted the throttle, the motor thrumming.

"And don't think for a minute fixing me up with Rita makes everything okay between us. You are going to pay."

Officer Sunshine, or Rita as she preferred when off-duty, yanked on the leash again. Buster mounted up behind her on the bike. He gripped the sissy bar behind him, but with another flick on the leash, he wrapped his arms around her waist.

"Pay," Buster mouthed as they roared off, Rita aiming the big bike for the street, Buster's head thrown back. A moment later they were gone, too.

Franklin got out. He threw the distributor cap into the clownmobile. The back end of the bus was already gone down that long, lonesome highway.

chapter seventeen

FRANKLIN LIVED ON HIS OWN, now that Buster had 'hung up the old nose,' the way he'd so often threatened. Or, more likely, the way his new girlfriend Officer Sunshine threatened. That was clear enough to Franklin.

She and Buster had an amazingly symbiotic relationship. Buster gave up chasing other women, and she let him run the siren when they parked in the police cruiser and made out. Franklin had to admit it seemed to work for the two of them.

Franklin moved out of the apartment and into a tiny caretaker's trailer just beyond Funtime's main gate. He took over as part-time custodian for the park, still shut down for the season.

The trailer sat in a patch of high weeds a few dozen yards from the entrance gates. A garden hose provided running water to the tiny sink in the trailer's kitchenette. The sink drained into a nearby storm culvert through pieces of PVC pipe connected with duct tape. The trailer had electricity, but it lacked a sewer hook-up. He used the employee locker room for the toilet and showers. Not all that homey, but tolerable, and it did get Buster and Rita out of his hair. Which was something.

Along with the trailer, the job provided a little extra cash each month. A big help, since Franklin remained as choosy as ever about the gigs he took. He still gave a pass to anything with eligible women involved. He was interested, of course. The problem? Not a single, solitary female he'd encountered in the last few months looked anything like Lucy. Or sounded like Lucy. Or smelled like Lucy. Or put him in fear of his life like Lucy. Or dominated his imagination like Lucy. If he ever happened to run across such a person anywhere in the tri-state area, he'd hand over his heart to her in an instant. She could do whatever she wanted with it. Not a lot of candidates at the kiddie parties or supermarket openings he worked.

But so far, Franklin would bet the ranch no such creature existed in the flesh, outside of Bakersfield. That was home to the only known specimen of perfection as far as he knew.

Dozens of times since watching that bus disappear with Lucy on it, Franklin opened a road atlas. He measured the miles, measured his meager means, measured his self-confidence. More than once, he worked up the determination to follow her. Especially after a gig where he had to fend off a clown junkie. He would empty the props and gadgets from his big flowered carpetbag. He'd throw in extra underwear and a toothbrush, determined for sure this time to follow her. Determined for sure this time to search until he found her.

Until he got a look at himself in the mirror as he wiped off his make-up. She hadn't bothered to get in touch. Or to reach out in any of a dozen convenient ways. If she'd wanted him to know how to find her, she'd have said something, written something, done something. So he'd decide, not this time. Next time. He'd unpack the underwear and the toothbrush. He'd put the gadgets and props back in the big flowered carpetbag. He'd go another day.

He'd kept the scrapbook. It didn't seem as important now, but he paged through it every now and then for the pictures of Lucy. There weren't many.

His favorite was a strip of five pictures taken while she hid in a photo booth at some carnival in Idaho. A clown ended up in a dunk tank filled with carbolic acid. She must have noticed them in the slot and grabbed them up to avoid incrimination as she fled.

The other was a picture Franklin added. A picture cut from the local paper. A news photo of her and her mother, caught by a photographer as they arrived at the courthouse in California. Extradited to California where the mayhem started.

Life was back to normal. As normal as it could ever get. For a clown. No reason not to. Franklin started his day in his clown get-up. He headed over to the Big Top to commiserate with the other clowns out of hiding now the Slasher was behind bars. They'd wait for the phone to ring, and for Red to hand out gigs. Like old times. The Slasher's career and capture brought a new level of notoriety and work these days. Most callers asked for Franklin, but Red spread the gigs around.

The weather this morning had turned chill, getting colder. Franklin appeared at the door of the little trailer, all togged out in his clown duds. He slapped his chest and breathed deep the fresh morning air. Then, because you never waste a classic set-up like that, Franklin doubled over in a coughing fit. To put a button on it, he pulled a cigarette from its pack and clipped the butt between his lips.

Franklin didn't smoke anymore but hadn't quite given up the oral fixation. He kept working on it. He didn't carry a lighter or matches.

Franklin pressed the button on the key fob, unlocking the doors on the clownmobile. He climbed in behind the wheel, fired it up, and headed toward the back-end of town.

The Big Top was busy again. Not like before, but better than it had been with the Slasher on the loose. Clowns were back to hanging out, kibitzing, and waiting.

Franklin came in to the now customary shower of peanuts. He was both hero and goat. Hero for helping nab the Baggy Pants Slasher, goat for letting a lucky find like Lucy get away from him. He never said anything, but everyone seemed to know.

Franklin took his usual spot on the stool at the end of the bar.

"Hey." Red gave him a nod.

"Hey." Franklin scooched the stool closer, balancing the tips of his shoes on the rail. He placed his pack of cigarettes on the bar.

Red pulled out a bundle of mail and set it down in front of Franklin. Since moving out of the apartment, Franklin had his mail forwarded to the Big Top. The little trailer didn't have mail service, which helped to keep some of his more questionable fans in the dark about where he lived.

On one side there were the bozophobes who cursed Franklin's part in ending the Slasher's rampage. They sent him hate letters, threatening to do unmentionable things to his body. On the other side were the bozophiles who celebrated Franklin's part in ending the Slasher's rampage. They sent him nude selfies and offered to do unmentionable things to his body. Any pictures of good looking women he threw away. The rest he gave to the other clowns. Serve them right for sticking their red rubber noses in his beeswax.

Franklin sorted through the letters, sniffed some, wrinkled his nose at the odor coming from others. He set up two piles—the 'phobes and the 'philes. He'd reached the point where he knew without opening them which were which.

Red held up a trash can. Franklin dropped the 'phobes in.

Franklin took one plain white envelope and tore the end, blowing to open it up. He drew out a plain piece of paper glued with words and letters torn from magazines.

"'I will have you clown,'" said Franklin, reading aloud. He turned it to show Red.

"One of your prison pen pals?" asked Red.

Since her incarceration, Gladys had inspired a handful of women in lockup with her to write him. Franklin figured they were harmless. Most of them were doing twenty-five-to-life. He'd write back, send them photos of himself in makeup. They seemed okay with it.

Franklin checked the envelope for a return address. He should have realized it belonged in the 'phobe pile.

"'Frazierass, Alaska, 99605,'" read Franklin. "Of course. Wonder why this one crawled out of the woodwork?"

Franklin tore into another envelope. He read the letter written on lined paper pulled from a wirebound notebook. The shreds of paper from the ragged edges fell on the bar top. "And here's why." Franklin lifted the pages up for Red to see.

"'Dear Franklin,'" he read, "'sorry to be writing with bad news—well, bad news for you, good news for me. My boyfriend Big Eddie just visited, and I told him all about you. Showed him pictures and told him about us. I may have exajerated—'" Franklin stopped and pointed. "Misspelled 'exaggerated.'" He went on, "'exajerated about you and me and a conjugal visit I told him we'd had together. I was trying to make him jealous cause he don't come see me like he used to. It worked! Boy, was he ever mad!'" Franklin pointed to the word. "Look how many times she underlined 'mad.'"

"That's a lot."

Franklin went back to reading, "'He says he's going to find you and tie a knot in your—'" Franklin stopped. "Okay. I think we all have that picture fixed firmly in our heads."

Franklin took up the white paper with the threatening message.

"I guess we have to add Big Eddie from Frazierass, Alaska to the bozophobe pile."

"I don't think he's really from Alaska."

"May have a summer house there, you know?" Franklin held the letter up to the light. "I guess I can always hope he'll get his tongue stuck to a polar bear or something."

"You plan on telling Officer Joe?"

"I guess I should." Franklin was through playing super-hero.

The phone rang.

"Big Top," growled Red. "Yeah? Okay, where?" Red made notes on the pad by the phone and tore it off.

The clowns in the place surged toward the bar, encircling Red.

"Birthday party at the Bowl Rite. Regular clown didn't show."

"Anybody we know?" Noodlenick called out from the crowd.

"Some rookie. Not one of us."

"Dang rookies!" the crowd of clowns cried out.

Red handed the slip of paper to Franklin.

"Hey, Red! What gives!" they shouted.

"Have to send my best." Red winked at Franklin. "Make it up to them."

Franklin slipped off the stool and pushed the stack of mail to Red. "Keep these warm for me. I'll be back."

Franklin moved through the gang and into the sunlight. Like old times.

There were some clowns who didn't like bowling alley birthday parties. When free beer flowed to keep the adults happy, the dads hung around, sucking down the suds. Soon enough they'd get to heckling. One of them always decided to go all super-clown on them and show how funny the old man could be. The more beer inside, the funnier they felt outside. Way funnier than some pie-face in the stupid shoes. Franklin swore he'd get tickets printed up some day to hand out. They'd say, 'Thanks to alcohol, your jokes are closer to stupid than they appear.'

As a public service.

Still, Franklin enjoyed parties in the bowling alley. They let him fool around on the lanes like he'd done as a kid with his mom and Buster.

And, of course, the free beer.

Franklin stood outside the entrance to the Bowl Rite, his bowling bag in one hand and his flowered carpetbag of props in the other. He took a breath, worked the door open. He went bounding in, blowing a whistle and sliding to a stop near the scoring table festooned with balloons. The place was empty except for the party kids, their moms, and a handful of dads.

Kids bounced and squealed. Franklin did his sweat-wipe gag and sent the kids scattering to escape his soggy wet gloves.

Wheezing through a kazoo, Franklin imitated a circus calliope as he ya-ta-doodley-doodled music for his gags.

He opened the bowling bag and pulled out a ball drilled with dozens of finger holes. He held it up, flummoxed at the choice of holes, twisting and turning it for just the right grip. As he closed his eyes to stick his fingers into a random set of holes a spring-loaded worm popped out of one hole. The kids yelled directions as he held the ball to his chest, grabbing at the worm. It popped in and out of sight, evading his grasp. Until he got a brilliant idea. He turned the ball over, put his mouth to a hole and blew the worm right out of the ball and sent it whistling across the room.

The kids cheered his victory, and he put the ball back, blowing a raspberry at the disappointing ball.

With a confident wave of his arms and a posture reeking of braggadocio, Franklin stepped to the ball return. He reached for another ball. But his gloved fingers slipped and slid over the ball, unable to turn it to reach the holes. He tried again. He licked his fingers and tried a third time. No luck. Then, another brilliant idea. He pulled a toilet plunger from his carpetbag, and with a great, spinning wind-up, plunged the suction head down on the ball. Satisfied, he twisted the plunger and ball until he could reach the finger holes.

Gripping the ball, he summoned the birthday girl and went to hand her the ball. As she took it into her hands, he appeared to let go, the weight pulling them both over. Franklin recovered and stopped the ball inches from his toes. Boy, that was close. Until Franklin let go to wipe his brow in relief. The ball landed on his foot.

Franklin howled. The kids howled. Yep, pain is still funny.

He rolled the ball around the floor until he could line up the finger holes again. He lifted the ball, slotted his thumb and middle fingers, sighted down the lane. He managed a decent delivery, until the release, sending the ball banging along down the lane, bouncing off the gutter's kiddie bumpers. It finally collided with a single end pin. Franklin pumped his fist and strutted like he'd picked up a seven-ten split.

The kids laughed and pointed while Franklin preened, ignorant at the source of their glee until they made him understand he had to knock them all down.

Oh, squeaked Franklin, slapping his forehead and rocking. He held up a finger for them to be patient and watch.

Waiting for the ball to roll back, Franklin put his face in the air stream of the hand drier. His lips fluttered, his mouth going like a Labrador with its head hanging out the window of a station wagon. His ball banged out of the chute and collided with the other balls in the return. Franklin took it up and hiked it through his legs. The ball rolled so very slowly until it reached the one-three pocket and knocked down the rest of the pins. A trick he'd learned as a kid with his mom, kept sharp for these sorts of occasions and a sure-fire hoot when it worked.

Like that? Franklin gestured to the kids, and they howled their approval.

He bounced in a victory circle, then sat at the scoring table. He waved for the kids to shout out their names. As he wrote them on the scoring pane, he doodled houseflies, flowers, worms, hearts, and puppies. When he finished he got up and with a flourish handed the marker to a mom. At the last moment, Franklin swiped his handkerchief over the seat as she sat down causing her to pop up again. Franklin, embarrassed at the near disaster, draped the handkerchief over his head.

Stepping away from the party, Franklin hid behind his hat to sneak a swig of beer from one of the dads. Franklin went back to moving between the lanes. He whistled amazement and wheezed encouragement. He shushed for silence and he offered a helpful nudge of the ball to the littlest kids.

A few teenagers huddled out of the way in the video arcade, blasting away at bad guys. Likely older siblings trapped into attendance by insistent party moms. Franklin slipped in to watch. The kids ran out of quarters, so Franklin dug deep, stood by the moto-cross game, and offered to take them on. The tallest teen, smirking at a clown's chances against the likes of him, climbed aboard the left-hand bike. Franklin took the right-hand bike. They inserted the coins and powered up the game. The video bikes took off, Franklin jerking backward as if caught off-guard.

They ran through the course as Franklin played the showoff. He rode no-hands, rode side saddle, rode standing on the seat. He still managed to keep his score even with the kid next to him. More evidence of Franklin's misspent youth.

From the corner of his eye, Franklin spotted a hulking brute of a guy in a black leather vest and black jeans. Stealing glances as he rode, he saw the guy wore shades, had a blonde beard, shaved head, and tiny gold rings in both ears.

Franklin waved for one of the other teens to climb onto the bike and take over. As the skinniest one slipped a leg over, Franklin slid off the back and left him to finish his ride.

Franklin went back to the birthday party in time to hand out the treat bags and send the kids off to eat cake and ice cream.

The big guy took a seat at the far end of the lanes. He'd glance over toward Franklin every few minutes but kept his seat like he was waiting.

Franklin cavorted over the kids and their birthday treats while keeping an eye on the big guy.

A note slid into his hand, making him jump as if snake-bit. He recovered by dancing a limber-legged jig. He edged back out of the crowd of kids and opened the note. 'How about some clowning around later?' it read. He glanced up to catch the studious non-look from the redhead who had slipped him the note. A little bit older than the other moms.

Lots of jewelry. Hoop earrings, bangles for bracelets, and fingers full of rings. Including a wedding band.

Oy. How to slip away without getting shucked out of his clown suit by an overheated redhead? She kept slipping glances his way. She managed to stay bent over, gathering up discarded party favor bags, gift wrapping, and ribbons. Bending and stretching. Bending and stretching. Aiming her backside at him or giving him glimpses down her blouse as she tidied up.

His mind a blank, he glanced around in time to see the big guy heading his way.

Oy again. How to slip away without getting broken into little pieces, dressed in a clown suit.

The big guy stopped and stood outside the party room, sighted down his finger to point at Franklin. He crooked his finger for Franklin to come closer.

Franklin figured it would be better if they didn't get blood all over the birthday cake. He sighed and stepped in close to the big guy. If he cut the distance the guy had for swinging his fist, it might hurt less.

"Hey, buddy," said the big guy, with a voice sounding exactly like a Harley Davidson's unmufflered dual-fire ignition growl. "Got time to roll a few with us before you go?" He jerked a thumb toward the other end of the lanes where more leathered-up guys and gals had gathered. A bikers' league.

Franklin blew a quick note of relief and gave the guy his 'anything for a pal' face. A bozophile, like gold, is where you find him.

The big guy took Franklin over and called out, "Hey! Look what I found!"

"Not another one!" said a short, blonde woman wearing a denim jacket over a tee-shirt, and cutoff shorts.

"We haven't been able to put the last one back together yet," said a smiling, stringy-haired guy with a black moustache and goatee.

"We can always use him for parts," said another bald biker, a red handlebar moustache.

"This is the clown 'at caught the Slasher!" said the big guy. He laid a large, be-ringed hand on Franklin's shoulder. "Took some balls, right?" He laughed again and shoved up his sleeve, showing off a happy circus clown tattoo. Its iconic colors held back the sea of dark-inked mayhem tattooed all over the big guy's forearms and neck.

"Driller." The big guy offered his hand to shake. Franklin took it, and Franklin being Franklin, shrank down onto one knee in fake pain at Driller's grip. They loved it. Pain, the sure-fire crowd pleaser, no matter how old the kids might be. Franklin waggled his boneless hand, flopping it up to his mouth to suck on the fingers. He smiled around at the group as he nursed the circulation back into his fingers.

He did for the bowling bikers all the bits he'd done for the kids. The wormy bowling ball, the plunger gag, stealing sips of their beers with a very long straw. Okay, he didn't use that one for kids, but it worked for this crew.

In return, they fed him shots and beers. And kept him out of reach of the red-hot red-headed momma.

Past midnight outside the darkened amusement park, Driller rode up on his Harley. He had Franklin wedged behind him against the sissy bar.

The few security lights along the fence were working again, though barely lighting the patch of ground around Franklin's little trailer.

"Whoa, spooky, man," said Driller, leaning forward to let Franklin dismount.

"But I call it home." Franklin worked to untangle himself from the Harley. He hopped backward to slide his leg over the seat and settle himself again on solid ground.

"Thanks for the ride." Franklin hitched up his pants, gave a shake of his head, and blew out a long, long breath. If anyone asked him right now what was inside his clown suit, he'd tell them, alcohol. Lots of alcohol.

Franklin pulled up his sleeve. "And thanks for the tattoo!"

"Better'n cash. Money don't last. A tat'll last you forever."

Franklin went to lift the gauze pad bandaging his arm.

"Don't peek, man, it's a surprise."

Franklin smoothed the pad and nodded, his eyes closed, holding a finger to his lips. "Our secret."

Driller gave Franklin a wave and twisted the throttle. The motorcycle roared, and Driller rode off down the road, Franklin waving bye-bye.

Franklin figured he'd have to take the bus into town tomorrow and retrieve the clownmobile and his stuff. But, considering the hospitality of Driller and his bowling buddies, he'd be lucky to remember where he'd parked it. Then again, Chumleyville wasn't all that big. He'd find it eventually.

Franklin made it through the door and into the trailer. In less than an instant, Franklin had stripped out of his costume and stood once more in the doorway of the little trailer. Now he wore his tattered old bathrobe and carried a towel, soap, and a big bottle of baby oil. He still wore his wig and make up. He considered himself ready for anything.

He unlocked the side gate in the cyclone fencing and headed for the funhouse and the showers. He stopped, turned back, and looked both ways. He snapped the lock on the gate. He gave a tug to check that it was secure. Then he turned back toward the funhouse. More muscle memory than caution.

In the locker room, Franklin dropped his towel, soap and baby oil on the shelf over the sinks. He started the water running. He'd picked up the baby oil, ready to squeeze out a dollop to wipe off his clown face. He spotted something odd reflected in the mirror. He turned around to see that someone had written on the wall in red tempera paint.

'I Will Have You Clown,' it read. The paint, now dry and flakey had dripped, blood-like. It had not been there when he showered and dressed at the start of the day.

Machinery began clanking next door in the funhouse. The music and sound effects started up. Franklin's sense of self-preservation, exhausted by the liquid generosity of the bikers, was gone. Franklin knew he should be wary of an abandoned amusement park coming to life on its own. But the unreasonable courage powered by quality booze made him fearless.

The chilling squeals and piercing shrieks from the funhouse carried into the locker room.

The cars jostled and jinked against the guide rail. They passed through the cobwebbed doors and into the ultraviolet spookiness beyond.

Franklin stepped inside as the next car bumped through the doors and did the hard-left turn through the ride. The doors hissed closed behind him. The white of his makeup and the pate of his wig glowed in the black light. His head appeared to float along without a visible body.

Franklin eased forward, walking along the edge to avoid getting clipped by a car coming up behind him. The sounds of the ride's catastrophes covered his footsteps. He knew when to expect the make-believe horrors as each passing car rolled over a switch. He waited as the howling, cadaverous creature on scissor hinges shot out, arms flailing. He paused for the giant insects, tendrils of fabric flapping inside the cars. He walked by scenes of mutilated mannequins flashing to life as the cars passed through. Cartoon torments and goofy terrors surrounded him as he moved along. He strained to see in the half-light if one of these mechanical creatures might now be alive.

Franklin reached the last stretch of the ride. He saw all the same, hokey scares. Nothing out of the ordinary. He'd reached the out-of-place pink and white door, at odds with the surrounding fake stone, gothic beams, and blood-spattered walls.

The doors flew open to reveal Zelda's boudoir, with Zelda standing in her bath.

The Zelda figure turned, opening the towel.

Looking exactly like Lucy. But naked.

Franklin's brain reacts lightning quick despite the uncounted jiggers of giggle juice. He sees her exactly as he's imagined her to be. What strikes Franklin as the most amazing thing? She has no tan lines.

"Franklin?"

A talking Zelda-Lucy. Franklin's imagination gave up, and naked Lucy evaporated.

A talking Zelda?

"Franklin!" It turned out to be a not-at-all-naked Lucy.

Lucy stood with the towel opened and underneath she wore jeans and a tube top to bare her shoulders. That's why she seemed topless under the towel. He would have to give his imagination a stern talking-to about this.

"Before I relax completely," said Franklin, "is it safe to assume you're the one who wrote on the wall in the men's locker room?"

"Yes."

"How long have you been waiting here?"

"Longer than I planned. I lucked out getting someone to keep you busy while I figured a way to get in here. I didn't think they'd keep you so long."

"Big guy in a black leather vest? Blonde beard? Earrings?"

"Yes."

"They all voted to have me tattooed. Democracy in action. I guess it's one way of keeping me busy long enough." Franklin swung his bicep up for her to see.

"A tattoo!" She stepped out of the tub and came over to him. "Let me see." She lifted the gauze pad.

"Did it hurt?"

"Nah. They got me sufficiently liquored up first. I didn't feel a thing."

"Eww." Lucy studied the tattoo.

Was she reacting to the blood, and the tattoo was okay? Or was she reacting to the tattoo, forever carved into his skin, and the blood was okay?

"It's supposed to be a surprise."

"It will be." She smoothed the pad back into place. "It does something for you. But it's not what I had in mind."

"It's worth it. As long as it's not me seeing things again."

"Red told me about the lady pen pal and her boyfriend, Big Eddie."

"Yeah. But I'm guessing you sent the note with the cut-out letters."

"Yes. Sorry. I'm surprised you came alone."

"Hey, who's in here!" came a shout.

Franklin's faced squinched up. "I didn't."

Officer Joe pushed through the doors with the next car in line. He aimed his flashlight at Lucy and Franklin.

"I left a key for him."

"What'n hell's going on in here, Franklin?"

"I thought I heard a zombie, Joe."

"Oh, I see." Officer Joe studied the two of them in the beam of his flashlight. He snorted a short laugh. "Remember to shut everything down when you leave." He swung the light away and went back through the doors. If it's possible for a person to smirk with their entire back, then smirking is exactly what Officer Joe's back did.

When they were alone again, Lucy said, "There's something I've been wanting to do ever since I had to kiss you that night at the bus stop."

"I can't wait to find out."

Lucy lifted a wet, soapy sponge and wiped away Franklin's makeup.

"You always carry around a bucket of water and sponge?"

"Only on special occasions."

Lucy leaned back to examine his bare face.

"In this light? Not as bad as I thought it might be."

"You've got me where I don't even remember what I look like."

"I'll let you see yourself later." She peeled off the wig and stroked his hair.

"Hey." Franklin pulled his head back the barest little bit.

"What?"

"When did you know?"

"Know what?"

"You're off in California, minding your very own business. Now you're here."

"Oh."

"So, when did you know?"

"When you left me at the gate out front and said, 'you don't count.'"

"I have to remember that line the next time I'm alone in a dark place with a scary female."

"At first, I thought it was more of your bullshit to get rid of me. Then, thinking about it, after all you did for me? Remembering the way you said it? Made it very easy to tell I counted more than anything."

"Don't let it go to your head."

"Why else come all the way back here?"

"I think I have to kiss you," said Franklin.

"Okay. But hold my hands. I'm still not a hundred percent down with being this close to a clown and not imagining how best to inflict gruesome bodily injury."

He took her hands and readied his mouth but didn't move toward her. "You'll have to come kiss me." Franklin would have added 'because I'm still not a hundred percent down with leaning lips-first into one more heartbreak.' But it came out, "because Driller and his friends did a bang-up job with all that whiskey."

As Lucy came closer, Franklin said, "You know what I hope?"

"What?"

"I hope I can feel this."

Her lips found his. Yes, he could feel it.

♦ ♦ ♦

In a darkened tent, a sliver of light bled through the gaps of the closed flaps.

Lucy hissed at Franklin, "I don't think I'm ready."

"You're ready."

"I'm not feeling comfortable with this."

"Good. You get comfortable, you get lazy," said Franklin. "Stop wiggling. Relax."

"Easy for you to say. I've never, ever done this with a clown before."

"I've never done it with someone who hated clowns before. Ready?"

"Ready," said Lucy, but not sounding anything like it.

Lucy made a *whoa-whoa'ing* sound as Franklin began a gentle rocking underneath her.

"Hey," Lucy breathed out a whisper.

"What?"

"Have I told you how glad I am it's you and not Buster down there?"

Music started and the flaps of the tent slapped open. Franklin let go the stanchions he'd used to stay steady, keeping himself and Lucy upright on his unicycle. He pedaled into the sunshine, with Lucy riding on his shoulders. Kids clapped as they rode around the little barricades of the makeshift circus ring.

Lucy let go of Franklin's chin, first with her right, then with her left. Helping Franklin balance, she worked up a smile behind her newly-painted clown face. She thrilled to the wind whipping through her fringe of yellow hair under her flower pot hat.

Franklin had a smile on his face. A real smile, not just the one painted on.

SCOTT PARSON writes fiction that embraces the comic, the surreal, and the romantic. He moved to New York City to be an actor where he added juggling, fire-eating, and swordplay to his resumé. After playing Shakespeare and touring the hinterlands, he moved from acting to writing. He still lives in Manhattan on the Upper West Side with his wife and daughter and sends fruit baskets to his son in grad school. Find out more at www.scottparson.com.